turn on

DARCY BURKE

OLIVERHEBERBOOKS

Turn On previously titled So Good Copyright 2016, 2025 © Darcy Burke

Cover Design by Wicked Smart Designs

Published by Oliver-Heber Books

0 9 8 7 6 5 4 3 2 1

For my parents-in-law, Linda and Roger, as they celebrate 50 years of marriage.

Your happy ever after is inspiring and amazing—and still going strong.

Turn On

Cameron Westcott has spent eight years recovering from heart-break by keeping romantic entanglements casual and simple. He's never minded being called a manwhore, but after two years immersing himself in his new winery, he might be ready for the next chapter. Especially when he meets a sexy wine distributor —only she says she isn't interested.

Following a bitter divorce, Brooke Ellis relocated to Ribbon Ridge to rebuild her life. Things will never be the same for her, and she's coming to terms with that reality when she meets charming, persistent Cam. She can't imagine a happy ever after given his reputation, but he makes her feel so good.

As the sparks between them intensify, they're both hesitant to commit for very different reasons. Or are they really just sabotaging their own futures? If they can trust each other—and themselves—they may realize that what they share is too good to let slip away.

Chapter One

July, Near Ribbon Ridge, Oregon

Cameron Westcott frowned at the serpentine line stretching before them. To their left, a forty-foot-long bed of hot coals roasted salmon that was speared on long, arched pikes. The heat wafted over the crowd of people waiting to go in to the dinner, making the already hot summer night even warmer.

But Cam didn't care about the temperature. He wanted a good seat. The annual salmon bake at the International Pinot Noir Celebration was a fun, casual event where the wine flowed freely, and the attendees came from all walks—wine connoisseurs, winemakers, wine critics, and, most importantly, wine lovers and buyers. It was the perfect place for Cam and his partners: his best friend and two of his brothers, to offer a sneak peek of their pinot noir.

Cam craned his neck to try to gauge how far back they were from the entrance. "We should've gotten here earlier."

Cam's younger-by-two-years brother Luke, nearly always

the coolest head in the room, clapped his shoulder and gave it a quick, hard massage. "Relax. Hayden will save us a spot."

Hayden Archer had been Cam's best friend since first grade. He was also the winemaker at their winery, West Arch Estate. Cam was the business and sales manager, Luke managed the vineyard, and their youngest brother, Jamie—who stood just behind them looking at his phone—was the chief financial officer.

"Yeah, you're right." Cam forced himself to do exactly what Luke said—relax. He'd been working crazy hours the past few weeks as they geared up for their first fall season as an official winery. They'd purchased the vineyard two years ago, but this was the first year they would have everything in place: a facility with a tasting room and their inaugural vintage, albeit small, of pinot noir.

The line suddenly started to move more quickly. The closer they got to the entry, the more they could see the dozens of round tables with their battery-operated candles and two bottles of wine each and the long rectangular tables that held the amazing buffet and carving stations. It was always a beautiful setting, a fairylike dinner in an oak grove at the local college.

Their wine wouldn't be poured by the roving servers nor would it be set out on the tables, but Hayden had a cooler with their whites and a rolling tote with their fledgling pinot. Like many other winemakers, he'd whip the bottles out and share them with everyone at their table and anyone else who wandered by.

Cam's phone vibrated in his pocket. He pulled it from his khaki shorts and looked at the screen.

Hayden: *Running late, sorry.*

Cam glanced at the tables that were rapidly filling. By the time they got inside, they'd be scrambling for a good spot. He typed a response into his phone.

Cam: *We're screwed for a decent table.*

Hayden: *Liam just nabbed two seats for me and Bex, but the rest of the table's full. Sorry, bro.*

Liam was Hayden's older brother and a master at networking.

Irritation curled along Cam's spine, but he inhaled deeply, getting a nose full of campfire scent for his efforts. This was no big deal. So they weren't sitting together. It would still be an amazing evening. Besides, once people started milling about, they'd all end up in the same place.

He turned to his brothers. "Hayden's running late, but he's got two seats saved thanks to Liam. We're on our own."

"Damn lucky Archers." Luke said this without heat, his dark eyes crinkling at the edges.

The Archers were the first family of Ribbon Ridge—literally, since their ancestor had settled the town—and most things they touched turned to gold. Cam wasn't jealous, though, and neither were his brothers. Especially when they were in business with one of them, and their older half-brother was married to another.

Jamie sidled closer. He looked between Cam and Luke. "So what's our plan? Split up and find something?"

"Just go for whatever's closest to the center," Cam said. "Ideally we'll find a table close to Hayden, but that may not be possible."

Luke nodded. "I'll find Hayden and check the surrounding area."

"And I'll just look for anything center-ish," Jamie said.

Cam edged closer toward the gate. "Sounds good."

At last, they reached the entry and rushed inside. Luke took off in one direction, while Jamie went in another. Cam scanned for empty seats and saw a few at a table near the edge but still relatively close to the center of things.

Just as Cam reached the table, a trio of women did the same. He set his hand on the back of a chair at the same moment one of them did.

The woman was probably a few years shy of thirty—a bit younger than him—and drop-dead gorgeous with shoulder-length, golden blonde hair and sharp blue-green eyes. If Cam wasn't so eager to claim the seats, he'd hit on her.

Hell, he'd probably hit on her anyway. *After* he took possession of the chairs.

She smiled at him, and she was even prettier. *Yes, definitely hitting on her.*

"We're taking these three," she said, glancing at the other two women—a petite brunette and a lean, athletic beauty with long, dark hair.

"I think I was here first," Cam said, flashing his most disarming smile.

Her eyes darkened a shade, but then she batted her lashes. Her gaze raked him from head to toe, firing his blood. "I don't think so, but anyway, a real gentleman would surrender."

Surrender.

For some reason, that word evoked an incredibly erotic response in him. He pictured himself surrendering to her in every way and decided that would be just fine with him. Okay, not *every* way. He wanted this damn table. A quick look around showed that the only seats left were in the corners.

He leaned toward her. She smelled of vanilla and bergamot —he'd gotten pretty good at detecting fragrance over the past eight years shilling wine. "A lady wouldn't resort to flirtation to steal seats."

"It's not stealing if I was here first." She arched a slender, sculpted blonde brow. "Which I was."

He met her brow arch with one of his own. "In your opinion."

Luke walked toward them. "You find something?"

Cam kept his hand on the chair. "I did."

The blonde glanced at Luke. "That is up for dispute."

Luke dipped his gaze toward his phone. "Jamie found us seats. Come on."

Cam didn't want to give in so easily. And not just because he wanted this table. He wished there were enough seats for all of them. That way he could get to know this stunning woman.

She looked past him at Luke, and her smile became more radiant, if that were possible. "Thank you."

Luke's mouth curved up. "My pleasure." He turned. "Let's go, Cam."

Cam reluctantly let go of the chairback. He took a small step toward her and lowered his voice. "You win this round."

She brushed the lush waves of her hair over her shoulder. "Oh, you think there'll be another?"

He dipped his gaze over her. She wore a coral-colored sleeveless top with a pair of long gold necklaces and white, cropped pants with strappy wedges. She had great style—precisely the type of woman that caught his eye. "Definitely," he said.

She set her small clutch purse on the table and flashed him a saucy look. "Hold my chair for me?"

Damn, she was a flirt. He couldn't stop a grin from stealing across his lips. He might be sitting in the nether regions of the grove, but he had the sense it was going to be a great night.

He held her chair out while she sat, then scooted her in. He dropped down and whispered close to her ear, "I'll be back later."

She looked at him over her shoulder. "I don't see a need for that."

What? Hadn't she just given him all sorts of signs that she was interested? He opened his mouth to ask why, but his phone vibrated. He quickly read the screen. Both his brothers were asking where the hell he was. They were having trouble defending his seat.

Resigned that he had to go, Cam settled for a parting shot. "I see plenty of need," he said. "And I'll show you later."

As he pivoted to walk away, he nearly tripped. Had she just rolled her eyes? He looked back at her, but she'd turned toward the table so he couldn't see her face anymore. His phone buzzed again.

Luke: *STOP FLIRTING AND GET YOUR ASS OVER HERE.*

Cam walked out to what felt like Siberia, to a table in the darkest corner of the grove. He surveyed the sad gathering—all guys. "Wow, great seats."

Jamie reached for one of the open bottles of wine on the table and poured pinot blanc into their smaller white-wine glasses. "At least we're together. It's not like we'll be here all night. We'll move around after dinner."

Luke set his phone next to his place setting. "You'll have ample opportunity to get back to the hot blonde."

Cam sat down between his brothers. "Maybe."

Luke threw him an incredulous look. "Maybe? Where's my brother the player? She was totally flirting with you."

"Yeah, I thought so too, but then she gave me the brush-off."

Jamie shrugged. "Maybe she was just flirting to get the seats. You were arguing over them, right?"

"She said as much," Luke said. He gave Cam a pitying look. "Can't win 'em all, bro."

Now it was Cam's turn to roll his eyes. He was used to his younger brothers giving him crap about his love life, which wasn't really an accurate description since love never came anywhere near the vicinity of it. "Whatever. Plenty of dateable women here tonight." Just not at their table.

Luke laughed. "Dateable? You're going to actually date someone for the first time in, what, seven, eight years?"

"Yeah, since what's-her-name." Jamie snapped his fingers.

Even though Jamie hadn't said her name, which Cam didn't allow since she was his own personal Voldemort, the mere mention of her set Cam's teeth on edge. "I date."

Jamie looked unconvinced. "I guess, but is it really dating when you have no intention of seeing someone more than a handful of times?"

That wasn't fair. Cam had seen plenty of women more than a handful of times. During the six years he'd worked for Blackthorn Cellars traveling around the country, he'd seen a couple of women regularly. Granted, neither of them had lived in Ribbon Ridge and the long-distance, casual nature of those relationships had suited all parties. "I've dated plenty of women." Just not exclusively, and he'd always been up-front about it.

"Hear that, Luke? *Plenty* of women." Jamie waggled his brows before dissolving into laughter.

Cam drummed his fingers on the table. "You can tease me all you want, but how many women have I been with since we started the winery?" He'd thrown himself into this endeavor, and yeah, since he wasn't traveling anymore, his options had narrowed. But he also didn't miss that lifestyle.

Luke stroked his hand along his perpetually stubbled chin. "Good point. Guess we should stop calling you a player and a manwhore and the like. How about we start calling you asshat instead?"

Cam grinned. "That's the best you can do?"

Jamie angled himself toward Cam and Luke and set his elbow on the table. "Speaking of the winery, I hope this pinot we're launching is ready."

Hayden had acknowledged it was going to be close. This was a small batch from the grapes they'd harvested almost two years ago—their first yield from the vineyard. Most of the fruit had gone to contractual obligations held by the former vineyard owner, but they'd had enough left over to produce just under ninety cases. It was meant to be a teaser for what would come next year—their haul from the entire vineyard, which was currently sitting in oak barrels in their new winemaking facility.

"It's ready," Luke said firmly. Before coming back to Ribbon Ridge two years ago, he'd worked for a few vineyards in Sonoma. Between him and Hayden, West Arch had the best winemaker/vineyard manager duo in the entire Willamette Valley. At least in Cam's opinion, and he was pretty sure he knew enough about wine in this region to make that call.

"I'm stoked to see what people think. That's why I'm bummed we aren't at his table." Or even close to it. On his way to the back of beyond, he'd seen Hayden and Bex setting up a few tables away from the seats he'd given to the ungrateful blonde.

Actually, she *had* been grateful. To Luke, he recalled. To Cam she'd been cool—after obtaining her victory.

The buffet tables opened up, and they stood to get their dinner. As they waited in line, they chatted with people they knew and made new acquaintances, all the while talking up West Arch. The three of them lived and breathed their start-up, and Cam was thrilled to be doing this with his brothers and his best friend.

Well, most of his brothers. They had an older half-brother who was married to Hayden's sister. Dylan was a contractor with a very successful business of his own. In fact, he'd built their winery, the bones of which had been completed just before last fall's harvest. Dylan would've been here tonight to support them, but he and Sara were doing what they did most Saturday nights—doting on their new daughter.

Just as they headed back to their table with their loaded-up plates, Hayden intercepted them, grimacing. "Hey, sorry about the table situation."

"No worries, man," Luke said, smiling. "We like our secluded, all-male table. Later on when we're shitfaced, we can act like complete assholes, and no one will care."

This provoked laughter from everyone. "Cool," Hayden said. "Liam schmoozed his way into our four seats."

Cam snorted. "Of course he did." Liam Archer worked a room better than anyone Cam had ever met. As a kid out of college, Cam had studied him and employed many of his same techniques when he'd started out selling wine.

Hayden glanced at their plates. "Hurry up and eat so you can come join us. That is, if you can tear yourself away from your new man club." His mouth tugged into a half-smile.

"Very funny." Cam inclined his head toward his best friend. "Let's call *him* asshat instead."

Hayden blinked. "Who are you calling asshat?"

Luke jabbed a thumb toward Cam. "Him, actually. He's trying to deflect. It seems we can't rightfully call him manwhore anymore."

Hayden laughed. "Why, because he's calmed down a little since we started up West Arch? Nah, I think we can still call him a manwhore. Just because he's been refocused on the winery doesn't mean he's ready to change his ways. Right, Cam?" He gave Cam's arm a slap before taking himself back to his rock-star table.

"Asshat," Cam muttered.

Luke and Jamie started back toward the outer limits, and Cam made to follow them. Instead, he collided with someone and had to clutch his plate with both hands, lest he lose his dinner to the ground.

"Hey, watch it!" He looked over at the person who'd run

into him, and couldn't keep his jaw from briefly dropping. "You."

"*You*." The blonde dipped her fiery gaze to the dirt and grass beneath their feet. "You made me drop my focaccia bread. I've been looking forward to those carbs all day."

"*I* made *you* drop it? Are you hell-bent on casting me as a villain tonight?"

She cocked her head to the side. "If the label fits..."

He narrowed his eyes at her. "You're a piece of work. First, you flirt with me to steal my seats, and instead of being gracious in victory, you give me the cold shoulder. And now you're trying to steal—or at least ruin—my dinner too."

Her eyes widened, and she sucked in a breath. "Like I ran into you on purpose!"

Satisfaction burned through him. "Ha! You admit you ran into me."

She let out a groan, and damn, it should *not* have been sexy. But it was.

She glared at him. "You're a menace."

Something about the way she said it made him slightly uncomfortable. It was as if she actually meant it, and how could she? They didn't even know each other. He wanted to change that. Because, holy hell, he was attracted to her.

"I'm not really. If you'll let me—" He'd been about to say buy you a drink, but you didn't have to buy any of the wine at this dinner. "I'd be happy to pour a great wine for you later."

"Thanks, but no thanks. I need to get back to my friends." She pulled her plate in close. "You go first."

He didn't want to take no for an answer, but he had a rule—three strikes, and he was out. That gave him one more chance with her. He'd save it for later. "By all means, ladies first. My feet are rooted to the ground until you move." He gave her a bow, something a *gentleman* would do.

Her gaze turned skeptical, but she moved. As she passed by, she gave him a bemused look. He watched her until she sat down at her table. A moment later, she turned her head, registered that he hadn't budged, then quickly turned back. But not before he'd caught a blush in her cheeks. Or maybe that was just his wishful thinking at this distance. Either way, he looked forward to trying that third time and just hoped he didn't strike out.

Chapter Two

"He's still watching you."

Brooke Ellis didn't mean to look, but she did. And there he was staring at her in all his handsome, self-assured glory.

She snapped her head back around and forked a bite of salmon into her mouth.

Her friend Naomi, seated on Brooke's right, sighed. "And now he's gone. You should've invited him to sit with us."

As it happened, there was an empty chair on the other side of the table. Both Naomi and their other friend Jana had remarked—several times—that the people at the table would surely shift so that Brooke could sit with him.

"I am *not* inviting Cameron Westcott to sit with us."

Jana paused in eating. "Wait, you know him?"

Brooke had successfully changed the subject when her friends had tried to bring up the attractive guy who'd clearly been hitting on her. She'd known as soon as she saw him exactly who he was. "Remember that wine sales guy I've mentioned a few times, the total player? The one with the reputation for having a girl in every city in his territory?"

Jana's blue eyes widened. "That's him?"

Naomi sipped her wine. "Who cares? He's hot. And interested in you. When was the last time you had sex?"

Nearly three years ago. But who was counting?

"She has a point," Jana said. "In fact, he's the perfect guy to end your dry spell since he won't expect anything. I think you should hit that."

Naomi lifted her glass in a toast. "Ditto. And if you don't, maybe I will. Or maybe I'll go for the taller one. They looked like they might be related." She glanced between Brooke and Jana. "Brothers, maybe?"

Brooke speared several leaves of romaine on her fork. "I have no idea. Nor do I care."

Jana grinned. "You're so full of it. I saw you checking him out, and whether you want to admit it or not, you were flirting with him."

"Until she shut him down cold." Naomi's teasing gaze turned serious. "Seriously, you deserve a good time. Why not give him a shot?"

Because he was a player, just like her ex-husband. And look how their marriage had turned out. She inwardly cringed because that wasn't a fair assessment. Yes, Darren had looked elsewhere, but their marriage had hit the skids long before that had happened.

"I am not giving a guy like Westcott a shot at anything." Although, Naomi raised a good argument *if* Brooke was looking for a one-night stand or a casual fling. Which she wasn't. "I'm focused on my job right now. They took a chance on me, and I don't want to blow it."

About fifteen months ago, she'd moved to the area from southern Oregon. Following her divorce, she'd needed a fresh start—new surroundings, new job, new outlook on life. She was still waiting for the new outlook. Yeah, maybe she did just need to get laid.

Jana tipped her head to the side and looked at Brooke as if she were bonkers. "Spending an evening with a super cute guy, having a great time... How is that going to mess up your job exactly?"

"Westcott has a reputation that I don't want to be associated with. The wine industry isn't that big."

"Okay, I guess." Jana didn't sound convinced. "Since you're both in sales, you probably want to keep your distance."

Brooke poked at the roasted potatoes on her plate. "Actually, he's not in sales anymore. He and his brothers started up a winery." Ugh, why had she mentioned that? Now they'd continue to harass her about him. But maybe she could divert their attention. "That had to be one of his brothers with him."

Naomi's head came up, her eyes widening slightly. "Brothers? How many?"

"There are three of them, I believe," Brooke said, relieved they were taking her bait and abandoning their objective to hook her up with Cameron Westcott.

"Excellent, one for each of us," Naomi said, lifting her glass.

Jana grabbed her wine to toast Naomi. Their glasses met over Brooke's plate, and they laughed. Then they turned to look at Brooke, their gazes demanding she join in their toast.

Brooke just chuckled and shook her head. "I'm out, but you two have fun."

It wasn't that she didn't want to date anyone. Okay, yes, it *was* that she didn't want to date anyone.

The pain of her failed marriage *had* started to dull, however. The harder she worked, the more she was able to block out her sadness and even look toward the future. Maybe it was time she got back in the game. At least for a short stint.

But not with Cameron Westcott. He *was* hot. *Too* hot. And confident. And charming.

She *had* been flirting with him, and without even realizing it. He'd sparked something within her, something that had lain dormant for the past few years. Something she'd missed, if she were honest with herself. And when did she bother to do that? Burying her feelings had become her favorite pastime. One she'd gotten *really* good at.

Jana sat back in her chair and sipped her wine. "If Naomi's got her eye on the tall drink of water and Brooke is going to pretend she doesn't want to get to know Cameron Westcott, I clearly need a target of my own." She turned her head to Brooke. "Did you say Westcott had brothers, plural?"

"Yes, although I'm not exactly sure how many." She tried to think of what she knew of their winery. "Actually, I just remembered that Hayden Archer is the winemaker. You know the Archers, right?" She looked at Naomi.

Naomi rolled her eyes and shook her head. "Yeah, duh. Now I feel stupid. I see Tori at races sometimes. I forgot her brother's a winemaker. With that hottie, huh?"

"And his brothers," Jana said. "If there are more Westcott brothers running around tonight, I call dibs."

Brooke waved her fork at them. "You can have all the Westcott brothers."

Naomi looked at her intently, all humor gone from her expression. "Brooke, you have to get back out there. This isolation isn't healthy."

Brooke couldn't help but feel defensive, especially since Naomi wasn't wrong. "I'm not isolated. I'm out here with you guys, aren't I?"

Jana exhaled. "Okay. We'll stop bothering you—for now." She leaned close and lowered her voice to ensure the last bit was just between the three of them. "But I still say Cameron's fuckability factor is off the charts. You're crazy not to want a piece of that."

"Agreed," Naomi said. "In fact, I think it's past time I went in search of hottie number two. She picked up her nearly empty wineglass and downed the contents before standing up.

Jana jumped to her feet. "I'm going with you to find hottie number three. Come on." She grabbed Naomi's hand, and they headed back toward the wine tent.

Brooke frowned after them, wondering why they hadn't invited her to tag along. Then she saw the reason coming toward her table. Her "friends" had seen Cameron Westcott headed her way and had decided to meddle by vacating the area. *Bitches.*

Brooke finished off her wine for fortification as Cameron neared the table. He carried his glass, which was also empty, and a bottle of wine. "May I take this empty seat, or are we going to have another knock-down-drag-out over it?"

She blinked up at him. "Nothing got violent. At least not until you tried to plow into me near the buffet."

He sat in Jana's chair and set his glass on the table, scooting her plate with the stem just before a worker plucked it off the table. "I thought we'd established you did the plowing."

"I misspoke." She looked at the bottle of wine in his hand. "Is that your wine?"

He set it on the table between them so she could read the label. "It is. I thought you might want to try it. I assume, since you're here, that you like wine."

She liked the look of their label. The font was stylish and sophisticated, and the graphic was simple but elegant—an archway with the sun setting behind it. She ran her fingertips over the embossing of West Arch Estate. "Classy branding."

"Thanks. I'll take credit for that."

She half smiled at his arrogance. "Why does that not surprise me?"

He grinned. "Fine, I'll share credit with my pal Evan Archer. He's the creative director at Archer Brewing and so far, I guess, at West Arch. He designed the font and created the graphic, but it really was my idea."

"It's very nice. Makes sense you would have a handle on wine branding, considering what you used to do."

He froze for a moment, studying her. "Wait a sec. You know who I am. I didn't put it together when you asked if this was my wine, but you know me."

"Yes, you're Cameron Westcott."

"Well, damn. I'm afraid you've got me at a disadvantage, because I don't know you."

She liked having him at a disadvantage and suspected he wasn't terribly familiar with the sensation. "Pour me a glass of that pinot, and maybe I'll tell you."

The wine was already open and just had a cork stuck in the top, which he pulled out. He laughed as he splashed the garnet liquid into her glass. "Maybe, huh? Why only maybe?"

"If your wine sucks, I'm ditching you immediately."

He laughed again. "Fair enough."

She vaguely realized she was flirting with him again, but decided it was harmless. People flirted all the time. Hell, flirting was a huge part of her job. Wine didn't sell itself.

She picked up the glass and swirled the wine around the bowl.

"Hold on," he said. "Are you really qualified to say if our wine sucks?"

She stared at him, the glass on its way to her lips. "I'm a wholesale wine distributor, smart-ass."

His eyes widened briefly, and then he sat back in his chair, a grin playing across his sexy mouth. "Then by all means, judge away."

She sniffed the aroma first and picked up a strong cherry

along with licorice and cola. She sipped and let the wine linger on her tongue. It was young, but it had great promise. She took another whiff before glancing at him. "My name is Brooke Ellis."

His lips spread into a full, satisfied grin. "I guess that means our wine doesn't suck, Brooke Ellis."

"No, it doesn't." In fact, it was quite good. Or it would be, anyway. "How much of this do you have?"

"Less than a hundred cases."

"*That* sucks."

He sat forward in his chair, his face animated. "Does it? I have to admit I've been excited about this wine, but nervous too. You really like it?"

"I do." His enthusiasm and uncertainty were both alluring and endearing, two things she hadn't expected this player to be. And he *was* a player—she shouldn't forget that.

She took another sip of the wine, liking it even more on the second drink. "How many cases do you have from the last harvest?"

"Don't know yet. The pinot is all still in barrel. Hayden's mulling what to bottle. We'll do some single vineyard, but he's planning an estate blend too." His excitement was palpable. It had to be incredibly exhilarating to start your own winery.

"Did you bring anything else tonight?"

"A couple of whites—a pinot gris and a chardonnay. You want to taste them? They're over at Hayden's table." He inclined his head to where a group of people stood milling about.

She hesitated but decided there was no harm in drinking wine with him. Plus, she wanted to meet the winemaker. "Sure. Looks like there's a bit of a buzz going on over there."

He stood up, smiling. "Just what we want." He held her chair, pulling it back as she stood.

She slipped the strap of her small clutch over her wrist and picked up her glass. Her friends' purses were still on the table, but they weren't her responsibility since they'd ditched her.

Brooke sipped her wine as they made their way to the other table. The man Cameron had been with earlier was there—evidently, Naomi hadn't been able to track him down. Or, perhaps more accurately, she'd found someone else.

Cameron stopped next to him. "Brooke, this is my brother Luke. He's the vineyard manager."

Brooke shook his hand. "Hi, I'm Brooke Ellis. I work for Willamette Distributors."

Luke nodded. "Good company. Nice to meet you."

She saw the resemblance between them in the dark shade of their hair, their wide foreheads, and the supple curve of their lips. Luke's eyes were a dark brown, while Cameron's were green. And where Luke had a faint beard, which a lot of women found sexy, Cameron was clean-shaven, which Brooke found even sexier. Overall, Luke exuded a casual, outdoorsy vibe, while Cameron looked more formal, from his expensive sandals to the crisp, pressed lines of his button-down shirt grazing his lean hips. He also smelled amazing, like clove and pine. She'd tag him at least slightly metrosexual, but in an exceedingly masculine way. Cameron Westcott was, unfortunately, precisely the kind of guy who did it for her.

Damn.

Cameron tapped another guy on the shoulder. He turned, and Brooke knew immediately he was another Westcott. He and Cameron were exactly the same height, possessed indistinguishable noses, and the set of their eyes was identical, though this one's were hazel.

"Brooke, this is our youngest brother, Jamie."

Jamie smiled, and she realized that together, all three brothers could probably power every string of lights hanging from the trees with the wattage from their smiles. Wow, what a cheesy thought.

"Pleased to make your acquaintance," he said with a slight bow.

Brooke smiled at him, her shoulders arching. "Very gallant."

Cameron rolled his eyes. "He lived in England for a couple of years and came back with these obnoxious manners."

Brooke gave him a prim stare. "I think they're nice."

Jamie laughed. "Score one for the little brother." He nodded toward the glass in her hand. "Did you try the pinot?"

She nodded. "It's excellent." She finished what was left in her glass. "I was hoping to sample the pinot gris or the chardonnay."

"Get the pinot gris first. It's running low." Jamie turned and reached past a woman to tap a man's arm. "Hayden, hand me the pinot gris."

The man, who Brooke surmised was Hayden Archer, gave Jamie the bottle. "Last one. Be judicious."

"Pouring for a wine distributor," Luke said, gesturing toward Brooke.

Hayden pivoted and stepped toward them with a smile. "Hi, I'm Hayden Archer."

Brooke took his hand. "Brooke Ellis, Willamette Distributors. Your pinot is amazing."

"Thanks. I'm glad you like it." He took her glass and went to grab a bottle of water from the table. "Can't let you drink the whites without a clean glass." He swirled water in the bowl and tossed it on the ground. "Much better." He handed it back to her, then took the bottle from Jamie to pour it himself.

As with the red, she swirled the liquid in her glass. She sniffed and picked up pear, lemongrass, and spearmint. When she tasted it, the flavors of starfruit and apricot danced across her tongue. She savored the swallow and took another. It was an incredibly refreshing wine for a hot summer night. "This is outstanding."

Hayden grinned. "Thank you. I appreciate that."

A voice interrupted them from the other side of the table. "Hey, Hayden, I hear you're pouring the best pinot gris in the place."

"Excuse me." Hayden gave her a warm smile before taking off around the table.

"This is a great night for him," Cameron said, proud of his friend and proud of West Arch.

Jamie raised his glass in a toast. "It's a great night for all of us."

Luke lifted his too. "That it is."

The three brothers tapped their glasses together, and Cameron looked at Brooke. He nodded toward her glass, and, mesmerized by his stare, she joined in.

"To West Arch," Cameron said. "And making new friends."

Friends? Yeah, okay, she could do that. But nothing more.

"On to the chardonnay?" he asked her.

"Definitely." He found a bottle on the table, and she finished her pinot gris to make room for the chardonnay.

He gave her a healthy pour. "We have plenty of this. It's still a bit young, but I think it'll be pretty damn special in about six months."

She tasted it and agreed with him. "Don't hate me, but I like the pinot gris more. That's a personal preference, though. Chardonnay has never been a favorite of mine."

"Me neither, actually." He lowered his voice. "I have a secret love for off-dry Riesling. I convinced Luke and Hayden to plant some last summer."

She liked Riesling too and proceeded to take him down a rathole of her favorite producers. She blushed as she realized she'd been talking for a few minutes without a break. "Sorry, I'm kind of passionate about wine."

"I like that—wine and passion are two of my favorite things."

She stared into his green eyes, fringed with ridiculously long, dark lashes, and thought she could dive right into their depths and never come up for air. Damn, that was even cheesier than her thought about their smiling. Then again, she'd already had a few glasses of wine since they'd arrived.

Wine. That was why she was here. Not to flirt with a guy with a horrible reputation. "Well, thanks for the wine. I appreciate you introducing me to it."

"It was my pleasure. Is there anything else you want to taste? I know a bunch of folks."

She tried not to laugh. "Um, I do too. Anyway, I should let you get to your adoring fans. You guys are attracting quite a buzz and rightly so."

She started to turn, but he touched her arm and moved closer. His scent was all around her, and he was near enough that she could feel his warmth. Her body instinctively gravitated toward him, but she willed herself not to bend. Not with Cameron Westcott. Hell, not with anyone. Ugh, her friends were right—she needed to get back out there. Except she wasn't sure she knew how.

"Stay with me. It'll be fun." His voice was low. Seductive. Dangerous. "Later we can cozy up by the bonfire."

Oh, he was *good*. And Jana was right about his fuckability factor—off the freaking charts. Her heart had sped up, and the sound of it beating seemed to flood her ears. This wasn't good. She wasn't ready. Not for this. Definitely not for him. "No, I think it's best if we say good night. Thanks for the wine."

His brow furrowed, but he let his fingers slip away from her arm. She felt a tinge of loss but vowed she wouldn't regret this.

"Can I call you?"

Damn, he was persistent. But she hadn't built a wall around herself since her divorce just to see it torn down in a single evening. "No." The lines in his forehead deepened. "Look, I'm sorry if I gave you the wrong idea. I didn't mean to be...flirty. But I'm not interested. *At all*."

He exhaled and took a step back from her. "Cool. I get it. See you around." The words were clipped, but not rude. He was trying to be a gentleman, because, well, maybe he *was* a gentleman, and since she'd given him the brush-off, he was doing his best to hide his disappointment.

Ugh. Now she felt bad. She turned from him before she could change her mind. Before regret took hold of her.

As she made her way back to her table, she realized it was too late.

Chapter Three

By the time noon rolled around on Friday, Cam and his cohorts—Luke, Jamie, and Hayden—were sweaty, disgusting messes. They'd spent the morning in the uppermost region of the vineyard, checking fruit, removing leaves, and pretty much getting as hot as possible. Not that Cam minded. He loved this job more than he thought possible. This morning, he was sweating it out in the vineyard, but later he'd be working in his office on a variety of things, from marketing to event planning and coordination to updating their website.

The four of them walked into the shade and air-conditioned comfort of the winery. Hayden turned as he took off his hat. "Too bad there's no salmon bake to look forward to tomorrow night." His exhalation held a wistful quality.

"Dude, you read my mind," Cam said, grinning. "I was just thinking about that. What a great night. We've had a lot of interest this week—the wine dinner next month is filling up fast."

"Excellent." Hayden shook his head and looked around at the other three. "I still can't believe this is actually happening."

Luke swept his hat off and wiped his forehead with the back of his hand. "Believe it."

Two years ago, Jamie had pitched the idea as a joke as they'd sat drinking beer in Hayden's family's flagship brewpub, The Arch and Vine, in the center of Ribbon Ridge. It hadn't been a serious discussion, but every one of them had walked away thinking about the possibilities. For Cameron, he'd been tired of traveling, of feeling disconnected. His parents, particularly his mother, had constantly hounded him about being gone so much, but in the early years, he'd needed that lifestyle. He'd thrived on the unexpected, the sense of adventure, and excelling at his job.

But the opportunity to start something with his brothers and his best friend had grabbed him hard and fast. He'd immersed himself in it ever since.

"How are things coming for the wine dinner?" Jamie asked.

Cam and Hayden were working on it with Hayden's brother Kyle and his sister Sara. The Archers owned and operated a luxury hotel, The Alex, in the hills over Ribbon Ridge, and Kyle, a world-class celebrity chef, managed the restaurant, The Arch and Fox, while Sara was the event manager for the entire property. It was a no-brainer for them to unveil the wines of West Arch there. The dinner would take place the weekend after Labor Day, just six weeks from now.

"Kyle and Sara are on top of the logistics," Cam said. "I'd like to get some high level wine critics in so I'll be working that angle."

Jamie threw him a humor-filled, teasing little brother look. "Is Brooke Ellis coming to the dinner?"

Cam knew Jamie was flipping him shit. "I didn't invite her." Not after she'd turned his overtures down flat.

Luke set his hat back on his head. "I was surprised she left before you. Or did you hook up later?"

"Nope."

Hayden looked at him in mock pity. "Damn, I think you're losing your touch."

Cam snorted, but there was a bit of truth in Hayden's words. Since Cam had noted that his love life had tamed over the past two years, he'd started to think about why. It had to be because he was too busy. Anyway, he wasn't a monk.

Jamie set his hands on his hips. "What happened there? She seemed kind of flirty when we were tasting the wine."

Yeah, Cam had thought so too, but she'd set him straight. He'd certainly tried—three times, and that was his rule: three strikes, and he was out. Total bummer because he'd really liked her. She was funny and smart. He could've talked wine with her into the wee hours. Now he was disappointed that he never would.

Cam lifted a shoulder as he answered his brother. "It's no big deal. Just no connection there."

Luke blew out a breath. "Too bad. Man, her friend was pretty eager, though. She stalked me all night."

The tall one with the long, dark hair and the sultry eyes. Very attractive, and yeah, she'd hung around, even after Brooke had gone. "I saw that," Cam said. "What happened?"

Luke shrugged. "Nothing."

"You give me shit about being a player, but you're a regular hermit when it comes to female companionship."

Luke arched a brow. "And how would you know?"

Cam nodded toward Jamie. "Because you live with him, and you apparently hardly ever date."

Luke elbowed Jamie in the arm. "What the hell, bro?"

Jamie elbowed him back. "What the hell is right. You *don't* date. No big deal. I guess it's because of your ex back in California, but who knows, since you never want to talk about her."

Luke made a noise that was half snort and half scoff. "Whatever. I'm grabbing some lunch, then heading back out." He'd spend the rest of the day with his vines.

"I'll join you later," Hayden called after him.

Luke waved his hand as he started up the stairs to the uppermost floor, where they all had offices with bathrooms—and what Cam was most after: a shower.

"I'm running home for lunch," Hayden said. He and his wife, Bex, had built a house last year on a couple of acres just up the road. "See you guys in a bit."

Jamie turned toward the stairs that Luke had gone up. "I need a shower, and then I've got numbers to crunch."

"Ditto," Cam said. "On the shower anyway. Keep your numbers away from me."

Jamie was terrifyingly intelligent, with multiple master's degrees from the London School of Economics. He took care of everything and anything to do with money, and Cam had no doubt he'd see this winery turning a profit in no time.

Jamie chuckled as they went upstairs together. They parted at the top. Jamie's and Luke's offices were on the south side of the building, while Cam's and Hayden's were on the north. The center portion was claimed by a large space, some of which would go to employees they would hire down the road, plus a conference room overlooking the vineyard.

Cam went to his office and beelined for the bathroom he shared with Hayden. While toweling off after his shower, he heard his phone ring. Wrapping the towel around his waist, he dashed out and picked up the receiver, but it was too late.

He set the phone down and started back toward the bathroom, then froze at the sound of a feminine voice.

"Hello?"

The query came from outside his office. He went to his door, which was ajar, and peered through the space. At the same moment, Brooke Ellis's blue-green gaze connected with his.

And here he was in nothing but a towel. He stifled a smile at his luck.

"Uh, I can come back later," she said, clearly trying not to look south of his face and failing miserably.

"No, it's fine. Come in." He opened the door wider.

She hesitated.

"You can sit while I get dressed," he said.

Her eyes widened briefly. "Really, I can come back later. Or wait out here."

He laughed. "I wasn't going to get dressed in front of you. Unless you want me to."

Pink bloomed in her cheeks. "Clearly, I don't."

"I have chairs in here. And a couch." Her eyes widened again, and again he tried not to laugh. "That you can *sit* on while I go into the bathroom, *close the door*, and make myself presentable. Sound good?"

Still, she hesitated, but finally said, "Sure." She walked toward him slowly, and he couldn't help but appreciate the view. She wore a sleeveless red-and-white-floral sundress with red sandals. Her toenails were painted red too, and they'd been coral the other night. Yeah, he noticed things like that. Just like he noticed the sexy gold chain hugging her ankle.

She stepped into the office, and he gestured to the mini fridge tucked beneath a granite counter in the corner. "Help yourself to whatever," he said. "There's water, iced tea, and a Riesling." He winked at her before going into the bathroom to get dressed.

He hurried, half afraid she would leave before he could finish and curious as hell as to why she'd come.

When he went back out, she was standing at the floor-to-ceiling windows, which afforded a stunning view of the vine-yard and Ribbon Ridge beyond.

"This is gorgeous. How do you work? I'd just stare at this all day."

He moved to stand beside her. "Sometimes it's tough, I'll admit. But I do love my job, so that helps."

"I bet," she murmured, and he loved the dark, seductive sound of her voice.

He looked at her empty hands. "You didn't get anything to drink?"

She turned her head to look at him. "I didn't want to open the Riesling."

"Not one of your favorites?"

"Just the opposite. It would be a shame to open it now and have just one glass."

Cam grinned. "So, we'll have more than one."

Her lips curved into a half-smile. "I'm working."

He went to the fridge and grabbed a sparkling water. "Is that why you're here?" He downed half the bottle before sitting in the comfy leather chair that was angled near the couch.

She came to join him, perching on the dark brown leather sofa, where she'd dropped her shoulder bag. "Yes, actually."

"Bummer. I was hoping you'd changed your mind about going out with me."

She smoothed her hand over her skirt, which fell across her knee. "I don't remember you asking me out. You asked if you could call me."

"You are *such* a stickler for details."

"I'm a stickler for accuracy." She straightened, assuming a businesslike posture. "Anyway, let's stay on topic, shall we?"

Damn, he loved talking to her, even if they were sparring. Especially if they were sparring. She was sharp and engaging—flirty, even if she didn't mean to be. "By all means."

"I came to talk to you about your wine. Have you selected a distributor yet?"

He should've seen this coming, but he'd been too distracted by his attraction to her. "No. You think it should be you?"

"I do. I love your wines, and I think I have a good handle on how to sell them."

He didn't disagree. Her comments about them reflected a keen knowledge and a true love of wine. Still, he wanted to make her work for this. A woman he used to see had once called him sadistic because he'd taunted her too much in bed. Maybe she was right.

"Tell me how." He sat back in the chair and took another drink of water, all while scrutinizing her and thinking about his damn three-strikes rule. He wanted to ignore it and try again. Hell, he wanted to torch it to the ground and put everything he had into pursuing her, but he wasn't a stalker. Still, if they hired her as their distributor, they'd see each other often enough, and maybe that would be all he needed to wear her down. She couldn't be disinterested. Not with the way she flirted. And definitely not with the way she'd checked him out in his towel.

"My territory is western Oregon and Washington. I have great contacts. Before I moved here, I worked for the Southern Oregon Wine Collective."

Cam had worked with them a little when he'd been at Blackthorn Cellars. "That's a great outfit. Why'd you leave there to come here?"

She hesitated just long enough to make him curious. "It was a promotion." Her gaze darted toward the windows, and that slight telltale sign of nervousness made him even more curious.

"Is that where you're from—southern Oregon?"

"Yes, Medford."

He wished she would open up more. He wondered if she was just trying to keep things focused on business with him or if she was this closed off with everyone. "You go to Southern Oregon University?"

"I did."

"I went to Oregon State." He cocked his head and studied her a moment. She looked confident in the way she held herself and assured in the manner in which she spoke. Even so, he sensed an underlying uncertainty. "You don't like to talk about yourself, do you?"

"Not in this sort of environment, though I understand you wanting to understand my professional experience and expertise." She then launched into an overview of her accounts in her territory and how she went about selling wine. She also impressed the hell out of him.

"You really know your stuff," he said when she was finished. "But this isn't just up to me. I have to talk about it with my partners."

"Sure, I understand. Let me know what you decide. I'd love the opportunity." She grabbed her bag and stood up.

He jumped to his feet, sorry that their interlude was over. That meant they needed another one. "I'll talk to them as soon as possible," he said. "We're formally unveiling the pinot at a wine dinner in early September. It would be great to have a distributor in place to spark some buzz. How about we have dinner to discuss it?"

She'd started walking toward his office door, but paused and turned, her brow arched. "Tonight? I'm headed down to Medford for the weekend. It's my younger sister's birthday."

"Next week then. How about Tuesday? We could go up to The Arch and Fox. Or Georgia's." Those were the two best restaurants in Ribbon Ridge.

"Sure, I'd love to talk to the others in person." She flashed him a bright smile that made his stomach flip with its intensity and beauty. "That way they can see what a great salesperson I am."

Oh, he could see it, and he was completely smitten. He'd buy whatever the hell she wanted to sell him. She'd neatly turned what could've become a date into a business meeting with other people so that she didn't have to be alone with him. He couldn't help but respect her prowess. "You're formidable," he said as he held the office door open and gestured for her to precede him. "I'll walk you out."

She started down the stairs. "This is an amazing facility. When will you be open for tasting?"

He trailed her to the main floor. "Not until November. The tasting room's not done yet. Hey, do you want a tour?"

"I do, but I can't today. I have another appointment I need to get to."

He understood. The workday of a wine distributor was busy at best and positively frenetic at worst.

He moved through the unfinished tasting room and passed her to open the door to the parking area in front. "After you."

She walked by him, and he inhaled her sweet, intoxicating scent. It certainly looked as though he was going to blow right through his three-strikes rule. He couldn't seem to help himself.

She dug into her bag and pulled out a pair of sunglasses, then slid them on, shielding her magnificent blue-green eyes. What a shame. But he couldn't deny she was just as sexy with the Burberry shades.

He didn't have his sunglasses on him, so he used his hand to shield his eyes. "I'll see you Tuesday night—you didn't pick where."

"Georgia's. It's close to where I live. I'll meet you there at seven."

"Perfect." It was close to where he lived too, and he wondered if they were maybe neighbors. He surely would've run into her, but maybe she was new to the neighborhood. He wanted to ask—hell, he wanted to know everything about her—but decided to save it for Tuesday night. For their date. Because, sadly, his partners weren't going to be able to make it.

"See you then." She turned and went to her car, a fairly new, dark gray Acura MDX, and climbed inside.

He waited until she drove away before going back into the winery. That was when the reality of what he was doing hit him. He was pursuing her. But for what? He hadn't lied about not being a player anymore, but he also didn't usually feel this way about a woman.

And what way was that? Like he wanted to know everything about her. Like he wanted to talk with her long into the night. Like he wanted to share himself.

Cold dread curled up his spine. He liked women. Loved them, in fact. And he did his best to be honest and give them a great time for however long they were together. He never, ever wanted to hurt anyone, and he'd been careful not to do so. Eight years on, and his own pain still lingered, still made him want to keep things casual and...safe.

He'd be damned sure to continue that.

Chapter Four

Brooke walked into Georgia's just before seven on Tuesday. It seemed especially dim inside after the brightness of outside. The hostess greeted her, and Brooke said she was meeting the Westcotts.

Smiling, the hostess said, "Right this way." She led Brooke to a small table in the corner in front of a window. It was empty but only had two seats.

"You beat me here." Cameron came up behind her, and Brooke turned.

She narrowed her eyes at him, uncertain of his motives before looking at the hostess. "We'll need a table for five, actually."

"Uh, no, we don't," Cameron said. He went to the table and held out a chair for her. "I'm afraid it's just us. My brothers and Hayden couldn't make it."

She didn't believe that for a second but didn't say so. Not yet anyway. She threw him a skeptical glare but took the proffered seat and set her purse on the floor beside her.

Cameron sat across from her as the hostess handed them their menus and told them about the specials. He looked up at her and asked, "Can we have a bottle of the 2012 Bergstrom Pinot?"

"Sure thing." She turned and left.

Brooke peered at him over her menu. "I don't get to choose the wine? Or at least consult?"

He looked mildly offended. "That's a fantastic bottle of wine I ordered. You disagree?"

No, she couldn't disagree. "It might have been nice if you'd asked. I was in the mood for Beaux Frères."

"Then I'll order that too." He set his menu down and looked at her. "I'm sorry. Really. I should've asked what you wanted to drink." His lips twisted into a half-smile. "That's what I get for trying to impress you."

Now she felt shrewish. But could she blame herself when she was clearly being manipulated? "Where are your brothers and Hayden, really?"

He picked the menu back up and studied it. "Busy."

"Did you even invite them?" She should've contacted them herself.

He didn't look up from the menu. "I, ah, mentioned it."

She shook her head and repeated what she'd told him at the salmon bake. "You *are* a menace."

Now he lifted his gaze, and his eyes sparked with mirth. "I thought we'd resolved that you ran into me at the salmon bake. Or is this something you're going to hold over me forever?"

Forever. That intimated a shared future. Did that mean she'd won the contract with the winery, or did he have other... plans, of a more personal nature? She narrowed her eyes again. "You're not scoring a lot of points here."

He laughed. "Tell you what. You order my dinner. I'll eat whatever you choose."

It was a silly offer, but she planned to take it. She looked over the appetizers and entrées. "Any dietary issues I need to be aware of?"

"What, like am I vegan or gluten-free? No and no. I'm full glutton."

She glanced at him, and though he was seated now, she'd noted his slim khakis and the way they hugged his hips. "I don't buy that for a second. You're in too good a shape."

He grinned at her. "Glad you noticed. It's all that work in the vineyard. Keeps us hopping."

Great, now he thought she'd been checking him out. Which she had. She couldn't help it. He was very attractive with his perfectly styled brown hair, seductive green eyes, and sexy-casual sense of style. Plus, she knew that underneath his shirt he possessed a spectacular set of abs. Add in his killer smile, and she could very easily be in trouble.

Which was why she had to be on her guard.

Their server arrived then and poured the wine. Cameron indicated that she should taste the sample, which she did. He'd chosen exceptionally well, damn him. She nodded at the server, who filled their glasses and said he'd be back shortly to take their order.

Brooke perused the possibilities and considered ordering him the vegan risotto just to be a pain in the ass but decided not to.

"So what am I eating?" he asked, interrupting her selection process.

"I'm having the filet, and you're having the duck."

"Excellent, though I might've chosen the filet too."

"Too bad. You gave me full control."

He picked up his wine and gave her a sly, sultry smile. "You can have all the control you want." He held his glass toward her. "To relinquishing control."

She rolled her eyes but clinked her glass against his. "Your attempts at flirtation are lame and pointless. This is a business dinner. If we aren't going to talk about business, I'll go. I have plenty to do at home."

Though she'd moved into her loft four weeks ago, she still had a few boxes to unpack and pictures to hang.

He sipped his wine. "Okay, let's talk business. You've got the job."

Triumph surged in her chest. This would be a great account. "Thanks. You *did* talk to your brothers and Hayden, right?"

"Of course I did. We're full partners."

"And they didn't want to meet with me?"

He arched a brow at her. "They met you at the salmon bake and, given my background in sales and marketing, they trust my judgment."

That made sense. She still wished she'd had the chance to talk with them. "I was kind of looking forward to discussing the winemaking."

"You still can. Why don't you come by this weekend for that tour? We're there every day. Luke will take you around the vineyard, and Hayden will tell you more than you want to know about his process."

"I'd love that. How about Saturday around one?"

"Done."

She reached down to grab her purse. "Well, I guess we don't really need to have dinner, do we?"

"Wait." He gestured toward the wine bottle on the table. "We have all this fantastic wine to drink, and now I have my mouth set on that duck. Plus, it's not like we don't have things to discuss. I could give you a complete overview of our wine catalog—small though it is at present." He glanced toward the approaching server. "He's coming back to take our order. I'll leave my fate in your hands." He sat back in his chair and watched her.

He seemed dead set on letting her be in control, which meant she could conclude this evening right now. Except as soon as the server arrived, she placed their order.

When they were alone once more, Cameron sat forward. "I'm surprised. But pleased." His gaze brimmed with anticipation. "Thank you."

She was pretty sure he was looking at this as some kind of date, or at least half business, half date, so she cast him an arch look. "This isn't a date." Was she informing him or herself? She had to admit she liked Cameron, and she found his persistence... Well, she wasn't sure what she found it. But she didn't *dislike* it. "Tell me about your wines."

He smiled broadly. "Happy to."

He spent the next ten minutes telling her how they'd started the winery two years ago, and that they'd only claimed a small percentage of grapes from that vintage. They'd made some limited cases of chardonnay and pinot gris, and slightly more of a pinot noir—the one she'd tasted the other night. Last year, the entire yield was theirs, which had given them a good supply of the whites and would generate a handful of varieties of pinot noir.

His enthusiasm was infectious. Brooke smiled as she wrapped her fingertips around the stem of her glass. "I can't wait to come see the operation and taste everything you've got."

He started to smile and maybe open his mouth, but he took a drink of wine instead.

She narrowed her eyes at him. "Were you going to make some sort of innuendo?"

He set his glass down and sighed. "Guilty as charged. Sorry, I really am trying to keep to business. At the same time, I have to tell you that I'm incredibly attracted to you." He said this with a matter-of-fact tone, without intensity, without any layered nuance. It made her shiver nonetheless. "Sorry, I probably shouldn't have said that since we *do* have a business relationship, but you'll find that I'm a straight shooter. I figured I had two choices—ignore that attraction or come clean. The former seems kind of impossible, so I went with the latter." He grinned at her.

She was having a hard time thinking of him as a smarmy player when he was so forthright and charming. She was inconveniently attracted to him too. But she didn't say so. "I appreciate you focusing on business—and I would appreciate you *trying* to ignore your, uh, attraction. Because that's so not happening. That said, I, ah, I have to admit you aren't quite what I expected."

"Uh-oh. I'm not sure if that's good or bad."

"Good, I think. I expected you to be, I don't know...*cheesy*." She shrugged. "And I guess you are."

"I am?" He sounded incredulous but laughed.

"A little." She grinned. "But it's kind of cute."

His eyes sparkled as he smiled at her. "I'll take it."

Their dinners arrived, and the conversation turned to wine once more. She was shocked to learn he hadn't been to France.

He shook his head. "I know, right? And my best friend was making wine over there for a year."

She scooped a bite of garlic mashed potatoes. "Hayden?"

He nodded. "He interned in Burgundy before we started up West Arch. I'd meant to go but just couldn't get away that year. I take it you've been?"

"Yeah, a few times."

"A *few* times. I'm green with envy."

"Well, the first time was a college trip to Paris. But since then, I've been a couple of times. We hit Burgundy on the first trip and Bordeaux on the second."

He swallowed a bite of duck and washed it back with sip of wine. "Who's 'we'?"

Crap, she'd walked right into that one. But her marriage wasn't a secret. "Uh, my ex."

"Boyfriend?"

She cut a piece of steak. "Husband."

"Ah. A little more complicated. Why is he your ex?"

That wasn't a secret per se either, but it was firmly in the do-not-discuss-with-almost-everybody category. "Complicated is the perfect word. Also boring. You don't really want to hear about my ex-husband, do you?"

His lips split into a smile. "Actually, no, I do not. What I would like is a bite of that steak, since that's what I would've ordered."

She looked at the piece of meat on her fork. "I don't know. This is really good. I'm not sure I want to share."

"Pretty please? I'll give you a piece of duck." He batted his eyelashes for added persuasion, but it only made him look ridiculous.

Brooke giggled. "I don't actually like duck."

His forehead wrinkled. "You ordered me something you don't even like?" He chuckled. "Well played."

"Sorry. It honestly didn't occur to me that *you* wouldn't like it. You said you were full glutton after all."

"That's true. I love food, including duck, and I'll try pretty much anything. Just don't ask me to cook it."

"Is that right? I love to cook." She was ecstatic to have her own kitchen after sharing a house with Jana the past year. She'd moved in with her former college roommate when she'd first moved up here.

"Then you should cook for me some time, especially if we're neighbors. You said you lived nearby, right?"

"Yes. Do you want this steak or not?" She waved the fork at him.

"Oh, I want it."

She rolled her eyes as she leaned forward and held it to him to take the bite. "You can't keep yourself from flirting, can you?"

He chewed and swallowed, his lips curving into a satisfied smile. "That is amazing. You definitely have the better dinner. And clearly I *can* help myself. I did earlier, remember?"

She remembered. She acknowledged that she liked his flirtatious behavior. It wasn't over the top—yet. Still, she steered the conversation to something safer, if such a thing existed with Cameron Westcott. "Have you lived in Ribbon Ridge a long time?"

"My whole life. My dad's the middle school principal, and my mom's the head secretary at the elementary school."

"And you have just the two brothers?"

He forked a green bean. "Three, actually. I have a half-brother."

"He's not in on your winery?"

"He built it, actually. He's a contractor. Super busy now too —thanks to The Alex Hotel and the winery, he has more commercial projects than he can handle."

"Wow." Brooke remembered reading about The Alex when it had opened. It was a former monastery and current luxury hotel in the hills over Ribbon Ridge. It was owned and operated by the Archers, who also owned her building. "This really is a small town, isn't it?"

He nodded. "Totally. I assumed you were new here since I hadn't met you before."

"I only moved in about a month ago. I was living in Newberg before that."

He slid the rest of his duck onto his fork. "What drew you to Ribbon Ridge?"

"I just wanted a place of my own—I had a roommate before —and this was the first place I found."

"Seems like you're going out of your way to avoid telling me where you live." He chuckled again as he sat back. "Just so you know, I have every intention of asking to walk you home."

She actually hadn't been trying *not* to tell him. "It isn't a secret—I live in the lofts over on Second."

His mouth spread into a wide smile. "And I live directly across the street in one of the row houses."

Of course he did. She shook her head and tipped it down toward her plate, an answering smile tugging at her lips. She finally gave in and looked at him. "How convenient."

His eyes glinted with humor and something else that made her stomach flip. "Very."

She finished the last of her dinner, and he poured the remainder of the wine into their glasses.

He swirled the wine in his glass as he studied her. "I wondered if you moved here to get away from the ex. Was he the roommate in Newberg?"

"I thought we agreed that was a boring topic."

"We did, my bad. I find you infinitely interesting—even the boring topics." He took a drink of wine, and his gaze was intense, provocative.

"Maybe we should go back to talking about business. We should schedule a meeting—maybe next week—to discuss the quantity of product you want me to sell. I'd like to get started."

"Sounds good. We're doing a formal debut at a dinner at The Arch and Fox in September. If you have some people you think would be good to invite, let me know."

A few people came immediately to mind, but she'd put together a list for him. "Well, me, for one."

"Consider yourself seated at my table."

She laughed softly, expecting him to say something like that. "I'll get you a list tomorrow."

Their server returned to take their plates and asked if they wanted dessert. Neither had room, so Cameron asked for the check. After the server had left, he finished his wine. "I should've asked if you wanted a late harvest Riesling or a port."

"I'm fine. Don't get me wrong, I rarely turn down a good wine, but I should get home. I have an early start tomorrow."

The server brought the check, and Cameron paid it. "It's business," he said, glancing up at her with mirth in his eyes. "Not a date."

No, it wasn't a date, but it had contained date-like moments. She'd forgotten how nice those could be.

He put his credit card away and looked over at her. "Ready?"

"Yep." She grabbed her purse and stood.

He gestured for her to precede him from the restaurant. The sun was starting to set, casting the sidewalk in golden shadow. "It seems silly to ask if I can walk you home since we're going in the same direction."

"It does." She thought back to his arrival just after her. "Did you follow me earlier?"

"No, I made a stop on the way so I came from the opposite direction."

They crossed the street and made their way toward Second. She glanced over at his profile. She'd had a good time tonight. She liked him. A real date might be nice... But this was Cameron Westcott. Did he even do real dates?

She readjusted the strap of her purse on her shoulder. "So, tell me how you came to be a player."

He barked out a laugh. "You nearly made me trip. Not going to beat around the bush with that one, huh?" He looked over at her, smiling.

"Nope. I'm taking a page from your playbook and shooting straight. You don't deny your reputation?"

"Nope," he echoed. "I will say that I've mellowed a bit recently. I'm too busy with the winery."

"So if not for the winery, you'd be up to your usual shenanigans."

"Shenanigans... Yes, I suppose so." He lifted a shoulder. "Maybe not. I don't know. What do you mean by 'shenanigans'?"

She kept her gaze forward. "I hear you had a different girl in every city when you were on the road."

They turned the corner, and she stopped as they reached the door to her building.

He stopped too and turned toward her. "Not *every* city. And anyway, I don't travel anymore."

"Right. You're busy. Does that mean you don't date?"

He moved closer. "Are you asking me out?"

The scent of his cologne stole over her. The green of his eyes at this range was so deep, so captivating, she could easily sway toward him and... She straightened her shoulders. "No."

"Well, that's a damn shame." His words carried a dark, seductive tone of regret. "Guess I'll have to ask you out—since I wasn't clear about it before."

"No. Thank you," she rushed to add. "I had a nice time tonight, but I'd prefer to keep our relationship strictly professional."

"Too bad," he said softly. "I was sort of hoping I could kiss you."

Standing here with him in the early twilight, feeling the intoxicating burn of his stare, she was sort of hoping that too. But she hadn't done that in so long... And she wasn't ready. Okay, her body was totally ready, but her mind was still trying to figure out what the hell to do with Cameron Westcott.

"Cameron—"

"Cam. Everyone calls me Cam." He inched closer so that she could *feel* his proximity, and heat raced through her. "At least everyone who likes me."

"Cam, I—"

"Oh good, you like me."

She couldn't help smiling. He was good at that—making her smile. No one had been good at that in a very long time. Not even herself. Especially not herself. "I do. And... Well, ask me again sometime."

Had she just said that out loud?

"If I can kiss you?" He leaned forward, putting his lips against her ear. "Count on it." He stepped back. "Good night."

"Good night." She watched him cross the street to the row house on the end, directly across from her. She expected him to turn and look at her, wave or something. But he didn't. He walked inside and closed the door, leaving her to wonder if she should've listened to her body instead.

Chapter Five

After finishing the last bite of his dad's mouthwatering ribs, Cam wondered for the thousandth time why he couldn't cook. It just wasn't fair, not when his dad was so good at it. Maybe he should try again. "Dad, will you send me the recipe one more time?"

Cam's mom's head snapped toward him. Her green eyes, which Cam had inherited, widened in shock. "You're going to cook something?"

Everyone chuckled around the table, which prompted Emma to squeal in her high chair between her parents. Sara and Dylan both turned to their five-month-old daughter and made silly faces and nonsensical comments. Cam smiled as he answered his mom, "I'm going to *try* to cook something. Don't hold your breath."

Mom got up and started gathering plates. Sara joined her, saying, "Let me help you clear the table."

Dad jumped to his feet. "Come on boys. Sara, sit and enjoy your daughter." When Dylan stood, Dad waved him back down. "Not you. The other ones."

Dylan leaned back in his chair and grinned tauntingly at his half-brothers.

Cam picked up his plate and one of the serving dishes and bussed them to the kitchen, passing Dad on his way back out. Mom stood at the open dishwasher and shook her head at her three sons. "Look at all of you—*alone*. Couldn't one of you have brought a date tonight?"

Cam and Luke and Jamie exchanged glances, but it was Cam who spoke. "Don't look at me. You know I'm a committed bachelor. Jamie's the one with a girlfriend. Where's Madison?"

He shrugged. "Busy."

Mom frowned. "You've only brought her over once. Didn't she like us?"

Jamie set the dishes he'd brought on the counter. "We've only been dating a couple of months, and we're not that serious. But really, she's just busy tonight."

"I see." Mom pursed her lips as she started loading dishes in the dishwasher. "What about you, Luke? Why aren't you dating someone?"

"Because he's still hung up on Paige," Jamie said.

Luke scowled at him. "You're full of crap. I don't have time to date anyone. It's summertime, and I've got crops to tend."

Jamie smiled at him. "You're such a good target."

Luke punched him in the arm.

"Ow!" Jamie massaged his bicep.

Luke grinned. "You're a good target too."

Mom straightened. "Boys, knock it off." She added another dish and then lifted her gaze to Cam's. "Maybe if you're willing to try cooking, you'll be willing to try dating someone. It won't kill you, you know."

No, it wouldn't, but his heart had barely recovered from his last girlfriend, and he had no desire to put it to another test. At least not yet and maybe not ever. "Maybe someday, Mom, but like Luke, I'm busy with the winery right now. Sorry, but you're going to have to get your grandma fix with Emma."

That was what this was really about. She adored her step-granddaughter, but she was still just a "step." Mom had never fully embraced Dylan as her son, not when his own mother was still a big part of his life. On one hand, Cam understood her not wanting to intrude on Dylan's relationship with his mother, but on the other, Cam thought Dylan might have liked that, especially when he was growing up living in two households for a week at a time. It had been a chaotic upbringing, and Cam hated that Dylan had suffered because of it.

Cam supposed it probably played into his reluctance to settle down. Divorce was a common occurrence, and the breakup he'd gone through eight years ago had been just as devastating. He couldn't imagine going through that after marrying someone, especially if they had children.

"And why not?" Luke asked, addressing Cam's comment about getting her grandma fix. "Emma's adorable. In fact, why don't you go do the grandma thing, and we'll finish up in here?"

Mom stopped and looked at them. "Really? That's very nice of you." She smiled, and the warmth in her gaze was full of love and pride. "I have the nicest boys. Thank you." She hugged each of them and started for the dining room but turned back. "Wait, I bet Emma would like a cookie." She grabbed a box of some sort of baby biscuits from the pantry and left.

Luke wiped his hand over his brow. "Whew, dodged that bullet."

Jamie started filling the dishwasher, and Cam went to rinse dishes.

"I knew you weren't just being nice," Jamie said, laughing.

"Hey, whatever it takes to end the inquisition." Luke sent their little brother an arch look. "Unless you'd like me to call her back so she can ask you more questions about why Madison isn't here."

Jamie shuddered. "No, thanks. We've got a low-key thing going. I realized as soon as I brought her to brunch here last month that it was a dumb move. Mom hasn't stopped asking about her since."

Cam handed him a bowl for the dishwasher. "Madison didn't dump you after that, huh?"

"Nah, she actually thought it was cute. She felt flattered that Mom was so interested in her."

Cam wasn't surprised. Their mother could be intense, but she was also fun, and she had no trouble chatting people up. She had a great knack for finding a common topic and making people feel engaged and included. He'd employed some of her techniques in sales situations, and they'd worked well for him.

Jamie pronounced the dishwasher full, so Cam dropped a soap packet into it and programmed it to run later. "You know," Jamie said, "you're both using the winery as an excuse to live a monk-like existence. Cam, I get why you're doing it. I mean, it's been eight freaking years, but whatever. But Luke, from what I can tell, your breakup with Paige wasn't tough. Or is there something you're not telling us?"

Luke and Paige had been together for about three and a half years—most of them in California. They'd tried a long-distance relationship when he'd moved back here two years ago, but it had barely lasted a year. Luke didn't disclose much, so they all assumed the long-distance thing just hadn't worked out. Cam also assumed things hadn't been that serious since she hadn't moved with him. She worked for a winery. It wasn't as if there weren't any winery jobs around Ribbon Ridge.

Luke shook his head. "Don't do Mom's dirty work for her."

Jamie laughed. "Not guilty. Just trying to figure you guys out."

"Why, so you can write a dissertation on romantic relation-ships?" Cam asked. He was only half kidding. Jamie had told them just yesterday that he was considering pursuing a PhD.

"Ha. Very funny." Jamie leaned back against the counter and folded his arms. "I'm all about the money, man. No psychology or human development for me." Yes, he was a numbers guy through and through. In fact, he was probably the least likely of them to succeed in a romantic relationship given his overly analytical mind. He wasn't so great at demonstrating emotion.

"I'm thinking it's ironic that you're the one in a relation-ship," Cam said.

Luke grabbed a beer from the fridge and nodded. "Good call." He held up the bottle. "Anyone else?"

"Hit me." Cam held out his hand, and Jamie did the same.

"Let's not get all crazy and call my thing with Madison a relationship," Jamie said. "We hook up once or twice a week maybe. It's extremely casual."

Luke pulled the bottle opener from a drawer and popped his top, then handed it off to Jamie. "Is it exclusive?"

Jamie opened his bottle and rolled his eyes, grinning as he gave the opener to Cam. "Yes. I'm not Cam."

Cam was used to their teasing, but of late it had grown stale. Why did he care? They weren't wrong. He didn't do exclusivity. Not since She-Who-Shall-Not-Be-Named.

"True. My bad." Luke lifted his bottle. "To doing whatever the hell we damn well please."

Jamie stepped forward and tapped his bottle to Luke's. "Indeed."

Cam did the same but felt a strange knot in his gut. He'd spent eight years guarding himself from pain and heartbreak, but was that how he planned to spend his entire life? For the first time, he didn't really know.

Brooke crossed the finish line of the 10k two seconds before Jana. Naomi, who ran much faster than either of them and had likely finished at least five minutes ago, waved at them from just past the finish area.

After collecting their medals and grabbing waters, Brooke and Jana joined Naomi, who appeared rested and beautiful.

"You barely look like you ran a race," Jana said, her face still red. "I hate you right now."

Naomi laughed. "I run at least five miles every day. This is like a walk in the park for me."

Jana glared at her. "You're not helping defuse my hatred."

Naomi laughed harder. "Sorry."

Jana looked down at herself and made a face. "It's not fair. You have the legs of a gazelle, while mine are like a rhino."

Brooke laughed. Naomi was blessed with long, athletic legs. Her form was built for running, whereas Jana was curvier, and yeah, her legs were kind of short. "Not a rhino. How about a miniature horse?" Brooke suggested.

Jana transferred her glare to Brooke. "You're not helping either." She suddenly laughed. "Screw it. I need a beer. This after-party has beer, right?"

"Yep, and rum." Naomi rubbed her hands together. "And hot guys. I chatted with a trio who finished right behind me. They're waiting for us in the beer garden."

Jana nearly choked on her water. "Ack! I look like hell!"

"You look awesome!" Naomi said. "That shirt does amazing things for your boobs. Which are already amazing. You can envy my legs all you want, but your tits are, well, *tits*."

Brooke snorted. Saying things were "tits," meaning "fantastic," had become Naomi's latest catchphrase.

Jana tossed a bit of water at Naomi, and she jumped back,

laughing. "Yeah, well you can *buy* tits if you want them so badly. I'll never have your legs."

Naomi continued to laugh. "True."

With nothing more to contribute to this odd conversation, Brooke finished the last of her water. "I think I'm going to take off."

Both Naomi and Jana turned toward her. "No!" Jana said, her brows slanting over her eyes. "You always bail when we try to hook you up."

"Yes, because I don't want to be hooked up." Their incessant prodding was one of the reasons—maybe the primary reason— she'd moved out of Jana's townhouse and stopped hanging out with them as much. She'd invited them to the salmon bake thinking they'd maybe just want to have a girls' night. But no, they'd both been on the prowl as usual.

"You'd be a lot happier if you just got laid," Naomi said. "And these guys are *hot*."

She probably wasn't wrong—Brooke hadn't had sex in ages. But she also wasn't interested in just having sex with some rando. "Thanks, but I'll pass. See you guys."

She smiled and waved before she turned, hoping to take the sting out of her departure. She didn't want them to think she was mad. At the same time, she couldn't think of when she might call them to hang out again, which bummed her out. She'd latched on to Jana when she'd moved up here from Medford because she was the only person Brooke had known in the area. Then Jana had introduced her to Naomi, and it had seemed like she'd anchored herself with a couple of good friends. But now she realized that wasn't really the case. Maybe she'd have better luck in Ribbon Ridge.

She thought of Cam. Was he her friend? Maybe, but he was also a coworker. Neither the same as having girlfriends. Hopefully she'd find some, or she was going to get very homesick. And she didn't want to go back home. There were too many memories. Too many things she wanted to block from her mind, including her ex-husband.

She drove back to Ribbon Ridge and decided to stop for a coffee. Her favorite brew was at a little place called Stella's. It was a few blocks from her loft, so she drove straight there and was lucky enough to park right outside.

As she walked to the entrance, the door opened and out walked Cam sipping on a tall iced beverage. "Well, if it isn't Brooke Ellis," he said, smiling as he slipped his sunglasses on. His gaze dipped over her. "You already ran a race this morning?"

She looked down and realized she hadn't removed her bib with the race number. "Yeah, a 10k over in Newberg. And now I need a coffee if I'm going to make it through the day."

"Definitely—I know you have an important appointment this afternoon."

She chuckled. "With you. Yes, very important."

"Hey, I've been looking forward to it since we set it up."

Had he? She had too, if she was honest, which she wouldn't say out loud. He was already too flirty, and she shouldn't encourage him. But hadn't she done that the other night when she'd invited him to try to kiss her some other time?

She'd thought about that over and over and cursed her stupidity. She *didn't* want to hook up with some random guy... Granted, he wasn't random.

Yikes, what was she *doing*?

Time to change the subject to something safer. She nodded toward the cup in his hand. "What's your poison?"

"Iced caramel macchiato." He leaned close and lowered his voice. "Don't tell them inside, but I never order the same thing twice in a row—I like to keep them on their toes."

"Really?"

He laughed. "No, I just like variety."

In coffee as well as women. Ugh, where had that icky thought come from? The vulnerable part of her that dictated she keep herself free and clear of nasty romantic entanglements. Only, it kept her free and clear of *any* romantic entanglements. Her divorce had been final for well over a year. Wasn't it past time she moved on?

She pushed her attention back to their conversation. "Since you clearly come here often, what's your favorite drink?"

He blew out a breath. "Whew, that's tough. I love anything with caramel, but really espresso is my go-to. Here, try this." He handed her his drink.

Stupidly, she realized she was about to put her lips where his had been. She looked at him as she took the straw in her mouth but couldn't see his eyes behind the sunglasses.

"Are you trying to drink that in the most seductive way possible?" His voice had lowered but still held that sexy, flirty vibe.

Her belly pitched in response, and she couldn't suppress a smile. Nor could she avoid batting her eyelashes as she sucked on the straw. She handed it back and licked her lips, fully aware of how "seductive" she probably looked. Flirting with him was probably a bad idea, but she couldn't seem to help herself. "Delicious. I'm totally ordering that."

"I'd love to stay and keep you company—really I would." He sounded a bit pained. "But I have to get up to the winery. I'll console myself with the fact that I get to see you in a few hours."

Her stomach was still full of butterflies. His voice was so sexy, particularly when he flirted with her. "That you do. After I shower and make myself more presentable."

He moved closer and leaned toward her ear. "Newsflash, sweetheart, you look absolutely stunning as is, and I'd bet you always do. See you later."

His words sparked a delightful shiver along her neck that worked its way down her spine. She pivoted and watched him walk away down the street. Eventually, she turned and went inside, confident she'd never look at a caramel macchiato the same way again.

Chapter Six

The bright August sun hit Cameron full force as he stepped outside the front door of the winery a few minutes before one o'clock on Saturday. He slipped on his sunglasses and inhaled the scents of cut grass and blackberries. A bramble of bushes grew along the opposite side of the road, and this time of year, the air was full of the fragrance of ripening fruit.

At that moment, Brooke pulled into the gravel lot. He waved and walked to where she parked.

She stepped out of the car, and Cameron couldn't help but look his fill. Her blonde waves grazed her shoulders, and she wore fitted khaki shorts with a cornflower-blue tank. She was also sporting her Burberry sunglasses so he couldn't see her eyes.

She closed the car door. "Waiting for me?"

Absolutely. He'd meant what he'd said earlier—he'd been looking forward to this since they'd set the appointment. "You're right on time. And dressed for a hike." He dipped his gaze toward her boots. They looked worn. "You hike a lot?"

She shrugged. "I don't know if 'a lot' is accurate, but some." She kicked a pebble. "These are kind of old and beat up."

"We should hike sometime. Hayden's wife is really into it. We've taken some cool weekend trips."

Brooke turned toward the winery. "Where are we starting?"

He noted that she ignored his invitation. She probably wanted to keep to business, as she'd told him the other night. But then he'd walked her home, and they'd had that near kiss. Plus, she'd openly flirted with him this morning with that sexy straw situation. It seemed like a social relationship might not be out of the realm of possibility. He sensed she preferred to take things— if there was ever going to be a *thing*—slow. He could do that.

A tiny voice somewhere in the recesses of his mind asked how he could keep things casual and nurture a slow-burn relationship at the same time. He pretended that voice was talking to someone else.

"We'll start inside, if that's okay," he said. "Hayden will be here in a few minutes."

"Sounds good."

Cam held the door open as she stepped inside. Cool air greeted them, and he pulled his sunglasses off. "Hot one today."

"Definitely." She pushed her glasses to the top of her head. She wore very little makeup, and he stood by his earlier assessment that she was stunning anytime.

He turned his brain to the winery. "This is a gravity flow facility, which I'm sure you figured out. Top floor is business offices, and this main floor will be the tasting room—"

"This space exactly, right?" She walked over to the wall of glass doors that opened to the patio and pushed one open.

"Yes. The build-out is starting in a couple of weeks." He followed her outside onto the covered deck. "This will be a pretty sweet place to sit and have a glass of Riesling."

She flashed him a smile before returning her gaze to the panorama before them. "Gorgeous view—same as upstairs." It overlooked the vineyard and the town of Ribbon Ridge below. "Did you lose much vineyard when you built this?"

"A bit, but we were able to acquire about ten acres up the hill. We planted that last year. All pinot noir."

She turned and walked back inside. "Plenty of space here for tables and events."

He closed the door as he came in. "That's the idea." He went to the wall on the left. "The bar will be here—there's a kitchen on the other side." He went through a door, and she followed him.

She chuckled. "It needs a little work. A backsplash would be good."

He smiled. "It's in progress. For now, we only need the fridge, the sink, the dishwasher, and the microwave. This will be finished before they start on the tasting room."

"Who's they?"

"My brother Dylan's contracting company. We get roped into doing a lot too—keeps costs down, and frankly, we like doing it."

"Hello?" Hayden's voice filtered into the kitchen.

Cam turned toward the door. "That's Hayden."

They moved back into the tasting room. Hayden held out his hand. "Good to see you again, Brooke. Thanks for coming today."

"Thanks for having me. I really appreciate the tour."

He grinned at her. "Just sell a ton of our wine, please."

She peered at him and shot a glance toward Cam. "Do you have a ton to sell?"

"Not yet, but we will," Cam said. "I'll let Hayden tell you all about what he has planned. Let's start on the mezzanine."

The opposite side of the tasting room opened up to the fermentation level below, and a walkway with railings on either side stretched toward the receiving area and where they stored the sorting equipment.

Brooke strolled to the railing and looked down at the fermentation tanks, currently empty.

Hayden joined her and slapped his hands on the metal. "The railings are removable so we can move the grapes down into the fermenters." She took her hands off the steel, and he chuckled. "Perfectly safe, I promise. Come on, let's go down."

Cam rolled his eyes. "Don't scare her off, Hay."

Hayden tossed him a teasing look over his shoulder as he started down the stairs. "That's your job—but please don't do it."

Brooke descended between them. "You guys have been friends a long time, I take it."

"Since first grade," Cam said. "I've tried to get rid of him, even got him to go to France for a year, but he's like a bad penny."

Hayden snorted. "As if. You cried like a baby when I left and practically begged me to come back." At the base of the stairs, Hayden waited for Brooke to step down, then moved closer to her. He lowered his voice, but not enough so that Cam couldn't hear him, which was the point. "Don't let Cam fool you. His brothers both left Ribbon Ridge for long periods—years—but Cam could only bring himself to leave for days, maybe a week, at a time and only because his work demanded it. He's a diehard Ribbon Ridger. Since he left Blackthorn and his hectic travel schedule, some might even call him a home-body. I don't think he's ventured out of the state in the past two years."

Cam came off the stairs and joined them. "Hey, I was tired of traveling. And I have too left the state. We've taken several research trips to Washington and California."

Brooke seemed to be enjoying Hayden's teasing, if the smile

hovering on her lips and the glint in her eye were any indication. "I hear he hasn't even been to France."

Hayden nodded, his gaze full of false pity. "True story." He chuckled. "Come on, let's talk wine!"

Hayden guided her through the fermentation level. Her questions came fast and furious, and Hayden answered every single one of them. Cam didn't say much—the winemaking was Hayden's thing—but he appreciated her intellect and her passion for wine.

As they proceeded down to the settling level, Cam asked, "You sound like maybe you should have been a winemaker."

She turned her head toward him, her eyebrow arching. "Really? I never thought about it. I worked at a tasting room part-time in college, and that turned into a full-time job when I graduated. From there, I went into sales and distribution."

This sparked a conversation about southern Oregon wine and where she'd worked. By the time they finished up with the cellar, which included the barrel rooms and the bottling area, it was past time to meet Luke for the vineyard tour. Cam's phone vibrated—a text from Luke asking where they were.

Cam looked across the bottling line to where Brooke and Hayden were chatting. "Luke's waiting for us."

Hayden gave her a sheepish look. "Sorry, I get a little carried away."

Brooke shook her head. "Not at all. I asked too many questions."

Cam went to the exterior door. "No such thing." He texted Luke to meet them out back on the lower level. "We can go out this way." He slid his sunglasses back on as he held the door.

Brooke preceded them into the sunlight and dropped her glasses back over her magnificent eyes. Bummer. He liked watching them animate and sparkle as they discussed winemaking.

Hayden gave Cam a slight elbow as he walked by. He turned his head for a brief glance that included arched eyebrows and wide eyes that clearly said, *Dude, she's cool,* or something to that effect.

Cam knew she was cool. And smart. And attractive in so many ways that went far beyond her looks.

"Oh, I love this!" Brooke exclaimed as she moved toward the massive fire pit they'd just installed last month. She looked around. "Is this for guests? I don't see an easy access point."

Hayden put his sunglasses on. "For now, it's just for us, but we'll eventually add stairs from the upper deck and another deck, then more stairs leading down here. We may have evening dinners out here—but that's down the road."

Cam walked to the pit where she stood. "We reclaimed the brick from the house before we demolished it."

"House?" Brooke asked.

"There was a mid-century ranch, which Hayden and Bex lived in for a while. We'd planned to use it for something, but it had...problems."

"The extensive dry rot and the leaking pipes were problems. The rodent infestation was catastrophic." Hayden shuddered.

Brooke made a face that clearly transmitted what she thought of that—*disgusting.* "Oh dear."

"Unsalvageable as a whole, unfortunately, but we saved what we could."

Hayden nodded. "Some of the wood will be used for the bar in the tasting room."

"That's so cool that you reused stuff."

"Especially this brick," Cam said. "It predates that ranch house, even. When we went to pull the brick out, we found one buried near the foundation with the year 1879 and the initials BNR."

"That's cool. What does it mean?"

Hayden grinned. "No idea. But my sister-in-law Alaina is on it. She and her BFF are history nerds, and they've been working on establishing a Ribbon Ridge museum."

"That's so neat. I'd totally go to that." She froze for a moment. "Wait a second. Is that Alaina Pierce? I just remembered she's married to one of the Archers."

Alaina was one of the world's most famous actresses, despite doing only a supporting role in a single film during the past two years. She'd been too busy being a newlywed and a mom.

Hayden laughed. "Yeah, that's her. She's completely down-to-earth. She's just another Ribbon Ridger now."

Brooke glanced between them. "Huh. How long does the indoctrination take? I mean, I've only been here a month or so."

Hayden looked at Cam and shrugged. "Dunno."

"Being a Ribbon Ridger is a state of mind. Time's got nothing to do with it," Cam said. "There's a distinct pride that comes in living and working here."

"What makes it so special?" she asked.

Cam tried to think of something specific—maybe the annual Ribbon Ridge Festival, which had taken place a couple of weeks ago—but there were too many intangibles. For him, it was the only home he'd ever known, and it was the only home he ever wanted. "Did you go to the Ribbon Ridge Festival?"

"I did. It was great."

Cam wondered why he hadn't seen her, but it was a widely attended event, drawing more and more people from the Portland metropolitan area every year. It was silly to think he'd pick her out of a crowd. Except now he knew he absolutely could.

"It's gotten kind of commercial in the past decade or so," Cam said, "but the festival started way back in the nineteenth century. They had horse racing, dancing, and even a quilting bee."

"Sounds like something that museum you mentioned should highlight. Maybe you can bring some of that back next year."

Cam suddenly wondered why no one ever had. "That's a great idea. Hayden and I'll get right on that."

Hayden chuckled. "Yeah, sure. Right after we launch our wines, not to mention everything else on our plates."

"Good point. Sounds like a job for Alaina and Crystal, though." Cam looked toward Brooke. "Crystal's her friend."

"I figured. Maybe I'll offer to give them a hand. Sounds fun. And maybe it'll help me earn my Ribbon Ridge Club Card."

Cam let out a bark of laughter. "We totally need those. We'll get Alaina and Crystal on that too."

Hayden pulled his phone from his pocket and glanced at the screen. "Bex is bringing some food in a bit if you guys are hungry. I haven't had lunch."

"I ate before I came," Brooke said.

Cam didn't want her to go when the tour was over. He envisioned them sitting on the patio upstairs. "Then wine—I still have that Riesling in my fridge."

She smiled at him, showing straight, brilliant white teeth. "I'm not sure I can decline that a second time."

Luke came down the hill then, his hat pulled low over his eyes. "It's a good thing I love the sun."

"You're in the wrong line of work if you don't," Cam said. "Luke, you remember Brooke Ellis."

"Yep. Good to see you again." He slipped off his sunglasses and shook her hand. "Ready for a sweltering walk?"

"Absolutely. I tried to choose the right footwear." She held her foot out to show her hiking boot.

"Perfect. Though a hat would've been good."

She nodded toward his head. "I see that now." She looked over at Cam and Hayden. "Where are yours? You guys should know better. In fact, you should have a stock of them here—haven't you heard of swag?"

Cam chuckled. "We're looking at some—hats, shirts, all that. Maybe you can help me decide what to buy. Tell me what people will want when you go selling."

"Sure," she said.

Hayden pivoted toward the building. "I've got stuff to do inside. In the air-conditioning. Actually, Cam, I could use a hand."

Cam preferred to go on the vineyard tour, even without a hat. "I was going to tag along with them."

"Like you haven't walked every inch of this vineyard a hundred times. Come on." Hayden jerked his head toward the winery. "See you in a bit, Brooke."

Cam had no choice but to reluctantly follow Hayden. Brooke and Luke were already on their way toward the vines before Cam could say anything. He trudged back inside into the cool dark of the bottling room.

He tossed Hayden a glare. "What could possibly be so urgent on a Saturday afternoon?"

Hayden laughed. "Absolutely nothing, dick-for-brains—and I mean that literally. Someone had to save you from yourself."

Cam pulled the door closed behind him. "What the hell does that mean?"

"You were practically tripping over yourself. Where's the cool ladies' man we all know and love?"

Cam scoffed. "You'd give me shit no matter what, wouldn't you?"

Hayden slapped his shoulder. "It's what we do." He walked out of the bottling room and started up the stairs. "But seriously, do you like her?" He glanced back at Cam as they ascended.

"Sure. She's great."

"I mean like-like her. Don't you think it's time you had a

girlfriend again? I know we always give you crap about being a player, but you *have* sort of abandoned that way of life of late. I guess I thought that might signal that you're ready to let down your guard."

Cam scowled at his friend's back. He hadn't mentioned the reason for Cam having a guard in the first place, but it wasn't necessary. They both knew why.

"I'm never doing that, and if you think I should, keep your opinion to yourself."

They climbed in silence until they reached the fermentation level. Hayden stopped and turned. "Is it wrong for me to want to see you happy?"

"Isn't this the same crap your family pulled when you came home from France to find Bex ensconced in your house and working for your brewpub? They were all happily paired off and wanted you to get right back with Bex."

Hayden looked down at the floor, but Cam caught the smile pulling at his mouth. "Yeah, they did. And it pissed me off. But they were also right about me and Bex." He looked at Cam again, and his gaze was sincere, caring even. "Maybe Brooke isn't the right woman—believe me, I really don't want you screwing up a good working relationship if she turns out to be a fantastic salesperson. But the right woman *is* out there. Jennifer was the aberration, not the norm."

"Damn it. You had to go and say her name."

"Dude, everyone eventually said Voldemort too."

Cam knew Hayden meant well, but his love life was off-limits. "I think you should drop the conversation."

Hayden held up his hands in surrender. "Sorry. Just... I don't want you to have regrets."

"It's far too late for that," Cam muttered. "Listen, I'm heading up to my office for a few." He started toward the stairs.

Hayden called after him. "I'll let you know when Bex gets here with lunch."

Cam nodded but didn't turn. He climbed up to his office, feeling agitated. He hated that word—regret. Because he had plenty of experience with it. He strove to live his life so that emotion never knocked him down again.

Yeah, he liked Brooke, but he still didn't want a girlfriend. Luckily for him, she didn't seem interested—even if he was. He was content to flirt with her and keep things light. That was what he did best.

And that was what kept him out of trouble.

By the time they finished the vineyard tour, Brooke was hot and more than eager for that glass of Riesling Cam had promised her. Like Hayden, Luke had been an engaging and incredibly knowledgeable tour guide.

"I have the sense you pretty much live and breathe this vineyard," she said as they walked back toward the building.

"Guilty. But then we all do."

She could see that. The four of them seemed to have poured all of their passion—their very souls—into this endeavor. It was inspiring and honestly a little envy inducing.

"You guys are incredibly lucky to be pursuing your dream."

Luke blew out a whistle. "Don't we know it." He led her toward a doorway on the uphill side of the building. "You sound wistful. Selling wine isn't your dream?"

"I love it, really." She did. But it wasn't really her *dream*. Her dream—to have a family—had been shattered when she and Darren had divorced. She realized she didn't have a new dream, and that felt like a bit of an epiphany.

"But maybe it's not where you see yourself in five or ten years," he said.

She hadn't thought about that. She'd been too focused on taking one day and then one week at a time. She'd stopped seeing a shrink when she'd moved north, but she still had tough questions she ought to explore.

Oh, get over yourself! Thinking about the future should not send you into a tailspin. Not anymore.

Luke opened the door to the winery as she silently chided herself. They walked into a vestibule with a staircase—the one that led up to the offices, she was fairly certain.

"Oh man, does that feel good." Luke swept his hat off and closed his eyes briefly.

Brooke welcomed the cool rush of air-conditioning, despite the instant goose bumps rising on her heated flesh. It felt delicious. "Yes, it does."

"This way," Luke said, gesturing past the stairs to the main room.

A table had been set up, and a cute brunette was arranging food on it. She turned as Brooke and Luke approached. "Hi!" She brushed her hands on her jean shorts and came toward Brooke. "I'm Bex Archer." She offered her hand, which Brooke shook.

"Nice to meet you. I'm Brooke Ellis."

"So I heard. I'm so thrilled you'll be working with the guys. They need a woman's influence."

Luke chuckled. "As if you don't insert yours. And we have no issue with that." He leaned forward and kissed her cheek.

Bex tossed him a look of affront. "Hey, I'm too busy with my beer."

"I meant no offense. Don't listen to me. I'm overheated."

"Then I'm just in time!" Cam called from the base of the

stairs. He carried two bottles of white wine—the Riesling, which she could discern by the shape of the bottle, and another white.

Hayden came from the kitchen carrying a knife and some napkins. He handed the knife to Bex. "This is for the cheese."

She gave him a quick kiss followed by a smile. "Thanks, babe."

He smiled back at her, and it was obvious they were still in newlywed mode or just that sickeningly happy. Brooke had thought that she and Darren had been that happy once, and she supposed they had. But it hadn't lasted.

Bex put the knife down on a cutting board with the cheese. "Help yourselves!"

There was a fruit salad, a chicken salad, little rolls and crackers, a charcuterie plate, two cheeses, and a spread that looked like fig.

Brooke's stomach rumbled. Yes, she'd had "lunch" but decided a protein shake didn't really count. Hadn't she earned a second lunch after running a 10k and taking a brutal hike through the ninety-degree vineyard? "This is all for you guys?"

Hayden picked up a plate as he tossed Bex a wink. "My wife knows how to put out a spread."

"Did I hear lunch was ready?" The youngest Westcott, Jamie, jumped down the last few stairs and burst into the room.

"Damn straight," Luke said as he grabbed his plate.

Jamie came forward and shook Brooke's hand. "Good to see you again, Brooke." He was a couple of inches shorter than Luke, but the same height as Cam. His eyes were a mix of his brothers', with Cam's green and Luke's brown converging into a warm hazel. His hair was the lightest of the three, but still brown and thick.

"Nice to see you too."

Cam looked at Bex. "What, no wineglasses?"

"Oh, I forgot. I admit I wasn't thinking about wine." Bex threw Cam a smile.

"Your beer bias is showing," Cam said.

"I am not biased! You guys are the worst." Bex laughed, which took any sting from her words.

"I'll get wineglasses," Cam said, shaking his head good-naturedly.

"I'll help," Brooke offered, feeling a bit like a fifth wheel since they all knew each other so well.

He led her to the kitchen. Inside, he turned to her. "I know you said you ate, but how can you say no to that spread?" He opened a cupboard, which held three shelves of wineglasses stamped with their winery logo.

"I can't, so I won't." She joined him and took down two glasses. "How many do we need?" She started counting people in her head.

"Just five. Bex won't be drinking wine." Right, because she preferred beer.

Cam curled the fingers of his left hand around the stems of two glasses and picked up the last with his right before closing the cabinet. "Oops, almost forgot to get an opener."

Brooke transferred one glass to her other hand. "I'll get it. Where?"

"That drawer next to the fridge." He gestured with his head.

Brooke opened it and saw at least twenty openers. She laughed. "Um, you've quite a selection." Like the wineglasses, they were all emblazoned with their logo. "You misled me—you have *some* swag."

"Wineglasses, openers, and four- and six-compartment bags to carry bottles. That's pretty much it. I do have designs for several apparel items as well as a soft-sided cooler."

"Great idea with the cooler."

He pushed open the door and stood against it while she

walked out of the kitchen. "Thank you. I have my marketing moments."

"I'm sure they're more than moments. Your sales numbers from Blackthorn are legend."

He gave her a side eye. "Is that right?" He laughed. "Along with my reputation."

She appreciated that he had no problem with the way others saw him. He not only owned it—he seemed to wave it like a flag. "Yep."

They deposited the glasses on the table, and Cam poured Riesling for the two of them, while the other three guys drank a white blend from a local winery.

Brooke helped herself to a plate of food. "No Riesling for you guys?"

Jamie looked horrified. "Cam guards that stuff with his life. He only pours it for special people."

"I thought you'd want the pinot blanc. Was I wrong?" Cam asked.

"Nope, I'm good."

For a brief moment, it had seemed to Brooke that Jamie's comment was bait for Cam to say that Brooke *was* special. But Cam didn't take it. He'd missed a prime opportunity to flirt. Was it because they weren't alone?

They all dished up from the mini-buffet and sat around the table. Bex and Brooke traded the usual get-to-know-you questions. Brooke was surprised to hear how long Bex and Hayden had known each other—nearly a decade, though they'd broken up for a five-year period in the middle of that. True love, however, had won out, or so it seemed given the way they grazed each other's hands or exchanged little glances when they thought other people weren't looking. Or maybe they didn't care. Maybe they waved their love for each other as proudly as Cam flew his flirtatious flag.

Cam scooted his chair back and stood. "I'm going to sit on the deck for a few."

Luke stood and picked up his plate. "I'm heading back out to the vineyard. If anyone wants to *work*, I'll be in the chardonnay block. Thanks for lunch, Bex." He smiled at her before taking his dishes to the kitchen and then disappeared the way he and Brooke had come in.

Brooke finished her glass of Riesling and wanted to pour another, but she wasn't sure she should. Jamie and Hayden were deep in discussion about some piece of equipment Hayden wanted to buy, and Bex stood up and started clearing away the food. Brooke's gaze drifted to the deck where Cam leaned against the rail, his wineglass dangling from his fingertips.

Bex came around the table near Brooke's chair. "You should go out and join him." She spoke quietly so that only Brooke could hear.

Brooke glanced over at her in mild surprise. Was she trying to push them together? Brooke didn't really know what to say, so she stood up and helped instead. "Where do you want the food?" she asked.

Bex grabbed as many containers as she could. "We'll put it in the kitchen so the guys can snack on the leftovers tomorrow."

Brooke picked up some odds and ends and followed her.

Turning from the counter where she'd deposited her items, Bex winced. "I'm sorry. I didn't mean to be obnoxious. I just thought...well, Hayden said that Cam liked you."

Brooke opened the fridge and put away the food she'd brought. "Doesn't Cam like a lot of women?"

"Yes, but Hayden thought you might be different. And then when you went to help with the wineglasses, I'm afraid I jumped to the wrong conclusion that you maybe liked him too. Probably." She closed her eyes and briefly massaged her forehead. When she looked at Brooke again, her gaze was clear and honest. "I really am sorry. It's none of my business. I've known Cam a long time—just about as long as I've known Hayden—and I'd love to see him find a genuine girlfriend. Here, I've barely met you, and I'm being all pushy. Ugh!" She shook her head and smiled. "Terrible first impression. Forget I said anything. *Please.*"

Brooke could've been annoyed by Bex's desire to meddle, but she was actually charmed. "It's nice to know Cam has such good friends—he's lucky. And I get it. My friends keep urging me to get a boyfriend too." Okay, maybe not a *boyfriend.* She wondered how much she and Cam might have in common with regard to their unwillingness to seek commitment. Did he have an ex like she did?

Bex laughed and seemed to relax as she tucked the rest of the nonperishable food away in a cupboard. "I'm not sure *he* thinks he's lucky, but we can be a tough crowd, especially when you throw in the rest of the Archers. It's one big crazy—but happy—family."

That sounded nice. Brooke had two sisters, one older and one younger, both of whom were married with children. Between them and her parents, there was no shortage of people extolling the virtues of committed relationships. Never mind that Brooke had tried that already and crashed and burned.

She thought about joining Cam outside. Why not? She was suddenly quite curious about why he was a player. Plus, there was still some Riesling to drink. "I think I'll head out and help him finish the wine. Wouldn't want it to go to waste." She smiled at Bex. "I'd offer you a glass, but I have the impression wine isn't your thing."

Bex looked momentarily confused, her brow puckering. "Oh! The guys just give me crap because I'm a brewer, but I actually love wine. I'd absolutely be drinking some along with you if I wasn't three and a half months pregnant."

Brooke's gaze dipped to Bex's still-flat belly. A surge of envy followed quickly by a wave of sadness slammed into her. She'd never know what it would feel like to care for a burgeoning life inside of her. She'd never smile and nod knowingly at another woman who'd been there and done that.

Damn. Just when she thought she'd finally compartmentalized her infertility, the old feelings and the despair threatened to steal her breath, her equilibrium, her ability to simply finish a stupid conversation. *Come on, Brooke, you can do this.* "Congratulations."

She knew she ought to make some chitchat about impending motherhood, but she just couldn't do it. She could barely keep her face from crumbling.

"Thanks. We're pretty excited." Her hand fluttered against her belly. "We've been trying for a little while."

And they'd been successful. It was strange how one could feel happiness, jealousy, and grief in the span of a single second. "That's terrific."

Brooke's heart, already broken when she'd learned she couldn't carry or even have a child of her own three years ago, shuddered anew. Someday—God, she hoped someday—she wouldn't feel that awful pang of loss. It was dumb really. She shouldn't be able to miss something she never had, right? Just something she'd desperately wanted with all of her heart.

"You okay?" Bex asked.

Brooke focused on the other woman. Her gaze was intent, concerned. She tucked a lock of dark hair behind her ear as she took a step forward. Shit. Brooke wasn't doing a very good job of compartmentalizing at all.

"I'm great. I was just realizing that I promised a friend of mine I'd meet her in a little bit. I guess I got swept away by your amazing lunch spread." She summoned a smile and hoped it looked a hell of a lot better than it felt.

Bex nodded. "I hate when I forget stuff. Seems to happen more and more lately." She laughed softly.

Brooke had to leave. *Now.* "Thanks again for lunch. It was great to meet you." She turned toward the door.

"You too."

Brooke left the kitchen. Jamie and Hayden were no longer at the table, but Cam was still outside on the deck. She ought to go say good-bye, but she couldn't. She wanted—needed—to be alone. So she grabbed her sunglasses from the table and made her way to the front door.

"Aren't you going to tell Cam you're leaving?" Bex asked. She'd apparently followed Brooke out of the kitchen, which Brooke would've noticed if she weren't acting like a total idiot.

"Uh, he looks deep in thought, and I really need to run. You can tell him I'll talk to him next week. Thanks!" She rushed out before Bex could encourage her to stay or before that look of worry crept back into her gaze. Brooke had enough people—her friends, her family—who'd regarded her with pity over the last few years.

She didn't need any more.

Chapter Seven

Cam pushed open the door of Taste, a wine bar that was closed tonight for a private party for a newish winery—Allen Drake. Keen to sample the competition, Cam went to as many of these kinds of events as he could. Not that they were really *competition*. Sure, they all wanted to be the next big producer, but the community was mostly supportive, and a win for one was a win for all.

The event was already bustling, and Cam recognized most of the faces in the room. There were small, round tables in the center plus a bar that ran along the windows facing Main and First Streets. The primary bar, where Allen was currently holding court, was at the back of the room.

Cam made his way to Allen, whom he'd known for several years. He was a former salesman like Cam, who'd decided to try his hand at crafting wine. He smiled when he saw Cam. "Hey, you made it."

Cam shook his hand and grinned. "Of course. Is anyone else here going to tell you if it tastes like swill?"

The guy to Allen's right, whose name currently escaped

Cam, laughed. "Of course we will. In fact, I think your brother already did."

Cam darted a few looks this way and that. He knew Luke had planned on stopping by, but didn't see him. "Did Luke drink and dash?"

"Nah, he's around here somewhere, I think," Allen said. "He was looking for my vineyard manager. They might've gone in the back to get more wine."

Probably. Luke always pitched in to help.

Allen motioned for one of the employees behind the bar to pour a glass for Cam. She filled the bowl with a dark pinot, enough for a healthy taste. Allen put his fingertips on the base of the glass and slid it to the edge of the granite. "I might regret this, but give it to me straight. Even if you think it *is* swill."

Cam shook his head. "It won't be." He picked up the glass and swirled the liquid before inhaling its cherry and cassis scent. The nose was great, but would the taste hold up? He sipped and let the wine rest on his tongue a moment. He was immediately assaulted with cherry and then hints of coffee and truffle. The texture was silky, and the flavor lingered after he swallowed. It was, in a word, incredible. Jealousy snaked through him but was quickly overcome with happiness for Allen. "This is still young," he said cautiously. "But it's going to be a fruit bomb."

Allen watched him expectantly. "Yeah, I think so too. Anything else?"

Cam considered drawing this out, but he knew what it felt like to be anxious about your brand-new wine. He shook his head at Allen. "Dude, it's fucking awesome. You suck."

Allen's face split into a wide grin. He pushed his glasses up his nose and exhaled. "You almost had me going there."

"Almost?"

"Hey, your opinion matters. You really like it?"

"It goes beyond that. I'm considering a long-term relationship with it."

This made everyone howl with laughter. The guy next to Allen slapped him on the back. "Damn, Allen, now you know it's good if Westcott's going to give up his bachelor lifestyle."

Cam laughed along with everyone, but bristled at always being labeled the consummate bachelor. Which made no sense. He had no problem with his lifestyle or his reputation. However, since he'd met Brooke, he'd started to wonder... He shook the thought right out of his head.

Cam steered the conversation to Allen's wine—the quantity, when he was going to start selling it, what else he had to taste and so on. At one point, Luke emerged from the back and nodded toward Cam, but he didn't join the group. Instead, he and Allen's vineyard manager took a couple of stools by the window.

"*Hello.*" The single word, barely more than a breath really, came from the guy on Cam's left. He was young—an intern at one of the larger wineries near Ribbon Ridge—and his head was turned toward the door.

Cam followed his line of sight and immediately saw what had drawn his reaction. Brooke was standing just inside. She looked around the room, taking stock. Cam did the same—but only of her. Her blond hair was loose, hanging in silky curls to her shoulders. She wore a cobalt-and-turquoise-striped maxi dress with silver sandals peeking out beneath the hem. He was utterly captivated. Like the guy next to him, apparently.

"Excuse me," the intern said, taking off toward Brooke.

The jealousy Cam had felt for the wine earlier came back tenfold, and this time it didn't immediately dissipate. He watched as the guy approached Brooke and greeted her. She smiled at him, her eyes crinkling at the sides and her dimples creasing. Cam reacted deep in his gut, wanting nothing more than to walk over to her and stake his claim.

Only he didn't have one.

Over the past week, since she'd toured the winery and vineyard, they'd kept their communication strictly business—all e-mail. She'd left without saying good-bye last Saturday, and when Cam had pressed Bex for why she'd left, Bex had only said that Brooke had gone to meet a friend. He'd half expected her to join him on the deck so they could finish that Riesling together, but then he hadn't actually invited her. Because he was trying to keep things business-oriented instead of flirty, something he found hard to do when he was with her. Away from her, he could ignore that he was insanely attracted to her.

He turned to the bar and asked for a full glass of the pinot. Then he asked for another. Before he could think better of it, he swooped up both glasses and beelined for Brooke and her admirer.

As he neared, she saw him, her eyes widening briefly in recognition, then slanting at the edges as she smiled. She seemed happy to see him.

"Cameron! Just the guy I was looking for." She turned to the intern and flashed him an apologetic look. "You'll have to excuse me. I need to talk shop with one of my clients."

Always eager to help someone out, he glanced somewhat apologetically at the intern as he offered Brooke one of the glasses. "I come bearing wine."

"Excellent." She tossed the intern a look and said, "Ciao," as she looped her arm through Cam's. The connection was instant and magnetic and made him wonder if strictly business was going to be possible tonight.

He let her lead him across the room, threading through tables and skirting people. They passed Luke and his pal. Luke raised an eyebrow, not much, but enough for Cam to catch it. Cam didn't respond verbally or otherwise.

She stopped at the end of the bar along the window, at the two seats closest to the back corner. "He didn't follow us, did he?" she asked in a low tone.

Cam had only just recovered from her touch to find she was removing her arm. That was too bad. He looked back toward where they'd started. The intern was still standing there, wearing a bemused expression. "No, he didn't."

She exhaled as she perched on the stool. "Great."

Cam took the other seat with his back to the corner. "I take it you were dying to get away from him?"

She set her wineglass and clutch purse on the smooth wood top of the bar. "Yes. Thank you."

So she hadn't *really* been looking for him. Bummer. "Glad I could be of convenient service."

She smoothed her hair back and flipped the curls over her shoulder. "He was laying it on a bit thick. I mean, he's a kid. Just out of college."

"You refuse to date younger guys?

She gave him a pointed look. "I refuse to date players. And he's most definitely a player."

Cam couldn't help laughing. "So you attached yourself to the closest available...*player*. Who's maybe in a better age range?" He laughed a little harder, feeling more amused than he probably ought.

She giggled, then let go into a full laugh. "Okay, now that you put it that way, that was a really bad move on my part. But, in my defense, you haven't seemed like all that much of a player. Your lines aren't *too* cheesy, and I think we've settled into a good working relationship." She let her laughter subside. "Or am I wrong about that?"

"Nope, I'd say you got it right. Besides, as you can probably tell from my two a.m. e-mails, I'm a little too work obsessed right now to play at anything."

Her eyes sparkled in the orange glow coming from the evening sun glinting off the windows across the street. "You are! You work more than I do, which is saying something." She nodded toward the glass on the bar. "What's the wine?"

"Allen's pinot."

She picked it up and swirled the garnet liquid. "A full glass, huh? Not a taste?"

"I already tasted. Trust me when I say it's envy inducing."

Her eyes widened. "That good? Oh my. I might have to pitch my services."

She absolutely should. But again, he felt a pang of jealousy. Which was stupid. She wasn't an employee of West Arch. Her job was to sell wine from a variety of sources, and from what he'd seen so far, she was good at it. He liked her. And he liked Allen. Why not help them both out?

"Do you know Allen?"

She shook her head as she inhaled the aroma of the wine.

"I'll introduce you so you can talk him up."

"That would be great, thanks. I'm surprised you're willing to share." She flashed him a sexy little smile. Or maybe he just found everything about her sexy. Either way, he got a definite flirty vibe. Business-only was looking harder by the minute.

A server came by and offered them a small bite. "Goat cheese tarts."

Brooke set her glass back down and picked a tart from the tray. "Thanks."

Cam took one for himself along with a napkin and set them on the bar.

As the server left, Brooke sampled the tart. A look of starry-eyed bliss glazed her expression. "I love cheese, don't you?"

He laughed again. "You look like you're maybe *in* love with cheese."

"You'd be right. And I guess those are two distinct emotions, aren't they?"

He pondered that for the briefest of seconds before agreeing. "Definitely." He knew the difference between loving someone and being in love. He'd done both, and the latter was far more painful.

She gave him a sly look as she picked up her glass and swirled the wine around the bowl. "Are you speaking from experience?"

He was good at dodging these kinds of questions. Talking about Jennifer was something he never did. Period. He didn't like to give her lip service or brain space. She didn't deserve it. "Don't we all? By our age anyway."

She froze in lifting the glass to her mouth. "Crap, are we *old*?"

He chuckled. "I turned thirty a couple months ago. Is that old?"

She winced. "Was it hard? I don't have to face that until late next year."

He grinned, enjoying their conversation. "No, it wasn't hard. I'm digging thirty so far." He was exactly where he wanted to be in life, and that was a pretty good feeling. He glanced toward her glass. "Are you going to taste that or not?"

"If you'll stop distracting me." She gave him one of those saucy looks that made his gut tighten. She took a sip, and he watched her scrutinize the texture and the flavor. Her eyes narrowed, and her lips pressed together. Then she swallowed. "You weren't kidding." She took a longer drink. "I need to meet this Allen guy like *right now*."

Cam looked toward the bar to gesture for Allen to come over, but he wasn't there. He glanced around and made eye contact with Luke, who gave him another look that clearly asked, *What's up with you and Brooke?* Cam ignored that one too.

Why was everyone suddenly trying to pair him off? He understood Hayden—he was married with a kid on the way—and Jamie was seeing Madison. But Luke was single. It was clearly time to turn the tables and set Luke up with someone so he could mind his own damned business.

Cam finally located Allen standing at the other end of the bar. "I see Allen. Let me go get him." He started to rise, but she put her hand on his arm.

"Don't. I don't want to seem pushy. If he wanders by or you catch his eye, you can flag him down."

He arched his brow at her. "You aren't very cutthroat."

The edge of her mouth ticked up, and a ruthless glint flashed in her gaze. "I am, actually. I'm just kind of tired. It's been a long week."

He could relate to that. They'd had a couple of colossal headaches at the winery with the wrong bottles being delivered —and the supplier being a jackass about it—followed by significant irrigation problems that had sent Luke into a tailspin.

The server came by with another round of appetizers, and they helped themselves.

Brooke sipped her wine and looked at him over the rim of her glass. "That was some pretty crafty avoidance earlier."

He set his glass on the bar and rested his arm on the edge of the wood. "What?"

"When I asked if you spoke from experience of being in love —the cheese?"

He knew what she was referring to. That she'd called him on it was strangely alluring. Shouldn't it be annoying? He refused to cave. "Who isn't in love with cheese?"

Her eyes narrowed, and he recognized the shrewd assessment in her gaze. "You're doing it again—avoiding. Do you even realize? Either you've never been in love, or you have and you'd rather not talk about it."

He leaned back and studied her, a smile hovering about his mouth. "You've got me all figured out, don't you?"

"Ha! Not even close. You're a pretty closed book, Cameron Westcott."

"It's the latter," he said, surprising himself. And her, given the subtle rounding of her eyes.

"I see," she murmured. She inclined her head slightly. The movement coupled with her tone seemed to convey some sort of respect...as if she understood he'd revealed something important and meant to keep it safe.

Damn, he liked her.

"And you? Wait, I know the answer—I think. You have an ex-husband, so I have to assume you were in love. I can't see you marrying someone without that."

"Aren't most people who get married? I'm curious why you think some people marry for something other than love."

His past experience with Jennifer crashed into his mind— she'd married that other prick because he was wealthy and could give her the material things she desired. "Because they do. Some people are cold and selfish, and love never enters into it." He picked up his glass and looked at her over the rim. "But that's not you."

She cocked her head to the side. "You think you know me that well?"

He sipped his wine and set the glass back on the wood. "Based on your response a moment ago, I think you were in love with your husband. But I also think you're guarded and skeptical, and since you're divorced, you likely had your heart broken."

She pursed her lips briefly, again studying him intently.

"You know what I think? I think you just told me about you. *You* would only marry for love. The question is whether you were with someone who was cold and selfish, and"—her voice dipped —"you had *your* heart broken."

His insides seized up, and the blood in his veins turned to ice. How the hell had she come up with that? "Now, who's deflecting?"

She laughed. "Damn, you caught me. Yes, I was in love with my ex." She polished off her wine and glanced around for the server. "Think I can get another?"

"Absolutely." In that moment, he happened to catch Allen's eye. He came toward them, and Cam introduced him to Brooke. Cam slid from his stool and picked up their glasses. "I'll get more wine while you two chat."

He made his way to the bar and set the glasses down for a refill. Luke sidled up next to him. "Hey, brother. You and Brooke look cozy."

"Knock it off." He turned his head to look at Luke, who was grinning like an idiot. "I've decided *you* need a girlfriend."

Luke glanced over his shoulder. "Who, Brooke, maybe?"

Cam scowled. "No, not Brooke. Someone else."

"What's wrong with Brooke? She's great. Funny, smart. She's also insanely beautiful."

"I know what you're trying to do, so don't bother."

Luke turned, resting his elbow on the countertop. "What's that?"

"You think I need a relationship. I don't. I'm busy. I'm happy. I'm *good.*"

"No one's disputing that. But we all see what you apparently don't—you like Brooke. Believe me, I'd be the first one to say you shouldn't encourage anything given the work stuff, but for me, I'd rather see you happy in a relationship. And if Brooke's that person, I'm all for it."

What were they "all" seeing? "Do you guys have meetings about this when I'm not around?"

"Ha-ha. No. Don't be a jerk."

"I'm not the one playing matchmaker like we're in seventh grade."

"Fine. I'll shut up." Luke shook his head but smiled. "I just hope you don't pass something up because you're too stubborn to realize they aren't all bad apples."

One of the bartenders finally poured his wine—they were busier at the bar than when he'd arrived—and Cam picked up the glasses. "I do realize. I just don't want an apple, okay?"

Luke rolled his eyes, and they went their separate ways.

His brother's words rankled. Maybe because they held more than a little bit of truth. He didn't trust women. Hell, he didn't trust himself. How could he have been such poor judge of character with Jennifer? He had to be a complete moron not to see her for what she was after being together for almost two years.

Was he still a moron, though? No, because he'd done a damned good job of keeping himself from making another stupid mistake.

When he arrived back at his seat, Brooke and Allen seemed like old friends. Allen was just tucking her card into his pocket as he turned to Cam. "Thanks for introducing me to my new wine broker."

That shaft of jealousy poked him again, but he summoned a smile. "Great. I don't think you'll be disappointed." He handed Brooke her wineglass. "How many sales did you close for me this week?"

"Eight. And we're just getting started."

Allen grinned. "Damn. I look forward to seeing you Monday, Brooke. Thanks!" He nodded at her and gripped Cam's bicep before taking off.

Cam sat down. "You sealed that up pretty quick."

"Told you I was ruthless." She arched her brows at him, and again he caught a flirty vibe.

He suddenly wanted to ask her to come home with him. He wanted to wrap her in his arms and kiss her, and see if the attraction he felt—that others seemed to see—was as hot and thrilling as he imagined. But he didn't think she'd go for that. What *would* she go for?

"You said earlier that you refused to date players. Who *do* you date?"

She twirled her glass for a moment and watched the pinot cascade around the sides. She looked up at him. "Like you, I don't really date."

"I date, just not seriously."

"Right. I don't date at all. Haven't since I divorced my ex." She took a drink of wine, and her gaze seemed to dare him to chastise her for that. He had the sense most people did, and of course, he wouldn't. Not when he was dealing with his own peanut gallery.

"How long ago was that?"

"Almost a year and a half."

A paltry amount compared to his eight-year streak. "Eh, that's not so bad. Give yourself a break."

She set her glass on the bar and kept her hand curled around the base of the stem. "Thanks. My friends and family keep telling me I should get back out there, but it's just... different after you're divorced."

He knew exactly what she meant. Even though he hadn't been married, he'd been close. If he'd proposed a little sooner, he might've married Jennifer.

No, you wouldn't have. You didn't have the money or the stuff to keep her.

He shook thoughts of his ex away. She so wasn't worth it. "So you don't date, and you're good with that."

She moved her glass around slightly, again swirling the wine. "For the most part. Lately, I've begun to think that I should maybe at least *try*."

Lately. Because of him? He tried not to feel encouraged, but it was tough. Especially if he'd been reading her body language correctly tonight. "Hey, I'm not a role model, unless you're interested in casual dating."

"I...might be." She picked up her glass and took another drink, then set it back down with a clack. "Never mind. This is a terrible conversation for us to have. Like I said earlier, we have a great working relationship. I should not be asking you for dating advice."

He chuckled. "Is that what you were doing? Well, I would say you should do what makes you feel good. Just be clear about what you want going in."

"That's what you do?"

"Absolutely. I like to have fun, but there's nothing permanent with me."

She blinked at him. "Nothing? Ever?"

Not in eight years, and he didn't see an end to his current mindset. "Nope."

"Wow, that's actually a little disturbing."

"Is it? I know what I want, and if it doesn't float someone's boat, there's no harm done."

"I meant disturbing in that you don't seem to miss having a significant other. But yeah, that shouldn't be—it's good to know you can be alone." She gave him an intent but coy look. "Not that you've been *alone*. You've dated plenty of women whose boats were, I'm sure, *well* floated."

He grinned. "You're getting it now—alone, but not *alone*."

A couple of guys who worked in sales at different wineries joined them. They all knew each other and visited for a few minutes before Brooke excused herself to use the restroom.

When she was gone, one asked, "How long have you and Brooke been dating?"

"We're not." Cam sipped his wine. "She's distributing our wine."

"Nice," the other one said, nodding. "So you're definitely not dating?"

Cam's senses pricked at their interest. "Definitely not. But what do you care?"

The second one, Joe, lifted a shoulder. "Just wondered about her availability. I asked her out a while back, but she said she wasn't dating. When I saw her with you, I assumed her status had changed."

Status...as in whether she would date or not. It certainly seemed as though she was considering it. He could encourage Joe, but he didn't want to. Man, he was a selfish bastard.

"I don't know," Cam said. "You could try asking her out again."

"I might, thanks."

Cam finished off his wine, suddenly ready to leave. But he wouldn't go until Brooke came back. When she returned, she glanced toward his empty glass. "You having another?"

"Nah, I'm heading out."

The other guys looked at her expectantly, and when Cam vacated his seat, Joe took it. A tiny crease formed between Brooke's eyes for just a moment. She looked at Cam. "I think I'm going to take off too." She smiled at Joe and Sam. "See you guys."

They nodded at her. "See you, Brooke," Joe said.

Cam swung by the bar, where Allen was now sitting, and thanked him for sharing his wine. Allen shook his hand and Brooke's and restated how he was looking forward to seeing her Monday. On their way out, Cam caught Luke's interested eye and shook his head.

"Did you want to go say hi to Luke?" Brooke asked as Cam opened the door for her.

"I talked to him earlier."

"Ah." She waved at Luke and smiled before she preceded Cam outside.

"Thanks for letting me leave with you," she said. "You've proven an effective shield tonight."

He laughed. "I'm happy to be your shield. Although don't expect it to have a lasting effect. Joe asked if we were an item, and when I said no, he made it clear he was interested in asking you out. Again, apparently."

She exhaled. "I see."

"It's your own fault for being so attractive."

She cast him a side eye as they strolled down Main Street. "Is that right? What should I do, forgo makeup? Stop washing my hair?"

He doubted any of that would help. She was more than a pretty face—she was funny and fun. He had a great time with her. "You could try. Let me know how that works."

"Or, I could just say that we're an item. Why not? You're not dating anyone. I'm not dating anyone. It would keep the vultures at bay."

A laugh erupted from his chest. "They're vultures now?"

She giggled. "Not that bad."

"Do you really have a problem fending off interested guys?"

"Sometimes. Tonight was one of those times, I guess."

"Because you look incredible."

She walked in front of him and turned, taking a few backward steps. She smiled at him—that sexy, seductive little grin that made his motor purr. "Why, thank you."

"Now you're just being mean. You have to stop flirting with me, Brooke. I'm not a vulture, but I'm still a *guy*." Who hadn't had sex in a few months. He mentally counted and couldn't quite come up with the last date. Three? Four?

She fell into step beside him as they turned onto Second. "Sorry. You're just so fun to tease."

"Well, you're tempting the hell out of me. I like our working relationship, but I'd be lying if I said I didn't think about taking things a step further—keeping in mind my policy. Nothing long-term."

They'd arrived at the door to the lofts. She turned toward him. "Okay, I get it. Don't flirt with you unless I want it to go somewhere."

He hadn't said that, but maybe that was what he meant. He let his gaze dip over her. She did look incredible. And if she were any other woman, he'd invite her over.

She held her clutch purse in front of her and brought her gaze to his. "So...remember when I said you should ask me again?"

Oh damn, did she mean what he thought she meant? Now she was seriously fucking with him. "About kissing?" The question came out raspy. He cleared his throat.

"Yes. You should ask me again."

He looked up and down the street, for the first time giving a shit if someone was watching. Why? Because he was suddenly agitated. Anxious. But in a good way. Anticipation curled through him.

"Don't say that unless you mean it."

Her blue-green eyes shone with intent. "Oh, I mean it." She reached out and grabbed his hand, pulling him back under the cover of the doorway.

The force of her action propelled him forward until he was nearly pressing against her. He linked his fingers through hers. "You sure?"

"Anyone ever tell you that you talk too much?" She wrapped her free hand around his neck and tugged his head down.

"Never in a moment like this." He brushed his lips against hers and slanted his head.

Her fingers curled into his neck, and she arched up into him. Her mouth opened beneath his, and the kiss took off like a rocket.

Their tongues met, eager, almost desperate. Or maybe that was their hands and bodies. She pulled him so that he was snug against her. He let go of her hand and gripped her hip. Her hand splayed against his side, the heat of her palm blistering through his shirt.

Her fingers stabbed into his hair, holding his head as she did ridiculous things to his mouth and tongue. Lights danced behind his closed eyes. He felt every inch of her—the press of her breasts against his chest, the pulse of her wrist against his neck, the push of her pelvis along his. He wanted to bring her even closer so that he could nestle his cock between her thighs.

She ended the kiss to nibble on his lips and drag her mouth and tongue along his jaw, then kissed him again. Holy hell, he was burning for her.

The next time she pulled away, she leaned back against the wall beside the door, her breath coming in heavy pants. His did the same. "Brooke." The word came out dark and hard. Needful. "I should go."

She looked up at him, her gorgeous aqua eyes dilated and so damn seductive. He exerted every bit of willpower he had and stepped back, heedless of his raging erection. There was absolutely no help for it. "Unless you want me to stay." He hadn't meant to say it. He was trying so damned hard to be a gentleman.

"I do. But...you're right that you should go." She blinked, and it dampened a bit of the electricity zinging between them. "I'm probably going to regret this," she muttered.

He knew he would. "Good night."

He turned and dashed across the street before what little common sense he had left completely abandoned him.

Chapter Eight

Brooke watched Cam cross the street, her legs shaking and her heart thundering in her chest. Her brain forced her body to turn and go into the building. But even parts of her brain were rebelling, telling her to go after him.

When was the last time she'd been kissed like that?

She tried to think, but her mind was mush. Okay, not that mushy. She wasn't sure that Darren had ever made her feel that good. Overwhelmed in the best possible way. Absolutely quivering with need. She almost turned and went back outside.

Pushing herself to the elevator, she jabbed her finger onto the Up button. Waiting, she pulled her phone from her clutch and texted her older sister, Rhonda.

I just walked away from a totally hot guy. Give me a reason I should go spend the night with him.

The response came almost immediately.

Rhonda: *Because you SHOULD. GO NOW*.

Brooke: *That's not a good reason.*

Rhonda: *You haven't had sex in years.*

Brooke: *He's a player.*

Rhonda: *So? You aren't marrying him. Go have great sex.*

Brooke: *It's been a long time...*

Rhonda: *OMG!*

Brooke smiled, hearing her sister's voice yelling at her.

Rhonda: *You're looking for excuses. If you're asking me for permission, you already want to. So go do it. Will you regret it?*

The elevator chimed, but Brooke didn't walk inside. Instead, she crossed to the other side of the lobby and stared at her phone. *Would* she regret it? Maybe. They did work together, after all. Things could very well be awkward.

Or they could be amazing, and she'd feel better than she had in years. Just kissing him had made her positively woozy with want. She'd been fine with her solitary, celibate life, but right now she thought she might wilt if she didn't find satisfaction.

With Cam.

Nothing else would do.

She tapped into her phone again. *What about my...problem?*

Rhonda: *What problem?*

Brooke frowned at the phone. *Duh, my infertility.*

Rhonda: *Srsly?! You want to have sex with this guy, not start a family! You said he was a player!*

Brooke watched the dots on her phone, which indicated Rhonda was typing. And it was a long text.

You deserve a night of fun. You actually deserve way more than that, but whatever. Please let yourself out of grief jail or whatever the hell you've been doing the past few years and LIVE. I can't even imagine why you're hesitating. But then I don't understand a lot of your choices.

Like divorcing Darren because they couldn't have children. Only it had been more than that. The fertility problems had sent Brooke into a tailspin, and she'd pushed everyone away, especially Darren, who hadn't been that devastated by her inability to carry a child. She'd been so immersed in her sadness that he'd started screwing one of the legal assistants at the law firm where he was in charge of IT. She'd never told anyone about that. It had seemed like her fault, but suddenly, in this moment, she realized it wasn't.

Brooke: *If you're talking about Darren, I had a perfectly good reason for leaving him. He was screwing that woman he's still with.*

Rhonda: *WTF?! Why didn't you ever say anything?*

Brooke: *I just didn't.*

Because she'd been too locked up in "grief jail," as Rhonda put it. Everything had felt like her fault, like her inadequacy. So she'd taken it as such.

Rhonda: *If you don't go get laid right now, I'm driving up there and kicking your ass tomorrow.*

Brooke: *How will you know? Apparently I'm a pretty good liar.*

Rhonda: *I want proof. Send me a pic of his boxers or something.*

Brooke giggled. She had a tiny bit of a wine buzz, so this idea was probably funnier—and more stupid—than it ought to be.

Brooke: *Okay.*

Rhonda: *Okay, you're doing it? YESSSSSS! Go get him!!!!*

Brooke rolled her eyes with a grin and stuffed the phone back in her clutch. Then she turned and left the building, barely looking both ways across the sleepy street before she hurried over to his townhouse. The sun had gone down behind the buildings, but it wasn't fully set so that there was a warm, golden glow over everything.

She raised her hand to knock, but didn't. What if he didn't want her to come in?

Oh come on, *he was totally into you!*

But he'd been the one to break the kiss and suggest they should go their separate ways.

He'd also suggested he could stay!

That was true. And he'd certainly acted as though he was enjoying it. He'd clutched at her body and wrought sensations she hadn't felt in years, if ever. Plus there'd been the evidence of his insistent erection pressing at her core. Her knees felt weak as she recalled the pulse of lust she'd felt every time he leaned into her.

Without further thought, she knocked.

Nothing.

Her gut clenched. She knocked again.

Still nothing.

Doubt crept in and iced the surge of desire she'd just felt. Clearly she'd made a mistake. She turned, and her purse vibrated. She pulled out her phone.

Rhonda: *I hope you aren't reading this, but if you are, stop vacillating and do it!*

She hadn't been vacillating! She'd been arguing with herself. Surely the difference between those two things was somehow important.

Okay, one more try. She took a deep breath and knocked again. Hard. And long.

At last she heard footfalls. It almost sounded like running followed by a thud. She winced. After a moment, the door clicked and came open.

Cam stood there, a towel draped about his waist, his hair soaked, and his cheeks flushed.

"Uh." She couldn't seem to form words. She'd seen his chest before—that day at the winery. And it was just as spectacular now as it had been then. Nearly smooth, but with just the right amount of sexy hair curled in the center. And the muscle definition—that was eye-popping. "I seem to have a knack for catching you when you're just out of the shower." She took in the towel wrapped about his lean hips.

"Yes, you do. It's like you have radar. And a damn useful one at that."

Damn useful indeed. She couldn't seem to look up. Her fingers itched to touch him, and her mouth was dry with the need to taste him. Water droplets clung to his flesh, making him look even sexier. Finally, she lifted her gaze. He was staring at her, his green eyes dark and sultry. "Did I interrupt your shower, or were you done?" she asked, rather stupidly.

He shook his head. "You're not interrupting anything. I just, uh, I needed to cool off."

He'd needed a cold shower? Made sense, she supposed. She might've had to do the same if she hadn't come back over. Or found her vibrator.

For some bizarre, perhaps prurient reason, she dropped her gaze to his crotch. No tent. Shit, was she too late?

He opened the door wider. "I'm such an ass. You should come in. Please."

She blinked at him, wondering if that was a good idea.

He pulled her inside and closed the door. "I don't really want to stand in my doorway in nothing but a towel."

She blushed then, feeling like an idiot. "Sorry, my bad."

"Why'd you come over?"

"I, uh..." Her sister's voice sounded in her head: stop vacillating! "I came to have sex. If you want to." Life didn't get any more honest than that, did it?

His eyes widened, and she nearly laughed at his shocked expression. "I'm surprised."

"Clearly." She dipped a look at his towel again and saw the start of something...tentlike. "I was afraid I was too late."

"What? Why?"

She looked up at his face. "You were in the shower. A cold shower, I guess. And you weren't—" Her gaze fell once more. "You looked as though you'd taken care of business."

He paused the briefest of moments before laughing. "You thought I was masturbating?" He sobered. "Okay, you caught me. You did interrupt—thank God—and then I slipped on the hardwood coming off the bottom of the stairs. That tends to kill an erection."

Now it was her turn to laugh at the image of him falling. "Did you fall completely? I heard a crash."

"Oh yeah. Towel went flying, and I hit the wall. Totally unsexy. Hurt like hell too."

She giggled. "Where?"

He gestured to the wall across from the stairs and the floor beside it. "Here."

She giggled harder, her stomach muscles contracting. "No. Where did you hurt yourself?"

He joined her in laughing. He pivoted and stroked his hip. "My ass, if you really want to know."

"I do." She tossed her purse on a small table, which he'd apparently just missed in his catastrophic spill. "Let me see."

He arched his brow at her but said nothing. He let that side of the towel go, and it fell across his butt, revealing a perfectly sculpted cheek. With a red mark on the side.

She lightly touched him, caressing his warm flesh. Desire flared through her, along with a burst of anxiety. It had been far too long since she'd seen a naked man, let alone touched one. "That's going to leave a bruise."

He looked at her over his shoulder. "I suppose it would be horribly cliché to ask you to kiss it for me?"

She continued to stroke him. "Horribly." Nonetheless, she was considering it.

"Did you mean what you said? About wanting to have sex?"

She stared at the hard plane of his lower back, the mouthwatering muscles tapering from his ass to his hamstring. "Yes."

Now more than ever. She wanted to grip his flesh as he drove into her. "Were you really masturbating?"

He wrapped the towel back around his hips, surprising her. What had she expected? That he'd pick her up caveman-style and thrust her against the wall for a good, hard screw? God, that sounded divine. Her thighs quivered in response.

He turned, and the tent was in full effect now. "Guilty. What can I say? I'm not seeing anyone right now, and spending the evening with you is enough to get me pretty worked up, particularly because you're unapologetically flirtatious. And sexy as hell."

She licked her lower lip. "That towel is going to have trouble staying in place."

"Especially if you keep doing provocative things with your tongue," he growled, catapulting her into an even greater state of sexual agitation.

"I'd like to, but you seem hesitant." She was still waiting for her caveman moment.

"I just want to be clear. You remember what I told you earlier. This is casual. If we have sex tonight, you can't expect me to call you tomorrow." He tipped his head back, and when he brought it back down, his mouth dipped into an almost frown. "Actually you can, because we'll still be working together. That's the other thing to consider. Is this going to be awkward?"

Yes, that *was* something to consider. Maybe the biggest something. "I don't know. We're adults, and I'd like to think we can keep this separate. But maybe not. Or maybe it won't be great, and we won't have any trouble pretending it never happened."

He took a step toward her, his eyes intensely green. "I'd bet my life that won't be the case."

She would too. This was already one of the most exciting,

enthralling, utterly arousing evenings she'd ever had. At the wine tasting earlier, there'd been this sexy undercurrent that went beyond flirtation. She'd wondered if it had just been her, but perhaps not.

He suddenly broke their eye contact. He looked over toward his kitchen. She followed his line of sight but had no idea what he was looking at. When his gaze found hers again, the kinetic sparks were gone.

She tensed, wondering what had happened.

"As much as I'd love to continue this evening toward its certainly thrilling conclusion, I think we should stop." The planes of his face were taut, his muscles rigid. He appeared physically pained.

Disappointment curdled in her gut. "I see." Her gaze dipped to his towel tent. He was clearly still aroused. But he was pushing her away. Had she done something wrong? She *was* out of practice. She wanted to find a hole, crawl inside, and maybe come out next week. *Maybe.*

She picked up her purse from the table. "Sure. I get it." Only she wasn't sure she did. A guy who was notorious for his conquests had just turned her down.

She wasn't sure it got any more pathetic than that.

You are not pathetic!

No, she wasn't. She was, however, pissed.

"Good decision," she said, turning. "I'll talk to you next week."

———

Cam watched her walk toward the door, his mind churning for something to say that didn't sound lame or patronizing. He moved quickly—too quickly as his towel tried to slide off his hips. He was vaguely aware that his erection was still raging. And *that* wasn't awkward as hell.

He caught up to her as she turned the handle and put his hand over hers. "Wait. I don't want you to be upset."

She turned her head, and her eyes were blazing. *Too late.* "You just turned me down. How am I supposed to feel?"

He tried to think of what to say that would soothe the situation. He didn't want her to be mad. Or whatever else she might be feeling. "Like you dodged a bullet?"

She arched a brow at him in question, and the fire in her eyes didn't diminish.

"I'm bad news, right?"

She just stared at him. He was not handling this well at all. "Look, it's the work thing," he said. "You're a tremendous asset, and I don't want to mess that up. Your job is important to you— as it should be—and I don't want to cause problems for you."

Her eyes narrowed. "Or for you. At least take some ownership here."

He inwardly winced. "Okay. I like and respect you too much to muck up our working relationship."

Her upper lip curled. "Since I'm pretty sure you've screwed other people you had to work with, I'm not sure how to take that. I guess I should just be happy I rate higher than those other women. Poor them."

Damn it, she was right. He'd slept with plenty of women he'd worked with, but they didn't live here in Ribbon Ridge. Across the street. They weren't in his everyday world. Well, fuck if he didn't feel like the manwhore everyone had always joked that he was.

Before he could come up with a reasonable response, she dipped her gaze and let out a harsh laugh. "I guess your hand is getting lucky tonight after all. Have fun." She opened the door and left, closing it sharply behind her.

He stared at the wood, tempted to go after her. But what would be the point? The way his night was going, he'd probably lose his towel in the street and accidentally lock himself out. Absurdly, he laughed, but only for a moment.

Damn it.

That had been a lose-lose situation. If she'd stayed, their work relationship probably would've suffered. But wouldn't it suffer anyway? She was pissed and rightfully so.

She wouldn't stay pissed, though. At least he hoped not. She'd come to realize this was the right decision, even if he'd probably doubt it for the rest of his life.

That nasty word—regret—reared in his mind again. This was one he'd have to learn to live with. In the meantime, he was getting right back in the damned shower.

He took the stairs two at a time.

Chapter Nine

Brooke slept later than usual on Sunday, then puttered around her loft, emptying the last of her moving boxes and hanging a few pictures. She kept herself from looking out the window toward Cam's townhouse, lest she happen to catch him coming or going. She'd have to face him sooner or later, but she'd do her best to make sure it was later.

She made herself a salad for lunch and was just finishing up when her phone rang. Her immediate thought was that it could be Cam, and she perversely hoped it was so that she could ignore him. But no, it was her sister on FaceTime.

Knowing full well that Rhonda wanted an accounting of what had happened last night, Brooke answered the phone anyway. She wanted to unload, and Rhonda would be a sympathetic ear.

She propped the phone against her water bottle on the table. "Hey, Rhonda."

Her sister's smile greeted her. She wore no makeup, but she'd never needed it, and her light brown hair was pulled back in a high ponytail—her "mom do" as she called it. "Hey! I waited as long as I could. I'm not catching you at a bad time, am I?"

Translation: Are you still shacked up with the hottie?

"Would I have answered the phone if you were?" Brooke asked.

Rhonda laughed. "I guess not, but you *are* out of practice."

So out of practice. "Yeah, I'm so rusty, I completely crashed and burned."

Rhonda's jaw dropped. "WHAT?!"

Brooke smiled, glad she didn't have the phone next to her ear.

"What happened?" Rhonda asked, clearly agitated. She sat down, and Brooke could tell she was on one of the stools at her kitchen counter.

"He wanted to, but he decided to grow a conscience. He was afraid we'd damage our working relationship if we went down that path."

Rhonda held up her hand and set the phone down against something so that she was hands-free. "Wait a sec. You didn't tell me you worked together."

Brooke hadn't meant to leave that part out. She just hadn't been thinking clearly. Damn him and his stupid sexy smile and his annoyingly seductive charm. "I picked up his winery as a client a couple of weeks ago."

Rhonda mashed her lips together. "Hmm. That's no bueno, sis. I hate to say it, but that was probably a good move on his part."

Brooke scowled. "Wow, you are not making me feel better."

"I know, and I'm sorry. I'm sure he's an asshole. Does that help?"

"A little." Brooke couldn't argue with her sister's logic, much as she wanted to. It had been a good move. And one *she* ought to have made, not him. "It just sucks. I finally put myself out there, and it was a total fail."

Rhonda cocked her head and nodded sympathetically. "It wasn't a *total* fail. You said he wanted to sleep with you, right?"

Yes, he'd said as much, even if his towering hard-on and admitted masturbation hadn't been evidence enough. "It doesn't really matter, though, does it? In the end, he passed."

"Ugh, don't take it like that. I think it's cool that he respected you enough to keep things professional."

God, did she have to regurgitate what he'd told her? Brooke tried to keep her expression impassive while silently cursing the jerk who'd invented FaceTime.

But Rhonda knew her too well. She winced. "He said that, didn't he?"

Brooke sat back in her chair and crossed her arms. "Yep."

Rhonda blew her a kiss. "Sorry."

"I guess it bothers me that he's slept with other women he's worked with before. But somehow I fell short."

Rhonda's forehead creased for a moment. "Or...he likes you more than he liked the others, and he really doesn't want to mess up a good thing workwise."

"He did spout some nonsense about not wanting to screw up my job since he knows it's important to me."

"Doesn't sound like nonsense. It sounds like he made a tough call." She set her elbow on her kitchen counter and leaned her chin on her palm. "One you probably would have made if your uninformed sister hadn't pushed you toward him."

Brooke appreciated Rhonda trying to shoulder some of the blame, but Rhonda was right—Brooke should have been the one to call a halt. Instead, she'd ended up feeling as though she'd been dumped. Which was stupid. But the hurt of Darren's betrayal had replayed at the back of her mind, like a bad song that pops into your head and stays there for a day. Or more. The old feelings had meshed with the new until she'd just felt like she ought to swear off men forever.

"So...since you're not going to be getting lucky with the hot coworker, Mom wants to set you up with someone."

Oh no. Brooke uncrossed her arms, instantly alert and tense. "I do not want Mom to set me up."

She'd tried a couple of times to put Brooke "back on the horse again," as she put it. Only Brooke hadn't been ready, and she still wasn't completely sure that she was. She'd told Cam last night that she might be interested in casual dating. But she'd been flirting with him. Anyway, she'd said "might." After last night's debacle, she was ready to revise that to "no way in hell."

Rhonda dropped her hand from her chin. "I know you're skeptical, but this doesn't sound like a bad deal, especially since you're ready to move on. *Finally*."

Brooke bristled at that but said nothing.

"You know Mom's pal Joyce?" At Brooke's nod she continued. "She has a nephew who's been living in McMinnville the past couple of years. He works in admissions at the college. I saw a picture, and he's cute."

Brooke remained skeptical. Her opinion of cute differed from Rhonda's. Her sister liked tall, lean guys with glasses, whose wardrobes contained funny T-shirts and a lot of button-downs—including flannel—to throw over them. In her own words, she dug nerds. Brooke preferred men who were well put together and more traditionally handsome. She supposed you could call them movie-star variety like Ryan Gosling or Chris Pine. Or Ribbon Ridge-winery-owner variety. Like Cameron Westcott.

"I don't know. I'll think about it." That would buy her time to come up with an excuse.

Rhonda blinked. "You will?"

"I said I'd think about it, not that I'd go out with him."

"I heard you. It's just more than you've committed to in... well, ever."

"I committed to nothing. Do not get Mom's hopes up." Brooke suddenly felt claustrophobic. It was a beautiful day, and she needed some exercise. "I'm going for a jog. Thanks for the pep talk."

"Sorry, I kind of sucked at that. I'm proud of you for taking the next step, even if it wasn't successful." She leaned forward, her brows arching. "And no, that's not the same as calling it a failure."

Brooke rolled her eyes. "Yeah, okay. You sound like such a middle school counselor."

Rhonda laughed as she picked up her phone. "Because I *am* a middle school counselor."

She was also a younger-sister counselor. How many times had Brooke and their little sister Tracy commiserated over Rhonda's bossiness, aka "help"? Too many to count.

"I'm going now," Brooke said. "Really, thanks. I appreciate your support."

Rhonda smiled at her and blew another kiss. "I love you, sis."

"Love you too." Brooke sent a kiss back and disconnected.

Brooke took her dishes to the sink and went to put on her running shoes. After strapping her phone to her bicep and tucking in earbuds, she took the elevator down to the garage so she could exit the building away from Cam's townhouse.

She hoped he wasn't out and about on foot today. Ugh, why'd she have to move to such a small town? No, the real question was why did she have to have a crush on a player she would most certainly run into on a regular basis?

Yuck. She didn't want to have a crush on him. So she wouldn't. She turned up the music and clenched her teeth as she ran near the park. It was a beautiful afternoon, and there were several families enjoying picnics. An impromptu soccer game was going on and the playground was clogged with children. She turned her attention away and kept her gaze focused straight ahead.

Crossing the street, she breathed easier as she left the scene of familial bliss behind. She jogged by City Hall and the police station, nodding at an officer as she passed. A sandwich board sign at the edge of the sidewalk read, "Library Now Open!"

Brooke turned her head to where a small piece of the City Hall building had been carved out to form the new community library. She'd heard that it was going to open soon, but didn't know it already had. The door was open, and she couldn't resist the scent of books.

She pulled her headphones from her ears and draped the cord around her neck as she walked inside. A rush of cool air-conditioning turned the sweat dappling her forehead and neck to ice, causing her to shiver.

To her right was a small checkout counter, and next to that, a couple of self-checkout machines. To her left was a reading area, clearly designed for children, with small chairs and short tables with stubby legs. A mother sat in one of the chairs, her knees hitting her chest as she read to her daughter, who sat beside her. She was around three years old, and she was utterly focused on the pages of the picture book lying open on the table. The mother stroked the girl's dark hair—a small, instinctive gesture, one that she was probably unaware of but that cut straight to Brooke's heart.

She turned abruptly and nearly crashed into a young woman. "Oh! Sorry, I didn't see you. My bad."

The woman smiled, her pale blue eyes crinkling at the edges. "It's no problem. Can I help you find anything?"

Brooke surveyed the books the woman clutched to her chest —she clearly worked here. "No, thank you. I was just running by and wanted to stop in for a quick look. It's so great to have a library."

The woman nodded. "Isn't it? It's been a long time coming. Ribbon Ridge has needed one for years. Well, I guess they had one once around the turn of the century. It was more of a traveling situation with a small collection of books that circulated around the area."

"You know your history," Brooke said. The brick at West Arch and what Hayden had told her about it popped into her head. "Do you know anything about a proposed Ribbon Ridge museum?"

The librarian tucked a dark curl behind her ear. "You've heard about that?"

"Only that it's in development. I work with Hayden Archer, and he mentioned it. I know you're not Alaina Pierce—he said she was working on it with her best friend. Is that you?"

She shook her head, chuckling. "Goodness, no. I only know Alaina a little, mostly from when she comes in to The Arch and Vine. I work there part-time as a server. Used to be full-time until I was hired here as the librarian, which is what I've always wanted to do."

Brooke knew The Arch and Vine was owned by the Archers, so it made sense that this woman was familiar with them, at least as an employee. "I'm Brooke Ellis, by the way." She offered her hand.

The librarian shook her hand. "Kelsey McDade. Nice to meet you."

"You too. I'm pretty new to town, so I don't really know many people."

Kelsey flashed a smile. "Well, you know the Archers, and if you have their stamp of approval, you're good to go in Ribbon Ridge."

Brooke chuckled. "I know one Archer—Hayden. And his

wife. And I don't know them well. I'm distributing his wine, so our relationship is both new and strictly professional." She couldn't help but think of Cameron and how their relationship was exactly the same. Then she couldn't help but think about how that sucked.

"I know several of them since I've worked at the pub for a couple of years. They're good people. I like Hayden and Bex a lot. She makes great beer."

"So I hear," Brooke said. "I'll have to try it sometime. Maybe you can join me."

Kelsey nodded, smiling. "That would be fun."

Brooke tugged her phone from her armband. "What's your cell, and I'll send you my number."

Kelsey rattled off the number. "Have you been up to The Alex? That's where Bex is the brewer—at The Arch and Fox, to be exact."

"Just once. I went to a wine dinner several months ago." She thought back and tried to recall if Cam had been there. He had to have been, but she didn't remember him. It was odd, but she had a hard time believing she could be in the same room with him and not be aware of his presence. Which was really stupid.

Time to get back to that run that was supposed to be clearing her head.

"Hey, about that museum," Kelsey started, sounding a bit hesitant. "What else did Hayden say? I've been thinking it would be great to open a Ribbon Ridge history exhibit upstairs."

Brooke grinned. "What a terrific idea—goes right along with the library. I think people would love it. Hayden didn't say much, just that Alaina and her best friend were working on it or something. You should ask him."

"I will, thanks." Kelsey moved the books to her other arm. "I should've thought to talk to the Archers. They're the reason this library even happened. They gave a grant to the county to expand the library system here."

"Wow." Brooke didn't even want to consider how much money that might have been. But even she, who was new to town, knew that the Archers were one of the wealthiest families in the state. "I bet they'd be thrilled to work with you on it." Brooke's mind turned to the brick again. "I was up at the winery —Hayden's winery—last week, and they showed me this cool brick that looks like it had to have been from around the founding of the town. Actually, I have no idea when Ribbon Ridge was founded. The brick was from 1879."

"That's pretty close," Kelsey said. "Benjamin Archer settled here in 1856 after a friend of his—a fur trader—wrote to him about the beauty of the area."

"The brick had the initials BNR on it."

"Where'd they find this brick?" Kelsey asked.

"Near the foundation of a house they tore down on the winery property. They think it had to have come from an earlier structure." Brooke frowned. "They're planning to install it in the fire pit outside, but I think it needs to be somewhere protected."

Kelsey smiled, her brow arching. "Like a museum?"

"Bingo." Brooke smiled in return. "You should definitely talk to them. Soon."

"I will. And hey, if you're at the winery, try to put that brick somewhere safe!"

And just like that, Brooke's mood took a turn down Disappointment Street. Yes, she'd be at the winery, but probably not soon, if she could help it. "Sure, I'll do that. But you'll probably beat me to it."

"Well, with both of us after it, we'll get it handled."

Someone came from the back of the library and approached the front desk. Kelsey nodded at them. "Guess I should help this person check out a book. I'll text you about getting together. It was really nice to meet you."

Brooke pulled her headphones from around her neck. "You too. See you later." She waved as she turned and left the library.

As she started up her run, she pushed herself hard so that her mind couldn't stray to Cam. By the time she got back to the loft, she was hot and tired. But her plan had worked because she hadn't thought to alter her path to avoid passing in front of his townhouse. And that made her smile.

———

For what seemed the hundredth time that morning, Cam caught himself staring off into space, rehashing what had happened on Saturday night. He'd spent most of yesterday on a friend's boat, which had served to distract his mind from thoughts of Brooke and what he'd missed out on.

Had he really turned her away?

Yep, and his conscience kept reiterating that it had been the right thing to do. But that didn't mean other parts of him agreed. He liked her. A lot. He wanted her. *A lot.*

But he also respected her, and he knew how much she loved her job. Still, she'd been the one to offer...

Thankfully his brothers took that moment to interrupt his pointless musings.

"What's up?" Jamie asked as he sprawled in one of the chairs in front of Cam's desk.

"Just working," Cam said. He eyed both of them as Luke took the other chair. "What do you guys need?"

Jamie clasped the arms of the chair. "We wanted to touch base about the wine dinner. We're about a month out, so things are going to start amping up."

Cam leaned back in his chair and twirled his pen between

his fingers. "I talked to Sara this morning, and she's got logistics pretty well covered."

"How's the food coming?" Luke asked. "Shouldn't we have a menu to advertise yet?" He shook his head. "What do I know? I leave the marketing and whatnot up to you."

Cam snorted. "Thanks. We're close. Kyle's just finalizing the dessert." As the executive chef at The Arch and Fox, Kyle was working on just the right recipes to pair with their wine.

"He better hurry. Isn't Maggie going to pop any day?" Jamie asked.

They were expecting their first child in a couple of weeks. "Not quite yet, but yeah, the timing's not ideal." Cam chuckled. "He's well aware. I'll follow up with him this afternoon."

Jamie slapped his hands on the arm of the chair as he sat forward. "Remind him of our budget. Kyle likes to splurge."

"You know I won't be able to stop him, and he'll just insist on paying the difference."

Jamie grinned. "He can afford it. Before I go, what's the scoop on the guest list? I met a woman the other night that I'd like to invite."

Cam exchanged an interested look with Luke before they both turned their attention to their little brother. "Not Madison?"

Jamie laughed. "No, not Madison. Leah's the new CFO at Seven Wonders. She's a business contact." That was one of the largest wineries in the area.

Cam tossed his pen onto the desk. "We aren't inviting a lot of winemakers. We're focused on people who are going to buy or promote our wine."

"I know, but her brother writes for *Wine Spectator* so..."

Cam leaned forward. "Say no more. She's in. And great get. Any chance he'll come?"

"I said we'd love to have him. We'll see what happens."

Cam rubbed his hands together. He'd invited someone from the magazine to come, but they hadn't committed yet and at this point, he feared they wouldn't. This connection might help. "Excellent. Brooke's also working an angle at *Wine Enthusiast*." She knew someone there and was pretty close to getting her to commit.

Jamie stood. "Brooke's been awesome. She's picked up some great accounts. Good find, bro." He nodded at Cam before turning and heading out of the office. "Back to the grind."

Luke didn't leave with him. Cam looked at his middle brother and arched a brow. "No grind for you?"

"Always, but since Jamie brought up Brooke..." He let the question hang out there, and Cam had no doubt what he was getting at.

Still, he'd make him work for it. "What about her?"

Luke let out a quick chuckle. He leaned his elbow on the armrest. "You left with her the other night. What happened?"

"Nothing. She lives across the street from me. I walked her home."

Luke scrutinized him for a moment, as if he could discern what had actually happened. Cam stared at him in stoic silence, daring him to try.

"I just wanted to know if I need to worry that you might drive her away."

Cam flashed a purely sarcastic smile. "Oh, that's nice of you. No, I won't be driving her away. Our relationship is strictly professional."

"Yeah, right. I see the way you look at each other."

Cam stood, irritated by the conversation because their relationship *was* strictly professional and it *sucked*. "Can you drop it?"

Luke got to his feet. "Hey, I'm not trying to be a dick."

Maybe not, but he was doing an excellent job.

"My bad. You guys seemed like you might make a good couple, that's all."

They might've, but if they tried and it didn't work out, things would be awkward. No, worse than that. Things would be ugly, and he and Brooke wouldn't be able to maintain this working relationship. And the winery was far more important to Cam than any sort of romantic entanglement. Which he didn't need or want anyway.

Cam rubbed his hand over his eyes and looked at his brother. "Look, I appreciate you trying to be supportive or whatever it is you're doing, but leave it alone. Yes, we were attracted to each other and we discussed going out. We decided the working relationship was too important to jeopardize, okay?"

"How mature of you both." Luke laughed. "I'm not sure I'd have that kind of resolve."

Cam chuckled, letting his irritation fall away. "Clearly. Wasn't your girlfriend in Cali a coworker?"

"At first, yeah, but then she moved to another winery."

"Was that a mutual decision?"

"Sort of. The boss found out, and told us to figure it out." Luke glanced toward the windows. "He made it, uh, clear that he didn't want to lose me."

"Ouch. I bet she was pissed."

Luke laughed again. "Yes, but not enough to break up."

Cam knew that because Luke moving up here hadn't even been enough to break them up. They'd kept up a long-distance relationship for a year or so before he'd finally called it quits. And he hadn't dated anyone since. "You know, if you spent half as much energy on your own love life as you do speculating about me and Brooke, you might actually start dating."

"Hey, I date. I'm just busy. Like you."

"Exactly. Keep your nose out of my business and I'll do the same."

Luke threw up his hands. "So much for brotherly cama-raderie or whatever." He turned and walked to the door but paused before leaving. "You usually take this sort of poking better. It seems like Brooke means more to you than anyone you've...*whatevered* with."

Cam stifled a scowl because he feared Luke was right. "Would you go, please?"

"I'm going." He pivoted and went out the door, closing it behind him.

Cam went to his mini fridge and popped open a sparkling water. He stood at the window and looked out over the sloping vineyard. It was green and verdant amidst the yellows and browns of mid-August. A sort of oasis, and it represented their hard work.

That was what he needed to focus on right now, not Brooke. This introductory dinner next month was crucial.

And what the hell was he thinking, anyway? He wasn't long-term relationship material, which meant an inevitable breakup. He liked her too much for things to end like that—and maybe that was the *real* reason he'd called a halt. Either way, it had been the right decision.

Chapter Ten

After meeting Kelsey for a beer at Books 'N Brew, Ribbon Ridge's kitschy bookstore that served coffee in the morning and Archer beer in the evening, Brooke and her new friend made their way down Main Street to the edge of town to Ruckus, Ribbon Ridge's answer to a dive bar.

"Thanks for agreeing to come here instead of The Arch and Vine," Kelsey said as they cut into the parking lot.

"No problem." Brooke flashed her a smile. "I totally understand why you don't want to hang out at your job on your night off. Plus, I'm the one that suggested something more casual than The Arch and Fox." They'd agreed to go up and drink Bex's beer another time.

The night was warm and dry, typical of August in the Willamette Valley. Brooke was glad she'd put her hair up, but she was still heated after the walk.

"Have you been here before?" Kelsey asked as they approached the door.

"Not yet. Do I need to be prepped?"

Kelsey laughed. "No. It's just a different clientele from most of the other places in town."

Brooke could see that, judging from the motorcycles and four-wheel-drive trucks in the lot as well as the neon signs offering Keno and video poker. It reminded her of the family friendly restaurant by day and bar by night back home, where her family had enjoyed many an excellent burger. "Do they serve burgers?"

"No, just basic bar food. Pretzels, hot dogs, fries, and nachos. Although, don't expect their nachos to compare to The Arch and Vine."

"I haven't had them." Brooke had only eaten at the Archers' pub a couple of times. "They do have pretty good burgers though."

Kelsey opened the door, and music blared at them. "That they do."

Brooke walked in behind her. "Bar or table?"

"Definitely table."

They scanned the busy room. The tables looked pretty full. But Kelsey pointed toward an empty booth in the middle of the far wall. It was still cluttered with glasses, indicating it had been recently vacated. Brooke nodded, and they wove through tables and patrons to reach their destination. Between the music and the conversation, a deep hum filled the place.

They each slid into opposite sides of the booth and set about scooting the former occupants' detritus to the edge of the table.

"Why do I feel like I should bus this?" Kelsey laughed.

Brooke joined her, chuckling. "Resist the urge! It's your night off."

A server came by and stacked the glasses. "Sorry. We're busy tonight." She pulled a towel from a pocket in the small apron around her waist and wiped down the table. "Do you know what you want?"

They ordered a couple of beers, and the server took off.

"So what's going on with the history exhibit?" Brooke asked.

"I talked to Hayden, and he hooked me up with Alaina and her friend Crystal. They were pretty excited to hear about the brick you mentioned. Which reminds me, I totally forgot to ask Hayden for it." Kelsey shook her head. "Any chance you'll be up at the winery any time soon? Maybe you can grab it."

Brooke would probably have to stop by there sometime next week to pick up more wine samples. She was running low, but she knew she'd wait until the last possible moment to get more. As it was, communication between her and Cam had trickled to a bare minimum. They'd exchanged just a couple of quick e-mails this week about the wine dinner next month.

"Sure, I can do that," Brooke said. She went back to their topic to push Cam out of her head. "So what's your plan with the exhibit?"

"I guess there was some discussion about turning the Archer homestead into a museum, but Alaina and her husband are renovating it instead, and they plan to live there."

Brooke immediately wondered if that was where the brick had come from. "What's the Archer homestead?"

"It's a house on the current Archer estate that dates back to about 1890." Kelsey's mouth curved up. "Yes, too late for the brick—I can see you went to the same place I did immediately." She chuckled.

Brooke smiled. "I did. The initials on it—BNR—did anyone have a clue about them?"

Kelsey shook her head. "No, but they were going to hit the books and see what they could find. I've been doing a bit of searching too, but they have the bulk of the materials."

"What sort of materials?" Brooke looked up at the server as she arrived with their beer. "Thanks."

Kelsey curled her hand around the base of her pint glass. "Letters, copies of birth and death certificates, and property deeds. A random collection, I guess. I haven't seen it yet. We're getting together soon so I can take a look and put together some ideas for the exhibit."

"That sounds so fun. You're going to house it upstairs at the library?"

Kelsey took a quick sip of her beer. "Yes. You know, I'm sure we could use a hand if you want to help. I'm always looking for library volunteers."

Brooke instantly warmed to the idea. It would give her something to do that wasn't work-related. Between that and trying to restart her nonexistent love life, she'd be busy enough to forget all about Cameron Westcott.

"I'd love to help, thanks for asking." Brooke took a long drink of beer. "Maybe we should've ordered shots."

Kelsey laughed. "Is that right? Is there something you're trying to forget?"

Wow, she'd nailed that. "It's just been a long week."

Kelsey grimaced. "And it's not over yet. I'm working at the library tomorrow from ten to four, then at The Arch and Vine from five to close."

"Yikes! I'd say you need a shot—or several—but then you might not be able to function tomorrow."

"True. So rain check on shots?"

"Definitely. I'd say on your next day off, but I'm worried you don't have any." Even though Kelsey hadn't worked at the pub today, she told Brooke that she'd done a full day at the library.

Kelsey lifted a shoulder. "The library's closed on Mondays and Wednesdays, and I try not to work at the pub on one of those days."

"So one day a week." At Kelsey's sheepish nod, Brooke shook her head. "That's not enough! Why do I think this is the first social outing you've had in ages?"

"Because it is?" Kelsey waved her hand. "It's fine. I like to be busy."

"Clearly you don't have a boyfriend, and I'm guessing you don't even date." Wow, this sounded so familiar. No wonder they'd hit it off.

"No, and correct."

Brooke lifted her pint in toast. "Well then, we have that in common. Men suck."

Kelsey was quick to tap her glass to Brooke's. "Amen."

They drank deeply, and Kelsey was the first to jump in. "Anything you want to share?"

Brooke shrugged. "I don't want to be Debbie Downer. Suffice it to say I'm divorced."

Kelsey nodded, and her eyes were warm and empathetic. "I get you. I won't depress you with my story either. Not divorced, but a long-term relationship that ended badly." She shuddered.

"Sorry to hear that. You might think I'm crazy, but I've actually been thinking it's time to get back in the game. I have two sisters and an overinvolved mother who keep trying to set me up."

Kelsey laughed. "I thought you told me earlier that your family still lives in southern Oregon?"

"They do, but you think that would stop them?"

"One can hope. My family lives up in Washington, and it could be Siberia for all I see of them."

Brooke couldn't tell if that was a good thing or not. "And is that okay?"

Kelsey cupped her hands around her pint glass. "It's fine. It's just my mom and stepdad and my younger half-brother. He's still in high school, so they're focused on that." She took another drink of beer. "Are you eyeing someone in particular? To date, I mean."

An image of Cam in his towel at his townhouse rose in her mind. No, not him. "My mom wants to set me up with a guy in Mac. I think I'm going to say yes."

Kelsey inhaled and briefly cocked her head to the side. "You're brave. Not only putting your toes back in the water, but with a blind date?"

Brooke winced. "You're giving me second thoughts."

Kelsey's eyes widened. "Oh no! I'm sorry. You should totally do it. If your mom vetted him, he's probably great."

Probably. "I think he might be more my sister's type than mine."

Kelsey chuckled. "So she should date him."

"Except she's married. Both my sisters are. I'm the failure." Brooke took a long pull on her beer to cover up her discomfort. She hadn't meant to say that.

Across the table, Kelsey's gaze darkened with concern. Brooke averted her eyes and caught the door opening. *Oh hell.* In walked Cam and Luke Westcott. Of all the damned, rotten luck.

She drank more of her beer, nearly draining it. If she finished it quickly, she could suggest they leave.

"Well, when you decide to go out with this guy, let me know if you need a wingman," Kelsey said. "I'm happy to sit at a nearby table and rescue you if necessary."

Brooke bit her tongue before she said that rescue was necessary right now. She glanced toward the door, and damn it, the brothers made eye contact with her. And started walking over.

Steeling herself, Brooke polished off her beer.

Kelsey noted that Brooke's glass was empty and picked hers up. "I need to catch you."

She did. Then they could leave.

"Hey there!" Luke greeted Brooke as they approached the table. He looked over at Kelsey.

There was no avoiding introductions at least. "Hi," Brooke said, somewhat unenthusiastically and not caring one bit. "Luke, this is my friend Kelsey. Kelsey, this is Luke Westcott and his brother Cameron." She didn't make eye contact with Cam.

"You look familiar," Luke said to Kelsey. "Have we met before?"

"Probably. I work at The Arch and Vine."

He shook his head, smiling. "Duh. Now I feel like a tool for not remembering that."

She smiled at him. "Don't. We haven't ever introduced ourselves or anything."

"Well, no time like the present." He sat on the bench next to Kelsey, and she scooted over to make room. "You don't mind, do you?" He looked from Kelsey to Brooke and back to Kelsey again. "There aren't any other tables."

"We'll be leaving shortly," Brooke said. She finally shot a glance at Cam, who was still standing next to the table. Their gazes connected, and fire sparked through her. Damn it. Absence apparently made more than the heart grow fonder—it made unsatisfied aches burn.

Luke looked up at his brother. "Aren't you going to sit?"

Brooke moved as close to the wall as she could without looking ridiculous. Cam slid in beside her, and though they weren't touching, she felt his presence as though they were.

"What're you drinking?" Luke asked.

"Hefeweizen," Kelsey answered.

"And it looks like you're due for another round." Luke looked around for the server.

Shit. Wait, this was stupid. She could sit next to Cam and be fine. They were going to be doing this in the future for various work-related stuff, so she'd better get used to it. Besides, Ribbon Ridge was a small town. Things like this were bound to happen.

The server stopped by, and Luke ordered a pitcher. After she left, he looked at Brooke and Kelsey. "Are we interrupting girls' night?"

"Sort of," Brooke said.

Luke flinched. "Sorry. We'll leave you alone as soon as a table opens up."

Kelsey shook her head. "It's fine." She exchanged a look with Brooke that seemed to ask if that was okay. Brooke gave a slight nod. What could she do?

Luke darted a look at Cam, and Brooke could see the unspoken question in his gaze—*why aren't you talking?* She wondered if Cam was as uncomfortable as she was.

"So, Kelsey," Luke said, "you work at The Arch and Vine?"

"She's also the new librarian," Brooke said.

Luke looked confused.

Kelsey turned her head to look at him. "The library just opened up a couple of weeks ago, and I'm running it."

"Very cool. I didn't realize. Too wrapped up in work, I guess. I'll have to stop by."

The server brought the pitcher with glasses, and when Cam went to pour the beer, his elbow brushed Brooke's arm. She sidled closer to the wall.

Luke took a drink, then angled his body toward Kelsey. "Tell me about the library."

As they chatted, Brooke sipped her beer. She kept her voice low as she looked over at Cam. "Something wrong with you tonight?"

He glanced at her. "No, why?"

"I've never seen you this quiet. It's...weird."

He exhaled. "Sorry." He took a long drink. "I didn't realize... That is, I didn't know how...seeing you... Hell, never mind." He went back to drinking.

Brooke smiled, enjoying his agitation. "Is this a problem?" She blinked at him and made sure her tone was sugary innocent.

He scowled at her briefly, then took a deep breath. When he

turned toward her, he smiled, and the effect was devastating. Brooke's gut clenched, and heat pooled between her legs.

"Nope, not a problem," he said, appearing to completely regroup and change his attitude. "I guess I was still feeling bad about the other night, but you seem fine."

"Yep, fine." She knew she answered too quickly and wished she'd said something far more sophisticated. Like what? Maybe something like, *What are you feeling bad about?* as if she'd forgotten all about their near-sexy times. Damn, why did the good comebacks never come to mind at the right time?

Kelsey looked at her beer. "You know, I usually drink this with lemon."

Luke jumped up. "I'll get you some."

"You don't have to," Kelsey said.

"No, but I want to." He flashed her a smile, and Brooke wondered how long Kelsey might stick to her no-dating resolve. Assuming Luke was interested. Maybe Brooke just saw a Westcott smile and immediately assumed they were on the hunt. Ugh, that wasn't fair. Especially with regard to Cam. He'd been a gentleman last weekend, and she should thank him for that.

Brooke shook away the last vestiges of her irritation as Luke took off to get the lemon.

"Actually, I'm going to run to the ladies' room," Kelsey said. "Be right back." She left, and suddenly Brooke and Cam were alone. Well, alone in a boisterous bar.

Cam sipped his beer and cast her a sidelong glance. "You look great."

"Thanks. You too." He wore a crisp green T-shirt and dark gray shorts that had clearly been pressed. He always looked so put together. So bizarre for a guy, and such a turn-on for her.

He turned his head to look at her. "Thanks for your help with the wine dinner. The critic from *Wine Enthusiast* is a huge get. We really appreciate it."

"My pleasure." That word set off warning bells in her brain. She looked at his chest and recalled how sexy he looked when it was bare. She jerked her gaze back to his face but ended up staring at his mouth, remembering what it felt like on hers. Fighting a blush that would tell him more than she wanted him to know, she picked up her beer and drank.

Luke came back with the lemons. "Where's Kelsey?"

"Ladies' room," Brooke said.

Luke nodded. He looked between her and his brother, his gaze assessing. *He knows.* But what exactly? He'd watched them leave the wine tasting last weekend. Had he drawn his own conclusions, or had Cam filled him in? She leaned back against the wall and watched Cam drink his beer.

"Hey, I need to drop by sometime this week to pick up some more samples," she said.

"You're on fire," Luke said. "We hit the jackpot when Cam hired you."

Cam slid her an appreciative look. "We sure did."

Uh-oh. He was flirting again. They weren't supposed to do that.

She glared at him and muttered, "Knock it off," so that only he could hear.

He looked away and exhaled, appearing defeated. *Good.*

She sipped her beer, and the alcohol infused her with a welcome sense of relaxation. She edged away from the wall and settled back against the booth.

Kelsey returned then, and she and Luke picked up their conversation again.

"That's better," Cam murmured too close to her ear. He'd leaned toward her. "You looked like you might crawl through the wall to get away from me."

She turned her head and gave him an ultrasweet smile. "Careful, or I might do it again. Stop flirting with me."

He blinked one eye closed and scrunched his face briefly. "I tried, but I can't help it. Sorry."

"Try *harder*."

"Yes. I will. I mean it." He gave her a determined look, and she almost laughed.

"This really is hard for you, isn't it?"

"Only with you."

That was *not* what she needed to hear.

Time to save them both from temptation. "I think I should go." She made a show of yawning, even though it was all of, what, nine thirty?

Kelsey, bless her—she was clearly a great wingman—bought the clue. She looked at Brooke in question, read her nonverbal response, which Brooke delivered in the form of a pleading stare, and gave a slight nod. She drank more of her beer, taking it down to the halfway mark. "Yeah, time for me to head home too. Working two jobs takes a toll." She stood up. "Enjoy the table."

Luke smiled at her. "Thanks. It was nice chatting with you."

Cam slid out to make way for Brooke. She followed him, and as she stood, caught her foot on the base of the booth. She stumbled, but Cam clasped her waist and kept her from falling. "You okay?" He didn't let go, and his green gaze blazed into hers.

She pivoted—reluctantly, if she was honest—and his hands finally dropped to his sides. "Yes. Good night."

She turned and followed Kelsey from the bar. Outside, the temperature had dropped a couple of degrees, and there was a lovely breeze that felt divine against her flushed cheeks.

"What's the story there?" Kelsey asked as they walked back toward the main part of town.

Brooke looked over at her, not terribly surprised that she'd detected something. "With Cam, you mean?"

She hunched her shoulders briefly. "Sorry. If you'd rather

not talk about it, I totally understand. I just... You guys have crazy sparks."

"I know." What else could she say? "But we work together, so it's a nonstarter."

"That's too bad."

"Not really. He's a player. Even if we didn't work together, it would be a flash-in-the-pan kind of thing." That sounded terrific. Just what she needed, probably. "Which wouldn't be so bad at this point in my life, actually."

"Well then, that sucks. Maybe you should stop working with him. It's not like you'd have to quit your actual job, right?"

Brooke had told Kelsey about her job earlier, so she knew that Cam wasn't her employer. "True, but so far, West Arch has proven to be a good income stream. Not sure I want to give that up for a few nights of fun."

"Yeah, that makes sense." Kelsey shook her head. "Tough situation. Whatever you decide, I'm here if you need to talk."

Brooke smiled, glad that she'd met Kelsey and that it seemed their friendship was off to a great, solid start. "Thanks. I appreciate that."

They reached Second, where they would part ways, and Kelsey said, "So, I'll let you know when we're going to meet about the exhibit."

"Sounds great. See you then."

They exchanged waves, and Kelsey crossed the street while Brooke took off toward her building.

A few minutes later as she stepped into the elevator, she pulled out her phone and texted her sister. *Okay, tell Mom I'll meet the guy from Mac.*

Rhonda's response came as Brooke stepped into her loft. *Excellent! This is going to be great. I can just feel it.*

The only thing Brooke could feel right now was a pull to Cam's townhouse across the street. But that wasn't an option.

Yes, it was time to make some changes. Starting with putting herself back on the market.

Cam hefted the case of wine onto his shoulder as he stepped off the elevator onto Brooke's floor. He ought to have called or texted first, but he didn't want her to tell him not to come. He could've just left it for her at the winery to pick up, but he wanted to talk to her. The other night at Ruckus had been unnecessarily awkward. Things didn't have to be like that. At least he hoped they didn't.

But damn, he had to admit it was difficult being around her and not pursuing a romantic relationship. Difficult, but not impossible. He could do this.

He knocked on her door. A moment later, her voice came through the wood. "Who is it?"

"It's Cam. I brought your wine."

She unlocked the door and opened it to reveal her skeptical expression. "You didn't buzz up."

"Someone else was coming in the building."

She frowned at him. "You aren't supposed to do that."

He narrowed his eyes at her, fairly certain she wasn't teasing. "Do you want to call the police? Just let me set the wine down, if you don't mind."

She opened the door wider and gestured him inside.

Somehow they'd gone from uncomfortable to adversarial. He *really* didn't like that. He set the wine on the floor in her entry. He noted she didn't close the door. "Can we talk for a few minutes?"

She hesitated but ultimately shut the door and walked farther into her loft. He watched the sway of her hips, cloaked in denim shorts. They cupped her ass perfectly and had a sexy, tattered hem, like they'd been torn. He got an instant visual of ripping them off her and started to sport wood.

Down boy, he cautioned. He hadn't come here to do anything but apologize and hopefully smooth things over.

She turned to the right and walked into her kitchen, standing next to a long, rectangular island. "What do you want to talk about?"

He joined her at the counter, but left a few feet between them. He leaned against the granite edge and crossed his arms. "I wanted to apologize for the other night. Things seemed uncomfortable, and I really don't want them to be."

She blew out a breath and crossed her arms too. "I don't either. Any ideas on how we do that?"

He'd spent a lot of time thinking about that. Too much, probably. And his thoughts generally veered in the wrong direction, where he ended up undressing her in his mind and having spectacular sex with her.

Yeah, that wasn't helping.

"I'm hoping we can be friends. Maybe if we focused on doing friend things, the...uh, the attraction between us might fade." He nearly laughed at how stupid that sounded.

She arched a brow at him, and her expression seemed to echo his thoughts. "You really think that will work?"

"Hey, it's worth trying." He cocked his head to the side. "What do *you* suggest?"

She hesitated a moment before saying, "Finding someone else at Willamette to take your account."

So they could pursue a romantic relationship? The rampant desire he was trying so hard to rein in pulsed through him.

She dropped her arms, and her brow furrowed. "But I hate to do that. This is a good account."

He didn't really want her to do that either. She was great, and the business part of his brain didn't want to lose her. "So back to my friend idea, then." Which sounded even more unappealing than it had two minutes ago.

She laid her palm flat on the counter and seemed to study the granite. "It's not a no. I just don't know how it will work." She darted him a glance. "I do like you. As a friend."

He edged closer and uncrossed his arms. He mimicked her, putting his hand on the counter so that their fingers were maybe a foot apart. "I like you too. A little more than as a friend, but I'll take what I can get."

She straightened and looked at him, her blue-green eyes sharp and beautiful. "Maybe we should just get this out of our systems. I know you're worried about us working together, but it's sort of not going all that great right now anyway, is it?"

Their communication had become stilted, and even though she was still doing a great job, things were awkward. All in all, she had a fair point. But was she serious about the getting-it-out-of-their-systems part? He couldn't tell.

He offered a self-deprecating smile. "I was trying to be a gentleman. And look where that got me."

She laughed softly, and her eyes lit. He ached to touch her.

"I appreciate you trying to do that—really. Even if I was pissed at first. But it's good. You've actually encouraged me to get back out there. My mom and sister are setting me up on a blind date."

She could've kicked him square in the balls, and it might've had less of an impact. His chest tightened, and his insides swirled with turmoil. Apparently, she hadn't been serious about getting their mutual attraction out of their systems. "Well, that's progress, I guess," he said tightly. He stalled the incremental movement of his hand—which he'd only been partially aware of —on the counter.

Her eyes narrowed slightly and only for a second, as if she'd caught the nuance of his reaction. Shit, maybe it wasn't that nuanced. Maybe his face screamed his envy. Time to get the hell out of there. "So let's try the friend thing, then. I'm confident we can do it. You can even tell me all about your date when I see you next." He forced a smile before turning and starting from the kitchen toward the door.

"Hey, you seem mad." She caught his hand. "Don't leave mad. Friends don't do that."

He turned, his fingers twining through hers. "Friends don't do a lot of things. Like think about how they want to toss the other one on the counter and screw them senseless."

Her eyes widened and immediately darkened with desire. "See, I told you we should just get it out of our systems. I bet that's all it would take."

She *was* serious. "That's a line I would use. You're killing me with it."

She lifted a shoulder and ran her thumb along his palm. "Maybe it's fun to play the player."

The sexy lilt of her voice and the seductive glint in her gaze completely destroyed whatever willpower he'd been clinging to. He clasped her waist and spun her around so that her back was up against the fridge. She gasped softly, but her eyes slitted as he pushed his body into hers.

He massaged her waist and brought her hand up, pinning it against the stainless steel. He leaned in close and inhaled her spicy, floral scent. She stared at him, her eyes daring him to take the next step. He shouldn't...he couldn't...he *had* to.

Angling his head, he kissed her hard and fast. He let go of her hand and cupped the side of her neck. Her hands came up around his back and clutched at him. He felt his shirt bunch up as she tugged at the fabric.

Their hips pressed against each other, their bodies pulsing and seeking. The kiss was deep and lush, delicious strokes of tongues and fevered moans. He cocked his head the other way, searching for new ground, claiming every part of her he could find.

She thrust into him, grinding her pelvis and opening her thighs. Hot lust poured through him. Mindless, he found the hem of her tank and pulled it up, yanking it over her head as he broke the kiss for the briefest of moments.

Her breasts were flush against his chest, full and enticing. He cupped the underside of one, his thumb and fingertips skimming over the lace decoration of her bra. She arched her back, pushing her breast into his hand. He pulled his mouth from hers and bent to her chest. Slipping his fingers into her bra, he tugged it down to pop her breast free. God, she was beautiful. Perfect. He ran his thumb over her nipple and watched it peak. It beckoned him to taste, and he didn't need much urging. He licked at her flesh, lightly, teasingly. She thrust her hands into his hair and pressed him against her. He held her breast, capturing it for his mouth. Then he taunted her with slow, gentle licks before he closed his lips over her.

She moaned, her fingers digging into his scalp. He squeezed her flesh and used his teeth lightly, making her gasp. "Yes." The word floated from her mouth—a plea, a demand. Over and over, she prodded him with that word and with her body. Her hips continued to rotate into his, and her hands moved over him, seeking and claiming. She clasped his ass and pulled him tight against her. His cock nestled between her legs, finding her heat despite the clothing between them. He needed her now.

"*Cam.*"

It sounded as if she needed him too.

He reluctantly left her breast, and she clasped the hem of his shirt. He whipped it off and threw it aside, then pulled her away from the fridge long enough to unhook her bra. Then he brought her against him and kissed her again, reveling in being flesh to flesh with her at last.

He pinned her against the fridge, and she tilted her hips. The movement caressed his cock just right. He groaned and grabbed her ass, lifting her. She wrapped her legs around him, bringing him even closer to that sweet spot. He mentally cursed the clothes they were still wearing.

She twined her arms around his neck and kissed him as she squeezed him with her legs. He couldn't remember the last time he'd been this worked up. Not even last week when she'd interrupted him in the shower. This was utter bliss. This was heaven. This was Brooke.

He considered where to go next—he needed to get the rest of their clothes off. He interrupted the kiss long enough to form a single-word question. "Bedroom?"

She kissed him, her tongue sweeping against his. "Mmm, yes."

He mentally undressed her and then him and then—
Shit.

He pulled back slightly. She opened her eyes and gave him a dusky stare.

"I, uh…" He hadn't come prepared for this. "I don't suppose you have a condom?"

Chapter Eleven

Brooke flattened her back against the refrigerator. The irony of Cam not having a condom nearly made her laugh...until she thought about the fact that they didn't actually need a condom, assuming they were both clean.

As if he read her mind, he said, "I'm clean. I get tested every six months, and I haven't, uh, had a partner since my last test. If you're on birth control, we could forgo the condom—but only if you're comfortable with that."

She would've been. But she wasn't on birth control. *Because I don't need it.*

She unhooked her legs and pushed at his shoulders.

Lines creased his brow, and he stepped back. "What's wrong?"

She pushed her hair back from her face. "Nothing. I'm not on birth control, and I don't have any condoms, so..." *You should go.*

He wiped a hand over his forehead and blew out a breath. Then his eyes found hers, and they sharpened with hope. "I have condoms at home. I can be right back."

She bent down and picked up her bra and tank top, then

walked away from him to put them on with her back to him. "I think this is probably the Universe telling us to put on the brakes, don't you?"

"Uh..." He sounded confused. Or frustrated. Or both.

She hooked her bra on and wiggled into it, pulling up the straps. After she shimmied into her tank top, she turned. He was still standing there bare-chested, and damn if she wasn't sorely tempted to pick up right where they'd left off.

She took a deep breath to calm her speeding pulse. "The points you made last week—about not ruining our working relationship—are as valid today as they were then. Maybe even more so since things have been kind of awkward. You came here for a reset and that's a great idea. We got carried away, but thankfully had a good reason to stop."

He still looked a bit dazed, and it reminded her of how she'd felt when he'd called a halt last time. She didn't feel any sort of vengeance, though. It wasn't about that.

Then what was it about?

Her mind was crammed with thoughts and sensations—wanting him, feeling alone, fighting the sudden urge to cry because she didn't need any damned birth control. "I'm sorry about sending mixed messages. This is complicated, and we've been trying to uncomplicate it, right? Stopping...*this* is the right thing to do."

He nodded finally, then stooped to pick up his shirt. He tugged it on, and it seemed to be happening in slow motion, as if time wanted to give Brooke one more chance to ask him to stay.

She stiffened her spine and walked past him, turning down the entry hall to the doorway. "Thanks for bringing the wine. I really appreciate it."

He walked toward her, and she opened the door before he could do or say anything that would threaten her resolve. *If* he could. She was so conflicted right now, so agitated, that she didn't know if he could persuade her to go back to where they'd been five minutes ago.

"You're welcome." He walked over the threshold then turned around to face her. "I'm sorry. I didn't mean to upset you."

"I'm not upset."

He frowned briefly, but the creases on his brow stayed. "I'm not sure I believe you. But it doesn't matter. It was your turn to be the cool head of reason."

Relieved that he wasn't angry, she relaxed her muscles.

"I wonder, though," he continued. "Who's going to do that next time? I'm not sure I've got it in me." He gave her a half-smile. "See you later."

As she watched him go, she wasn't sure she had it in herself either. Which meant they'd have to stop meeting alone like this. No more visits to each other's homes. She'd tell him that when she talked to him next.

She closed the door and locked it, then leaned back against it with a deep breath. Her body still thrummed with desire, and her mouth was still imprinted with his kiss.

She didn't doubt that she'd missed out on what would've been a great night. But it had been the right thing to do. She'd just keep telling herself that until she completely believed it.

In an attempt to clear her head, she went to the case of wine he'd brought in and looked through the variety. No chardonnay. Damn. She would run out this week, which meant she'd have to pick up more. She'd arrange for him to put some aside at the winery, and then she'd drop by when she was pretty sure he wouldn't be there.

This plan made her feel better. It gave her hope that they could continue this work thing without falling into each other's arms.

But would that be so bad? What's the worst that could

happen? They'd have sex and things would become awkward? They were already there.

Hell, put like that, she was tempted to call him and invite him back over. But the shadow of that pesky question, "Are you on birth control?" hovered at the back of her mind. It was stupid. She didn't have to tell him about her infertility. Like Rhonda had said, it wasn't as if they were in this for the long-term.

She closed her eyes and groaned.

The other thing Rhonda kept telling her was also true—she so needed to get laid. Their mom had sent over the blind date's phone number yesterday. His name was Justin Weber, and she could text him right now.

Before she lost her nerve, she picked her phone up off the table and brought up his contact. She typed out a message introducing herself—he knew she had his number—and asked if he wanted to get together for a drink this week.

She tossed her phone back down, not expecting to hear back. She was surprised when it immediately pinged. Picking it back up, she quickly read his response: *Sounds great. How about tomorrow night?*

Wow, so soon. She wasn't sure she wanted to do that...but why? The sooner she made this leap, the better. She typed in her answer.

Sure, seven? How about Grape Central?

That was a wine bar in downtown McMinnville, where he lived. She didn't want to meet here. Ribbon Ridge was too small. Was she afraid they'd run into Cam? Again, she was being *so* stupid.

His response came fast. *Perfect. See you then.*

Mom had texted a picture of him with her friend—his aunt —so Brooke would be able to find him. She didn't know if he'd received a picture of her and didn't ask. She was suddenly exhausted.

She decided to take a long hot bath. And maybe find her waterproof vibrator.

Cam walked into Hazel, one of Newberg's best restaurants a few nights later, anticipating a fun evening of good food, lively conversation, and excellent wine from some of the area's top producers. He was also anticipating possibly running into Brooke, and he just wasn't sure how that would go.

There'd been radio silence since their aborted lovemaking session on Sunday, but he wasn't surprised. What could they say that hadn't been said?

How about, *screw the work thing and let's just have sex?*

Because, really, could things get any worse than they were? They tiptoed around the elephant in the room and despite their best intentions couldn't seem to help themselves. If he saw her tonight, he'd do his level best to say hi and move on. Hayden would be here soon, and he'd be an excellent distraction.

Cam made his way to the bar and picked up a glass of pinot from one of his favorite winemakers. When he turned, he nearly bumped into Kyle Archer.

He grinned. "Hey, Cam, good to see you. What're you drinking?"

"Hey, Kyle." Cam held up his glass, swirling the dark ruby pinot. "A. F. Nichols."

"Oh, he's great." Kyle nodded toward the bartender. "Same for me, please."

The bartender nodded back. "You got it."

"I didn't know you were going to be here," Cam said.

"Shouldn't you be home massaging your wife's feet or something since she's about to give birth?"

Kyle picked up his wine. "Yep. Phone's in my back pocket with the sound jacked up way too high, but I keep checking it anyway. I'm so excited, but nerve-racked as hell at the same time."

Cam sipped his wine. He couldn't identify, of course, but he recalled his half-brother Dylan feeling the same way before his daughter, Emma, was born. "Let me know if you need help busting out of here in a flash. She's got a bag packed, right?"

Kyle laughed. "In the car. We're more than ready. Maggie's so done being pregnant in the middle of summer."

"Yeah, it's been really hot this week." It had been in the nineties every day, which made Cam's current getup of slacks and a long-sleeve shirt rather stupid. But Cam didn't sacrifice looking good for comfort. At least not often. And he'd at least rolled up the sleeves to his mid-forearm. "I can't imagine how Maggie must be feeling."

"She was going to come with me tonight but decided it just wasn't worth putting on shoes." Kyle leaned toward him. "I should probably go home and give her a foot massage."

Cam chuckled and raised his glass. "To being the sperm donor instead."

Kyle lifted his wine. "Hear, hear. But don't let them hear us say that." He took a drink. "Actually, you don't have to watch yourself, free-agent man. Think you'll ever settle down?"

Cam shrugged. "Don't have any plans to."

"Right." Kyle nodded, likely recalling whatever story he'd heard regarding Cam and Jennifer. Since Hayden was Cam's best friend as well as Kyle's brother, Cam imagined Kyle had to know something. "You know, no one ever saw me settling down," Kyle said.

"No one ever saw you coming back to Ribbon Ridge," Cam

said wryly. Kyle had taken off for several years, during which he'd mostly cut ties with everyone here. After one of the Archer septuplets killed himself, Kyle had come home. Then he'd shocked everyone by falling in love with his deceased brother's therapist. And now they were expecting their first kid. "You're a testament to the unpredictability of life."

Kyle laughed. "Isn't that the truth?" His eye landed on someone at the end of the bar. "That's my pal who owns this joint. I need to go say hello." He clapped Cam on the shoulder. "Catch you later."

"Later." Cam turned and walked into the main dining room. It wasn't terribly large—the building was a renovated house—and encompassed a space akin to a living and dining room combination. Most of the tables had been moved out for tonight's mingling and were likely stashed upstairs in the private dining rooms.

What they had plenty of was wine. Much of the wall space was taken up with cabinets stuffed full of the best the Willamette Valley had to offer. Cam loved to peruse the labels. He always found a hidden treasure when he came here.

He sauntered toward a cabinet in the corner and stopped short when he heard a familiar laugh. When he turned, his gaze wandered to the back of the room and landed on the source of the lovely sound. Brooke.

She stood with another young woman, who was also laughing. He knew he ought to stay put, but his feet didn't get the memo. As he neared, Brooke saw him, her eyes widening briefly in recognition before she looked down at her wine.

"Good evening," he said to the other woman. She was younger than Brooke, with straight brown hair and gold-brown eyes. Cam turned his attention to the reason he'd come over. "Hi, Brooke."

She lifted her gaze to his. "Hi, Cameron. This is my

coworker, Elise. Elise, this is Cameron Westcott. He's one of the owners of West Arch Estate."

Elise smiled at him. "I know who he is." She offered her hand. "Nice to meet you. I've heard all about you."

"Uh-oh." Cam shot a glance at Brooke, wondering what she'd said.

Brooke shook her head. "Not from me. Elise is new. She started at Willamette, what, three weeks ago?" She looked at Elise who nodded.

"Not quite." Elise edged closer to Cam. "And I was teasing. I haven't heard *all* about you. Someone mentioned you in a list of eligible bachelors in the area."

Cam laughed. "I see."

"He's definitely eligible," Brooke said before taking a sip of wine. "And he's definitely a bachelor through and through." She finished what was left in her glass. "I'm empty. Excuse me while I get a refill." She smiled at him as she passed by. He noticed she was careful not to touch him. He also watched her backside as she walked away and recalled the feel of it in his hands. Damn.

"So what are you drinking?" Elise asked. "I'm new to this area—not the wine necessarily—but I've been working at a winery up in Prosser. Do you know where that is?"

"Sure, south central Washington. I've been there many times. Where'd you work?" He sipped his wine. "Oh, and this is A.F. Nichols. He's a small indie producer, but really great. Give him a try if you haven't."

"I will, thanks." She spent the next few minutes talking about her prior job, her dog, and the manicure she'd gotten that afternoon. With each topic, she moved closer until her arm was grazing his.

Meanwhile, Cam kept watching the doorway, waiting for Brooke to return from the bar. When it looked as though she wasn't coming back, Cam searched for an out. He didn't want to abandon Elise, so he eyeballed someone else in the room that he knew and drew her over to meet him. "Elise, come meet Henri Morin. He's the winemaker up at Synchronicity."

"Hello, it's my pleasure to meet you," Henri said in his thick French accent.

Elise shook his hand. "I love your wine!"

Satisfied that he'd made a good handoff, Cam excused himself and went in search of Brooke, despite his better judgment.

He found her in the bar area near the window, chatting with someone he didn't know. Cam went to the bar and refilled his glass while he wanted for an opening. A few minutes passed before her conversation partner departed, and Cam beelined toward her.

"You abandoned me," he said.

She arched a brow at him. "Not on purpose. I'm networking. That's why I come to these events." Her gaze dipped over him. "You look hot."

He grinned at her compliment. "Thanks."

She laughed softly. "No, you look hot in that outfit. Why are you wearing long sleeves? It's like ninety-six."

He held out his arm and glanced at the French blue fabric. "I like this shirt."

"I like it too, but you have to have a million others. I've seen what you wear—you have no shortage of stylish clothes."

He took delight in the fact that she noticed. "Anyway, it's not ninety-six now. The sun's gone down."

"True, but I'd say it's still upwards of eighty-five."

Probably. Why were they talking about the weather? Because it was safe, and so far it had prevented any weirdness like they'd had that evening at Ruckus. "You look cool and comfortable," he said, taking in her black spaghetti-strap dress that was longer in back than in the front. "Actually, *you* look hot

—and not the temperature kind." She couldn't be wearing a bra in that dress, but he couldn't see her nipples, so it had to have some sort of built-in coverage. But all he could think was that there was just one layer between him and paradise.

She didn't respond. Instead, she sipped her wine and looked out the window for a moment before asking, "What happened to Elise?"

"I left her with someone. She's fine."

"She was excited to meet you. In fact, she told me before you came over that she was hoping to meet you tonight. Your reputation precedes you."

He groaned. "Great. Why me?"

Brooke lifted a tan, sculpted, sexy shoulder. "Because you're attractive, very single, and like I said, your reputation is kind of unparalleled."

He wanted to know what she was getting at. Specifically. "In what way?"

"Just that you're known for giving a girl a good time—with or without sex, if you must know."

"Well, that's a bit of a relief. I don't really want to be known as just a manwhore." *Anymore.*

"But you kind of are, aren't you?"

He narrowed his eyes at her. "You're being rather saucy this evening. You know I've calmed down my...*behavior* for some time now. In fact, I'm living like a damned monk at present."

"You could change that with Elise, I'm sure. Why don't you ask her out?"

A chuckle rose in his chest. "I fell right into that one."

Brooke gave him a half-smile, but he saw the victory lurking in her eyes as she took another drink of wine. "In all seriousness, you should ask her out. Why not?"

Because he didn't want to go out with Elise. He didn't want to go out with anyone who wasn't Brooke. "She's not my type."

And she really wasn't, even if he *had* been looking. Which he wasn't. "Plus, I'm not sure I'm in the right head space to be dating anyone."

She looked at him in surprise, her eyelids fluttering. "I went on that blind date last night." She quickly averted her gaze, focusing on her wineglass, and he wondered if she regretted saying it.

Jealousy cut into him, leaving a hot trail of irritation. "How was it?" He knew his tone sounded clipped, but he couldn't help it any more than he could help asking. Which was stupid because he really didn't want to know.

"Fine. Forget I mentioned it. We should keep our personal lives personal."

"Like we did the other night?" He leaned closer and reveled in her scent. "That was extremely personal to me," he murmured.

"I need to use the ladies' room, excuse me."

It was a chicken-shit move—he could see the hunger and the hesitation in her eyes. He watched her go and ask the bartender where the bathroom was, but she didn't go straight to the back where it was located. Instead, she turned and went up the stairs.

Don't follow her. Don't follow her. Don't follow her.

He downed the rest of his wine, deposited the glass on the bar, and followed her.

He climbed the stairs and wove to the back, where another bathroom was located. He slowed as he approached, his mind warring with itself on whether he should stay or go back downstairs. He should really go.

As he was about to pivot, the bathroom door opened. She stood on the threshold and her gaze connected with his. "You followed me."

"Guilty."

"We're not supposed to do this. Unless you came up here to talk to me about work."

"I didn't." He didn't bother trying to mask the longing he felt. "I came here because I'm jealous that you went out with some other guy."

Her chest hitched, as if she'd lost her breath for a second. "You should go. We know what happens when we're alone."

And they were quite alone up here. No one would hear them...

"Yes, I should go." But his feet propelled him forward.

She didn't move, and her gaze was unflinching. "Don't go."

Then she reached out and grabbed him by the shirtfront and dragged him—not that it took much effort—into the bathroom and closed the door.

Chapter Twelve

As soon as she closed the door, Brooke pushed him up against the wood and locked the knob. She immediately started unbuttoning his shirt. "You shouldn't have followed me."

He stared at her, his green eyes blistering with heat. "You're giving me such mixed messages."

"Just because I said you *shouldn't* have doesn't mean I'm disappointed." She finished with his buttons and spread his shirt open, pressing her palms against his smooth, warm flesh. His chest felt even better than it looked. "Do I look disappointed to you?"

He clasped her waist. "God, Brooke." He pulled her into him and kissed her.

She curled her fingers into his chest and met his tongue. Lust—raw, pure, and devastating—raged through her. She pushed her hands up and cupped his neck as she pressed against him.

He broke the kiss and took a gasp of air. "I need to understand this. We can't keep starting up and...stopping. My body can't take it."

He sounded so adorably high-strung. She smiled and traced her finger over his lips. They were so soft and delicious. "Mine can't either. Clearly, we need to do this, and hopefully that will be the end of it."

His brow arched up as skepticism joined the desire in his gaze. "So we aren't stopping?"

She shook her head. "No." Then she kissed him again with wild abandon. There were no voices in the back of her head telling her to stop, no conscience saying she might regret this. Because she knew, without a doubt, that she wouldn't. Except...

She pulled back with a groan. "Tell me you have a condom."

His lips spread in a lazy, sexy grin. "Put a couple in my wallet after the other night. No way was I going to let that happen again."

"Smart man." She tugged at his neck and brought his mouth to hers.

They kissed ravenously, like starved animals led to a feast. His hands cupped her ass as he pulled her tight against him. She could feel the length of his cock and couldn't help but rotate her hips to create friction.

He moaned into her mouth and pushed away from the door. He interrupted the kiss and looked around. She licked along his jaw and spread kisses down his neck.

"God, I've waited for this. *Dreamed* about this. And we're in a damned bathroom."

She giggled. "There's a fairly sturdy-looking cabinet against the other wall."

He steered her in that direction. "Thankfully this bathroom isn't tiny." He reclaimed her mouth just before her backside hit the cabinet. He lifted her, effortlessly, and set her on the top. Something behind her jostled.

She reached back, and her fingers closed around a vase of dried flowers. "Do something with this before we break it." She thrust it into his hand, and he left briefly to set it on the counter next to the sink.

When he came back, he looked at her a moment, his gaze dark and fierce and full of promise. With both hands, he brushed her hair back from her face before lowering his head to kiss her again. This time was softer, less frantic, but every bit as passionate. His tongue made long, searching strokes as his fingers tangled into her hair. This was a kiss that made you swoon. A kiss you'd never forget.

She opened her legs, and he moved between them. She clutched his back, holding on to him tightly because if she didn't, she might just slide off the cabinet and form a puddle on the floor.

He pulled away, sighing. "I could do this all night. But we don't have a lot of time."

"I know. The bartender sent me up here because the other bathroom was in use. He'll send others..."

This galvanized him. He hiked up her skirt, baring her legs.

She undid his belt and his pants and said, "Condom," into his mouth.

He pulled his wallet from his back pocket. She watched as he withdrew a condom, then tossed his wallet to the floor. She pulled at the waistband of his boxer briefs until his cock was exposed. She couldn't resist running her hand along his length and smiled when he moaned again.

She helped him don the condom, and then his hands were on her. He pushed her thighs farther apart and went straight for her clit, teasing and rubbing the sensitive spot until she moaned. She tried to be quiet, but it was nearly impossible. "Someone's going to hear me."

"Baby, I'd like nothing more than to hear you scream my name." He slipped his finger inside her. "But don't."

She clutched at his hips. "*Cameron.*" Her whispered plea made him smile.

"That works. Just keep saying that." He stroked his finger into her and kept his thumb on her clit.

Damn, he was skilled. And she did precisely as he asked, murmuring his name over and over as pressure built inside her.

Then he was at her entrance, and his mouth was on hers once more. He pushed into her, and she slumped against him as sensation overwhelmed her. It had been so long since she'd done this, and probably forever since she'd wanted anyone this badly.

He began to move, his hips thrusting, his cock filling her. She pressed into him, her breasts flush against his chest. She clutched at his hips, urging him faster and deeper.

He braced his hand on the wall behind her and clasped her waist as he drove into her, increasing the pace. Pleasure assaulted her, and she knew if he wasn't kissing her, she'd be making a vociferous fool of herself. As it was, the cabinet began to rock and hit the wall.

"Hurry," she urged between kisses.

He gripped her harder and thrust even faster, increasing the knocking of the cabinet. Her muscles contracted as her orgasm started. Her eyes were closed, but she saw brilliant white light as he pulsed into her. A dozen more strokes maybe, and she felt him stiffen. She kissed him deeply, swallowing his moans and taking them into herself as spoils for a battle well fought—and won.

She hadn't meant for this to happen, but she was sure as hell glad that it had.

She held on to him tightly as they slowed their movements. He softened the kiss, tugging on her lip as he eased away from her. He caressed her cheek before turning toward the toilet to take care of the condom. She focused on adjusting her clothing and slid off the cabinet.

The toilet flushed, and when he turned back, his pants were done up. He bent and retrieved his wallet, then stashed it in his back pocket.

Brooke smoothed her hand down her dress and went to him. She started buttoning his shirt. "Thank you. That was nice."

"Nice?" His eyes still held a bit of their wild intensity. "That was fucking incredible. Please don't tell me it was just nice."

"It was amazing. And I have to admit, I feel much, much better." She didn't remember the last time she'd felt so...satisfied.

He laughed, dark and sexy. "I hope so. And I hope this means your date was a total bust."

It hadn't been great, but it also hadn't been a *total* bust. And she blamed its lack of greatness on Cam. She'd kept comparing Justin to Cam in her head, and poor Justin had consistently come in second place. He'd asked to see her again, and she'd said yes, if only because she thought she owed it to him to give him another shot. Maybe now that she'd exorcised her crazy lust for Cam, she could give Justin the attention he deserved.

She finished the last button and stepped back. "It was an okay date. It didn't end like this." Damn, he looked sexy. His hair was mussed, and now his eyes had this dazed, satiated quality. He looked like he'd just been screwed, and he'd liked it. Wondering how she looked, she turned to survey herself in the mirror. Her hair was also a bit ragged, and her cheeks were flushed.

"Great to hear." He leaned close to her ear. "You're gorgeous." He pressed a quick kiss to her temple, then looked at his reflection.

The sound of footfalls made them both freeze as they were tending to their hair. Brooke held her breath. The knob tried to turn, and this was followed by a knock.

"Just give me a minute," Cam answered.

"No problem." More footfalls. Was he walking away?

Cam took a deep breath and finished finger-combing his hair back into its style. He winked at her, then went to the door. After unlocking it, he opened it just enough to peer through the gap. "Coast looks clear," he said.

Brooke exhaled fully, and her shoulders dropped. He held the door open. "After you."

"Thank you." She preceded him and walked down the hallway toward the stairs.

He caught up to her and snagged her hand, drawing her past the stairs to a small dining room. "Hey. What now?"

Shit. That was the one question she'd been hoping he wouldn't ask.

He really hadn't meant to ask that. Wasn't that the reason they'd tried to keep from having sex, because it would open up a can of worms? "Forget I said that. I had a great time."

She visibly relaxed, and his ego took a minor hit. Had he hoped she'd fall at his feet? No, but he hoped they could do this again. He hadn't realized he'd feel that way, but now it seemed rather obvious. He liked her a lot, and it wasn't just about the sex or being physically attracted to her. She was fun to be with, and he respected her drive and work ethic. She also had a vulnerability that he longed to explore. Something about her brought out a desire to care for her, protect her even. He hadn't felt that way about someone in a long time. In fact, he didn't know if he'd ever felt that about Jennifer. But then it had turned out that she hadn't ever really opened herself up to him. Maybe Brooke would be different.

Cam pushed those thoughts away. They were dangerous and probably pointless.

Brooke untwisted the strap of her dress and smoothed it over her shoulder. "I had a great time too. But, uh, let's hope this is one and done. Out of our system. Probably for the best, right?"

"Definitely." Maybe not. He actually wanted to take her home right now and go for round two. No, he wanted to hold her hand and go for a walk. Something. Anything that would prolong this feeling of...happiness.

His blood turned to ice. Happiness scared the hell out of him. *That* he'd felt before. And he didn't like it when it was evoked by other people. That meant it could be decimated by other people too.

"Shall we go back downstairs?" she asked. "I stashed my purse in a corner. Hopefully it's still there."

"I'm sure it is. Let's go find out." He stepped aside, and she walked out in front of him, then turned and went down the stairs.

He watched her, remembering the feel of her against him, thinking that he'd never be able to look at her and not recall what it felt like to hold her in his arms.

He had a feeling that one and done was a pipe dream.

They didn't pass whoever had come up to use the bathroom, but as soon as they walked back into the bar area, Hayden approached them.

"There you are," he said. "Hi Brooke, how's it going?" He looked between them, and Cam couldn't decide if Hayden was trying to figure anything out. Since he and Cam's brothers seemed hell-bent on pairing him with Brooke, he had to assume Hayden's mind was churning ideas about why they'd come downstairs together.

"Good, thanks. Excuse me, I need to find my purse before someone walks off with it." She flashed Hayden a smile and quickly departed for the main dining room.

Cam watched her go because, really, there was absolutely no reason for him to accompany her. Except he wanted to.

Hayden pulled him toward the windows, away from the more crowded area near the bar. "I've been here a good ten minutes, and you've been...upstairs? With Brooke? Spill."

Cam knew there was no point in telling him to fuck off. Cam had butted in the same way when Hayden had tried to avoid falling back in love with Bex. As if they'd ever fallen out of love. Cam had sometimes wondered if he was still in love with Jennifer, if that was the real reason he hadn't moved on. But then his insides pitched with disgust, and he felt nauseated. Nope, he was pretty sure that ship had sailed right into the Bermuda Triangle. And good riddance to it.

"It's complicated," Cam said.

"I'm sure it is. Are you guys together or not?"

That depended on what he meant by "together," but Cam wasn't going to split hairs. "Not."

Hayden exhaled. "You usually tell me about your conquests. This is disappointing."

Cam narrowed his eyes. "Brooke isn't a conquest."

Hayden's eyes widened. "Aha."

Cam had fallen for that one. "You're a dick."

Hayden smiled. "Takes one to know one, but you know that."

Brooke came back toward them, waving her clutch. "Found it."

Cam hadn't expected her to come back. He was pleasantly surprised. "I said you would."

She nodded. "I'm going to take off. Oh, I keep forgetting to ask you something." She transferred her attention to Hayden. "That brick you showed me, I told Kelsey about it—she's the new librarian, and she's putting together a Ribbon Ridge exhibit. She'd like to include it. She's going to try to find out more about it with Alaina and Crystal."

"Right, I talked to her about the museum. It sounds great," Hayden said. "Of course the brick should go in the exhibit."

"I'm meeting with them tomorrow night, so I'll tell them, thanks."

"Yeah, anything we can do to help," Hayden offered. "Just let us know."

"Will do." She darted a glance at Cam. "See you guys."

Hayden lifted his hand. "Bye."

"See you," Cam murmured.

Hayden turned back to Cam. "You're sleeping with her."

"Not really." That was true, right? There had been absolutely no sleeping, and that phrase made it sound like what they *had* done was an ongoing thing. "No, I'm not. We, uh, we have some chemistry, but I think we resolved it." He highly doubted that, but maybe if he repeated it to himself over and over, it would come true.

Hayden didn't look convinced either. "If you say so. Whatever you do, don't drive her away. She's really good at her job."

Cam gave him an exasperated stare. "I know. But thanks for the reminder. Are you going to stand here and harass me about Brooke, or are we going to do what we came here to do and talk up our wine?"

Hayden held up his hands. "Hey, I didn't mean to piss you off. You really like her. That's great. I hope it works out."

"There's nothing to work out." Though as he said it, Cam couldn't help but hope he was wrong. "I'm getting more wine." He turned toward the bar.

Hayden clapped him on the back. "Right behind you, bro."

The next evening, Brooke walked into The Arch and Vine. Kelsey had invited her to meet Alaina and Crystal to discuss the Ribbon Ridge exhibit.

She glanced around the interior, looking for the others. The man behind the bar, which was situated in the middle of the space, nodded toward her. "You can seat yourself. Or can I help you with something?"

"I'm meeting some people."

The man, probably in his early sixties, adjusted his glasses on his nose. "You're welcome to look around. What are their names?"

He would know them, of course, especially since Kelsey worked here. "Kelsey McDade is one of them."

"She's back in the corner over there." He pointed behind him and to the left. "Go on over. I'm George, by the way. I don't know that I've seen you in here."

Brooke walked to the bar and offered her hand, which he shook. "I'm Brooke Ellis. I'm pretty new to town."

He grinned at her. "Well, welcome to Ribbon Ridge. There's plenty of room for charming young ladies like yourself."

She laughed softly, immediately liking his easy, warm demeanor. "That's good to hear."

"If you ever need to take a load off—your feet or your mind —just belly up to my bar here, and I'll get you on the path to feeling better. Or the beer will." He winked at her.

"Sounds like a deal I can't refuse. Thank you." She started to turn toward the back corner.

"Wait, you need a beverage," he said. "What can I get you?" He rattled off their beers on tap, and Brooke chose a blonde ale called Legolas.

George nodded. "Good choice." He grabbed a pint glass and went to the tap. "This is actually made up at The Arch and Fox."

Brooke supposed that meant that Bex had made it. "Bex Archer makes the beer up there, right?"

He brought the glass and set it on the bar for her. "You aren't that new to town."

Brooke chuckled. "I guess I've been here a couple of months now, and I've met Bex. I'm distributing wine for West Arch."

"Aha, that makes sense. Well, this one's on the house—don't be a stranger, now."

Brooke thanked him and made her way toward the sound of feminine laughter in the corner. As she approached the table, Kelsey caught her eye. "Brooke! Come sit." She patted the empty space beside her.

Brooke slid onto the bench and set her beer on the table. "Hi. Thanks for inviting me."

"Brooke, this is Crystal and Alaina."

"Nice to meet you," Brooke said.

Crystal had pale blonde hair and deep blue eyes. "Hi, Brooke, good to meet you too."

Brooke moved her gaze to Alaina Pierce. It was weird sitting here across the table from someone she'd seen on film. She seemed familiar, but of course Brooke had never met her before.

Alaina smiled warmly. "Kelsey told us all about you. Okay, not 'all' about you, but you know." She laughed softly and offered Brooke her hand to shake.

Tentatively, Brooke took it and shook. "I love your movies." She withdrew her hand in horror. "Sorry. I told myself I wasn't going to do that."

Alaina laughed. "It's quite all right. Kelsey says you're a wine distributor. Since you make sure good wine gets into my hands—that's pretty much how it works, right?—I appreciate your work as well."

Crystal laughed and looked at Brooke. "See what a dork she really is?"

Brooke relaxed as the starstruck sensation began to fade. "No, but I'll take your word for it."

"Oh, do," Alaina said. "I'm the biggest dork. Take this exhibition, for example. I'm completely nerding out. I'm even thinking I should go to college and get a degree in history. Or science. I love science."

Crystal shook her head. "See what I mean? She is so not going to college. She's too busy with a toddler running around and the odd film project."

Alaina exhaled. "It's true. But maybe someday. I can't make movies forever. I'm already over the Hollywood hill."

Brooke could hardly believe that. Alaina was as beautiful as she'd been in her debut film and had only gotten better with each role. "That's so lame. Male stars your age are in their prime, right?"

Alaina nodded. "For at least another twenty years. Jerks." She flashed a grin.

Kelsey looked over at Brooke. "We were just talking about that brick. Did you ask if we could have it for the exhibit?"

"I did," Brooke said. "I saw Hayden last night, and he was more than happy to give it to you. He offered to help in any way possible."

Kelsey grinned. "That's great. Should I arrange to pick it up?"

Brooke almost offered to get it for them—and she could because she needed to stop by the winery sometime this week to restock her chardonnay supply before she headed to the coast this weekend for a sales trip. Why was she hesitating since she had to go there anyway? She could arrange the pickup with Hayden, not Cam. Was she avoiding Cam? In person, yes. She might've said last night was one and done, but the way she'd thought of him almost constantly today told a completely different story.

Brooke sipped her beer. It had a smooth wheaty flavor. "I can pick it up later this week, if that works. When are you planning to open the exhibit?"

The three women looked at each other, and it was instantly apparent that they didn't know. "We're still figuring out what should go in it," Kelsey said. "It's kind of turned into a massive undertaking."

"Yes, and we're trying to not have it be the Archer show." Crystal chuckled. "But it just so happens that they have the best cache of historical documents and items."

"Well, they're the first family or something, aren't they?" Brooke asked.

Alaina nodded. "Yes, Benjamin Archer settled here in 1856, but others followed. He made frequent trips into Portland, where he met his wife. Her brother and cousins came to the area and were involved in establishing the town."

Brooke was intrigued by all this. "Is there a written history of Ribbon Ridge?"

"Nothing formal," Alaina said. "It's something the Archer family had planned to do, but it just hasn't happened yet. Crystal has actually offered to document it for them. She's not as busy working as my assistant since my career has taken a backseat to being a wife and mother. Plus, she's a terrific writer. I keep telling her to finish the screenplay she started, but she keeps finding other things to do." Alaina gave her friend a look that said they'd had this conversation many times.

Crystal returned the look with a mild, probably playful glare before taking a drink of her beer. She set the glass back on the table. "Maybe I *have* finished it. I certainly wouldn't tell you." Crystal looked pointedly at Kelsey and Brooke. "She's a real nag once you get to know her."

Alaina smiled broadly. "That's me. And hey, what's wrong

with encouraging your friends toward things that you know will make them happy?"

They sounded like Brooke and her sisters. "You've been friends for a long time, haven't you?" Brooke asked.

"Since we were kids," Alaina said. She briefly rested her head on Crystal's shoulder. "She's held my hand through so much. Is it bad that I want her to be happy?"

"Of course it isn't. You know I love you." Crystal turned and kissed her cheek, provoking a grin from Alaina.

Brooke couldn't help but smile in the presence of such a warm and deep friendship. She suddenly missed her sisters and planned to call them both later.

"So in the process of gathering information to write this town history, we've been trying to figure out what those letters on the brick stand for," Crystal said. "So far, we've got nothing."

"I assumed they were someone's initials." Brooke took another drink of beer.

"I think we all did, but we've pored over the birth and death records—well, those we have from those early years—and there isn't anyone with a first name that starts with B and a last name that starts with R."

"We've also scoured marriage records and still nothing," Alaina said. "There's a pretty good cache of letters too, and we're not all the way through them. But so far, no mention of anyone that would match the initials BNR."

"That's a little frustrating," Brooke said.

Kelsey pressed her lips together. "Tell us about it. Don't suppose you have any brilliant ideas?" She stared at Brooke hopefully.

Brooke took a moment to sip her beer and think. She knew next to nothing about Ribbon Ridge. Maybe she should start by exploring every corner of the town, starting with the oldest buildings and places. A lightbulb went off in her head. "Hey, have you guys been to the cemetery? Maybe BNR's death wasn't properly documented or the documentation was lost."

Kelsey's face lit. "That's a great idea! Nice going, Brooke."

Brooke smiled. It felt good to be helpful. "Thanks. Should we plan a field trip?"

Alaina cocked her head to the side. "It would be faster if we all went together to canvass it. But Crystal and I are headed to LA tomorrow, and we won't be back until Tuesday. Can you guys wait until then?"

Brooke looked over at Kelsey. "I can. I'm headed to the coast Saturday and won't be back until Wednesday."

"What time?" Kelsey said. "My next free day is actually Wednesday. Any chance we could make that work?" She glanced at Brooke.

"If we make it later in the day—say three or so—I can do that."

"Sounds good to me," Alaina said. "Crystal?"

Crystal nodded. "It's a date." She already had her phone out and was typing into it. "And now it's in my calendar. I'll send you all an invitation so it'll be in your calendars too."

Alaina grinned at Crystal. "I'm so glad you're here to keep us all organized."

Crystal chuckled. "Can't help it, even when I'm not working." She looked over at Brooke. "I just need your number, Brooke."

Brooke provided it, happy to have found a group of friends here in Ribbon Ridge. She had barely talked to Naomi and Jana since the 10k, but that was probably for the best. They were single women on the prowl and too overbearing in trying to jump-start Brooke's love life.

Alaina rubbed her hands together. "I'm so excited about this. Thanks, Brooke! And on that note, I need to get home and put my daughter to bed."

The familiar pain ripped into Brooke. She wanted to ask about Alaina's daughter but was afraid that it would only intensify her heartache. But she was also tired of letting that rule her life. "How old is she?" The question came out soft and tentative. Hopefully no one else noticed.

"Two and a half and such a spitfire." Alaina pulled out her phone and scrolled to a picture, then handed it to Brooke. "She looks just like her dad."

Brooke hadn't met Evan Archer but could see the toddler didn't have her mother's dark blonde hair. Her hair was dark brown and a bit wild. She stood in a small inflatable pool wearing a bright yellow swimsuit with flowers and a huge grin. "She's adorable." Brooke's gut twisted. She'd wanted that so badly—to be a mother, to share a picture of her own child, to feel that pride and that bond. She gave the phone back and didn't ask any more questions.

Alaina tucked the phone into her purse. "Thank you. I'm grateful for every day with her—she's such a gift."

Her words made Brooke's eyes sting with unshed tears. Her throat clogged, and she merely nodded.

"It was great meeting you, Brooke. I'm really looking forward to this project!" Alaina stood. "See you next week."

Brooke summoned a wobbly smile and forced words past the emotion jamming her throat. "See you then."

Crystal followed her out of the booth. "Alaina's my ride. Great to meet you, Brooke." She lowered her voice and looked at Kelsey and Brooke. "Us single ladies should plan a night out." She winked at them and grinned before turning and joining Alaina.

Brooke watched them leave and drank more of her beer, hoping it would blunt the ache.

"Everything okay?" Kelsey asked.

Damn, she'd picked up on something. Maybe they all had.

"Yep," Brooke answered. She liked Kelsey, but she didn't share her infertility with most people, especially those she didn't know well. A voice in the back of her head asked if Cam still fell into that category. How could he after last night? It wasn't just that they'd had sex. It was that they'd both finally lowered their guard.

Kelsey finished her drink. "Well, if you ever need to talk, I'm apparently a good listener. Or so my college roommate always told me. But maybe that was because she talked all the time and I didn't have a choice." She laughed, and Brooke joined her. She felt instantly better, and whether Kelsey had provoked that on purpose or not, Brooke appreciated it.

"Crystal and Alaina are really nice," Brooke said, moving the topic in a new direction.

"Aren't they? Alaina is so down-to-earth, and Crystal's hilarious. You'll see that the more you spend time with her." Kelsey tipped her head to the side. "Maybe when we go out for our single ladies' night out. Hey, did you ever go on that blind date?"

"I did, actually."

Kelsey watched her expectantly. "And?"

Brooke chuckled. "It was fine. Nothing spectacular, but it didn't crash and burn either."

"Are you going to see him again?"

She'd thought so, but then she'd hooked up with Cam in a bathroom, and now a second date with Justin seemed disingenuous. Never mind that she wasn't *with* Cam and didn't expect a repeat performance. Probably because in the recesses of her body and mind, she *hoped* for a repeat.

"I don't know. Maybe."

"That doesn't sound promising. Any chance Cameron Westcott is holding you back?"

Wow, she was good. But then she'd noticed the crazy sparks —that was what she'd said, wasn't it?—between them. Brooke considered brushing her off, as she'd done a few minutes ago, but she suddenly wanted to talk to someone about what had happened.

"Yes, I think he is."

Kelsey looked surprised, her eyes widening. "I see. Did something happen?"

Brooke couldn't withhold the smile from her lips. "You could say that. We, uh, had a moment last night."

Kelsey turned on the bench and faced her. "What does that mean?"

Brooke winced, her eyes squinting. "We had sex in a restaurant bathroom?"

Kelsey clapped her hand over her mouth and giggled. "That's a bit more than a 'moment.' You are too funny. Are you guys together now?"

Brooke shook her head definitively. "No. In fact, we both agreed it was a one-time deal."

"Yet you're holding back with the blind-date guy."

"A little." Brooke set her elbow on the table and put her forehead on her hand. "Ugh. What am I doing? I would much rather things move forward with blind-date guy—uh, Justin—than with Cam."

"And why is that? The work thing?"

"Yes, and—" And what? Cam's history as a player? Certainly, but he seemed to have relaxed that behavior from what she could tell. Or maybe it was something far deeper. Something she didn't want to explore. Something to do with her and her inability to give him, or anyone else, a family. She slammed back the rest of her beer.

Kelsey was still studying her, likely waiting for the rest of whatever Brooke meant to say.

"That's pretty much it—the work thing." Brooke was done sharing for the day.

"I understand. That's a bummer, though. Maybe there's a way around it?"

Only if Brooke gave the account to someone else at Willamette, and she didn't want to do that. She felt personally invested in their wine, and she wanted to be a part of its success. But if life had taught her anything it was that you couldn't have your cake and eat it too. "I don't see one, but really, it's okay. I'm pretty sure I got him out of my system. Talking to you has helped me see that. I think I'll give Justin a call."

Kelsey nodded. "Sounds good. I'm a little jealous, actually. I wish I was ready."

Brooke wanted to return Kelsey's kindness. "Anything I can do to help?"

"No, it's all me. I'll get there eventually. I hope." She smiled and glanced toward her empty glass. "Alaina must've paid the bill. Or maybe George comped it."

Brooke slid out of the booth. "He comped mine as a sort of welcome to town."

"George is the best. He's one of the reasons I'm still here in Ribbon Ridge. He made me feel welcome from day one—like family."

"That's so great." Brooke missed her family, but more and more she felt like Ribbon Ridge was home.

They parted and went their separate ways, and as Brooke walked to the store to grab something for dinner, she thought about what she'd told Kelsey, that she'd call Justin. Would she, really?

Or would she continue to obsess about Cam? She was fairly certain it would be the latter, unfortunately.

Chapter Thirteen

Cam stared at the prepackaged meals stacked in the deli refrigerator at Ribbon Ridge's sole grocery store. It was a perfectly fine store, albeit small, but didn't offer much in the way of variety for a single guy who didn't cook. If it couldn't be prepared in three steps or less, Cam didn't make it.

So what was it going to be tonight—pulled pork or pasta with meatballs? He glanced at the items already in his handheld basket: paper towels, cereal, a half gallon of milk, and a bottle of microbrew. Beer went better with the pork. "Winner, winner, pork dinner!" he said as he grabbed it from the reefer.

"Are you talking to that?"

He swung his head around at the familiar sound of Brooke's voice. Her hair was pulled up, and she wore cropped jeans and a fitted T-shirt. She looked casual and comfortable and heart-stoppingly sexy.

Cam took a minute to put his thoughts into coherent speech. "Uh, yeah. I always talk to my food. Don't you?"

"I try not to, actually." She held her hand up to the side of her head and twirled her finger. "People might think I'm *crazy*." She whispered the last word, and he laughed.

He glanced at her basket, which was full of veggies. "Look at you being all healthy."

"Sometimes a girl's just gotta have a big salad."

His stomach grumbled. Damn, that sounded good. "Boys too. But that's a lot of work."

She flicked a look toward her basket before tipping her head to the side. "What, chopping vegetables? That's not a lot of work."

"Yeah, it is."

Now she laughed. "Then you either have the wrong knife or you're lazy."

"Both, probably." He smiled, glad she'd approached him. It would've been easy for her to simply avoid him and any awkwardness. But this didn't feel awkward. It felt...good.

"Well, I can't help you with lazy, but the right knife is actually super important. You can cut much more efficiently if you have a good blade. I can't believe a bachelor like you doesn't have good knives. That's pretty much the only thing you can count on a guy to have, right? And maybe a grill or a smoker."

He shook his head. "I don't have any of those. Didn't I tell you that I don't cook?"

"Maybe? But you're serious, you don't cook, like, at all?"

"Nope, much to my mother's chagrin. My brothers are much better at it. Dylan is actually pretty good, or has gotten that way anyway. He designed himself a badass gourmet kitchen, and then he went and got married. All that domesticity breeds cookery, I guess." He shuddered but smiled playfully.

"Ah yes, domesticity. The arch nemesis of a confirmed bachelor like yourself. I'm tempted to invite you over to demonstrate how a good knife can change your life."

Tempted... He was tempted to do far more than that, but he reined himself in. They had a pact. Or an agreement. Or an assumption. Whatever. They weren't supposed to repeat what they'd done the other night, and if he went to her loft for salad making, he was pretty sure it would lead to lovemaking.

At least on his part. Maybe she really was over it.

"You could save me from prepackaged pulled pork."

She peered into his basket. "I've had that, and it's actually pretty good. Besides, you've already talked to it—it'll be sad if you reject it now."

He laughed again, loving her sense of humor. "I think it'll survive. Or not—I'll eat it tomorrow."

"In that case, you can come for salad." She looked down at her basket briefly, and he saw her lips press together. When she tilted her head back up, her gaze was determined. "Just salad."

"Just salad."

She watched him warily. "I'm quite skilled with that knife."

"I don't doubt it." He couldn't resist a grin. "You may not want to show me all your tricks."

She squinted at him for a second. "I can't tell if you're flirting. If so, knock it off or I'll rescind my invitation."

He held up his hand. "You win. No flirting."

She turned toward the checkout registers, and he followed. She seemed quite over their...whatever it had been. His chest felt suddenly hollow. Because he *wasn't* over it. He'd tossed and turned at night, his thoughts consumed with her touch and her scent. He longed to feel her against him again but was afraid that would never happen. Now he was even more sure of that.

This was stupid. He was in lust with her, nothing more. Okay, there was plenty more, but screw it. They could be friends. He *wanted* to be friends.

She started unloading her veggies onto the conveyer belt.

"Hey, I can pay for everything," he offered.

She tossed him a gimlet eye. "This is not a date, mister. I'll pay for my own salad makings, thank you."

She said it in a good-humored enough voice that he didn't take offense. He still couldn't help *wishing* it was a date. God, he wanted to date her.

Yes.

Maybe he could convince her to give it a try...

She cleared her throat loudly.

He looked down at the belt and saw that she'd put out a divider so he could unload his groceries. "Thanks." He transferred everything from his basket and set it under the check stand.

"Hi, Cam!" Marcia, the checkout clerk smiled at him. "What's for dinner tonight?" She looked at Cam's groceries on the belt as she scanned Brooke's items. "Pork again? You just had that a few nights ago."

He shook his head and gave her a wry, friendly smile. "Good to know you're cataloguing my meals."

She pursed her lips. "Someone has to. Your mother likes to know what you're eating." Marcia played in his mom's Bunco group, and Cam had known her for probably twenty years. "She'd also like to know that you're eating with someone." She looked at Brooke inquisitively.

Great, just what Cam needed: Marcia reporting to his mother that he was on a date or something. Wanting to date someone and wanting your family to know about it were two very different things. Mom would probably fall prostrate with shock if she thought he was dating—right before she harangued him for every detail. That her stepson was married and a father and none of her own sons were remotely close to that drove her nuts. Cam rushed to quell any misunderstanding. "Uh, we're neighbors, and we work together. We're not eating together." He inwardly flinched and thought about how to cushion that lie as soon as he and Brooke left.

Marcia frowned and then sighed. "Well, that's too bad. You'd make a cute couple." She winked at Brooke. "That's twenty-eight thirty-three. Brooke, right?"

Brooke nodded. "Thanks." She swiped her debit card and completed her transaction. Then she turned to Cam with a cool stare and said, "Nice seeing you. Bye."

Disappointment coursed through him as he watched her leave. He shouldn't be disappointed—or surprised, since he'd said they weren't eating together. She couldn't know he'd only said that for Marcia's benefit.

Marcia made more small talk as she scanned his items *slowly*. He tried not to be visibly antsy but had already swiped his card and entered his PIN long before she'd finished. At long last, she was done. He bid her a hasty good-night and left the store at a fast pace. He looked down the street and saw that Brooke was already across the street at the corner a block down.

He dashed out into the street without looking and stopped short at the sound of a horn blaring. The car hadn't come close to hitting him, but the driver held up his hands and clearly mouthed, *What the hell?*

Cam waved at him and mouthed, "Sorry!" before continuing across. He looked toward the corner and saw Brooke was waiting for him, her head cocked to the side. When he reached her, he saw that her expression was one of concern but also mild annoyance.

"Nice move," she said. "You have a death wish?"

"Definitely not. I was trying to catch up with you."

She arched a brow before pivoting and walking around the corner. "At your own peril."

Darcy Burke

He caught up to her. "Evidently. Hey, I didn't mean what I said back there. We *are* eating together—if you still want to."

Brooke didn't slow her pace. "Why'd you lie to Marcia?"

"She plays Bunco with my mom. She's already going to tell her that she saw me with you at the store, and my mom will get a zillion ideas." He rolled his eyes, wondering when their next Bunco night was so that he could avoid his mom's inevitable phone call.

"What sort of ideas?"

"That we're dating or whatever."

Brooke cast him a narrow-eyed look. "I'm pretty sure I don't want to know what 'whatever' is."

What did she mean? "I just meant that she'll draw her own conclusions."

"Oh, I know what you mean. Given your history, I can only imagine what those conclusions might be."

Shit, this was not going well. And they'd had such a great conversation at the store. He snagged her elbow and drew her to a stop as they reached the corner across from the entrance to her building. "Wait. Let me explain. My mom is desperate for grandchildren. My stepbrother just had a kid a few months ago, but their relationship is a bit strained, and she'd like a grandchild of her own blood—her words, not mine."

Brooke looked past him and started to cross the street. "That's too bad." She sounded terse and cool.

He realized he hadn't painted the best picture of his mother, and she wasn't a bad person. "My mom's a bit high-strung, I guess. She loves Emma—Dylan's daughter—really."

"I would hope so. She should feel blessed to have a grandchild at all."

"Yes." Cam followed her onto the curb outside the entrance to her building. "So, dinner?"

Brooke turned to look at him. "I think it's best if we skip it.

174

I'll e-mail you a link to a knife you should buy. Really, it will make a huge difference."

He longed to touch her, to soothe the creases in her forehead. He wondered if there was more to this than his idiot behavior. "I will. And hey, I'm sorry if I upset you. My family can be meddlesome, and I didn't want them to get the wrong idea."

"Absolutely. I don't want them—or you—to get the wrong idea either. We're coworkers. Friends. That's it. We'll have dinner another time." She gave him a warm smile, but he had the sense it wasn't completely genuine. "Enjoy your pork." She turned and went into her building, leaving him to stare after her.

Why did he feel like he'd just royally screwed up?

―――

By the time Brooke walked into her loft, her pulse was hammering a staccato rhythm. She'd kept herself together in front of Cam, but hearing about his mother had summoned those terrible feelings of inadequacy, of being...broken.

She set her purse and the bag of groceries on the kitchen island and walked into the living room. Any thoughts of dinner had fled during their conversation as she stared out the bank of windows toward his townhouse. She clenched her fists, angry with herself for her debilitating reaction. Why did this seem to be so prevalent lately?

Because she had a man in her life, something she'd strove to avoid since her divorce. Whether she wanted him there or not, Cameron Westcott was *in* her life. She liked him. She was attracted to him. She looked forward to being with him.

But there was no future for them. Not when he talked of a family who was champing at the bit for him to provide grandchildren.

Still…could there be a right now? Could she find a way to be with him in the present? A way that would allow them to enjoy what they had for a while and split ways amicably so they could continue their working relationship.

Sure, right after monkeys flew out of her butt.

She retraced her steps to the kitchen and fished her phone from her purse. She dialed Rhonda and waited anxiously for her sister to pick up.

"Yo, sissy!" Rhonda answered in a goofy voice she often used.

"I need help. Tell me how to make this work with Cameron."

"Whoa, you sound stressed. Let's just take a deep breath." Rhonda breathed deeply on the other end of the phone, and Brooke inhaled with her. "How to make what work?"

Brooke had told her about hooking up with Cameron in the bathroom, but had insisted it was a one-time thing and that she was okay with that. "A…relationship. A casual one," she quickly amended.

"Did you have sex again?"

"No."

"Then what's got you so wound up?"

"I ran into him at the grocery store, and we ended up talking about his family. Apparently, his mom is dying for grandkids."

Rhonda sighed. "And that sent you over the edge. Sis, you might need to find a therapist up there."

"I don't need a therapist. This is only bothering me because of Cameron. He's the first guy I've met since Darren that I… like."

"That's true." Rhonda made a high-pitched sound like she was sucking on her lip. "Okay, let's figure this out. You like him. He likes you. There's absolutely no reason to think this is a forever thing, hence any discussion about procreation isn't necessary. There. Done. Now go get him."

Brooke rolled her eyes but couldn't help smiling. She realized this was why she'd called Rhonda. Yes, she was oversimplifying things, but maybe that was what Brooke needed. She was the one making it into a Thing. "Say we get together—like date and stuff. We still work together. Remember when you thought my hooking up with him was a bad idea? What happens when one of us is ready to move on?" She didn't voice the fear she was desperately trying to tamp down—that he would dump her long before she wanted to dump him. He didn't do long-term, right?

"You break up like grown-ups. People actually do this. Look at my friend Kara. She and Doug broke up after four years together, and it was perfectly civilized. They even share custody of the dog."

Brooke knew Kara and Doug and Spreckles. They *had* made it work. Maybe she and Cam *could* do this. Assuming he even wanted to. "Cam might not be interested."

"You're making a lot of assumptions about him—about what he wants, about his dreams for the future, and whether he wants kids. Why don't you spend some time finding out the truth? Do that, and then you can bail if you see red flags."

Now Brooke felt a bit foolish. "It all seems so straightforward when you say it."

Rhonda laughed. "Because it is. You're caught up in it though, so of course it seems complicated to you. Just take a step back tonight and see where you are tomorrow. I bet you'll feel much more clearheaded."

"Yeah, you're probably right." Brooke exhaled, and this time she felt the stress start to dissipate. "Thanks, sis. I appreciate you talking me off the ledge. Again."

More laughter. "That's what I do. Okay, I need to tuck Isla in to bed. Text me tomorrow and let me know what happens!"

"Will do. Kiss Isla and Will for me."

"Of course." She blew a kiss into the phone. "Night!"

"Night." Brooke ended the call and set the phone on the counter, feeling much better. She still wasn't completely certain what to do, but she wasn't in a panic anymore. She could do this. She was ready for the next step.

She just hoped that step didn't send her tumbling off a cliff.

Chapter Fourteen

Cam scrubbed his hand over his face as he stared at his computer monitor. He'd reread this e-mail he was drafting to Sara at least twenty times and still kept thinking of things to add. He'd be better off just talking to her in person to make sure they captured everything that needed to be done for the winery dinner. She'd laugh and tell him he was obsessing. Which was probably true.

Just not about this.

He couldn't stop thinking of Brooke. He'd started texting her a dozen times today, but never sent anything. He didn't know what to say about last night. Things had taken a weird turn, and he was sure it was his fault. But that wasn't why he didn't text her. No, it was because he was pretty sure she'd given him a definite brush-off this time. She'd been friendly at the grocery store, but not necessarily flirty. Then when he'd become flirty, she'd started to distance herself. Then he'd stuck his foot in it with Marcia, and Brooke had completely left the building as far as he was concerned.

Time to figure out a way to move past her once and for all.

He sat straight in his chair and inhaled sharply before refocusing on his screen.

A moment later, his resolve took a major hit when a light knock on his door was preceded by Brooke stepping into his office.

Her gaze met his. Searching. Tentative. Beautiful in its clarity—he could stare into her eyes all damn day. "Am I bothering you?" she asked.

"No." He coughed past the cobwebs that had suddenly crisscrossed his throat.

"Oh good." She smiled softly and came farther into his office. "I, ah, came to pick up that case of chardonnay I need for next week. I'm headed to the beach tomorrow morning."

"You can't be working Labor Day weekend."

"Actually, my sisters are meeting me for a girls' weekend."

Cam sat back in his chair and rested his right elbow on the arm. "Sounds like trouble."

Now she grinned. "Probably. But that's how we Ellis girls roll."

"Damn, now I wish I could come along."

"It's a *girls'* weekend." She lifted a shoulder. "The condo's in Lincoln City."

The one owned by her employer—he knew it well. "Willamette's? I've been there for an after-party or two. Nice place. There's a hot tub on the deck." He sat up in the chair and dropped all pretense. "Am I nuts, or are we flirting? I am so confused. After last night—"

"I'm flirting. Are you flirting?"

"I'm trying not to. But you make it impossible, sorry."

"So do you." She laughed softly. "That's the other reason I'm here. I'm sorry about last night. I was trying really hard to keep things platonic, and then we made plans to have dinner at my loft, and, well, that just didn't seem like it would support the whole platonic thing."

He couldn't disagree with her there. He stood up slowly and circled the desk. "I don't disagree. But I was really disappointed. I also felt like a major jackass for saying that at the store. I was just trying to be private, I guess."

"I get it. This is a small town. I think I glommed on to that as a good reason to put the brakes on."

Cam moved in front of his desk to face her and leaned against it. "Makes sense. So we're flirting. And it seems like platonic is tough for both of us."

She dropped her purse into one of the chairs facing his desk. "It seems that way." Her gaze was hot and intense.

He swallowed, his body tightening with desire. He eyed her purse and tried to process why she'd dropped it. She planned to stay? She wanted her hands free? She was about to touch him? All of the above? His skin tingled with anticipation.

She took a step toward him. "I was thinking that one-and-done business didn't really pan out for me. How about you?"

"Not even a little bit," he rasped. Need catapulted through him. He put his hands on the desk on either side of his hips and squeezed the wood lest he launch himself forward and crush her against him.

"I was hoping you'd say that." She moved closer and laid her hand against his chest.

He was sure she had to feel the wild pounding of his heart. "So you're here to…?"

"Negotiate terms." She arched a brow at him and curved her lips into the sexiest smile he'd ever seen. "You told me that you make no promises, that you like to live in the present and take one day at a time. Is that right?"

He wanted to live in this moment forever. "Yes."

"Perfect. No expectations. No demands. And we have to agree that we can still work together."

"Yes, of course." He vaguely realized that he'd probably surrender his firstborn right now if that were part of her terms, but that was his Y chromosome talking. He meant what he said. "I respect and value you too much to let anything else happen."

"Then I guess we're settled." She started to remove his shirt, slowly, her fingers slipping the buttons through the holes.

"I guess so. And we're going to move on this now?"

Her hands stilled. She blinked at him, her head cocking to the side. "Unless you'd rather not?"

"I'd rather die than not." He swooped forward and clasped her against him as his mouth claimed hers.

She clutched at his shirtfront, her fingers digging into his flesh as they clenched the fabric. He held her against him, his head tipping opposite hers to kiss her deeply. Her tongue slid against his as she thrust into him.

She started in on his buttons again, her hands fumbling between them. She pulled back slightly so she could better complete her task, and as soon as the shirt was open, he shrugged it off his shoulders with her help. Her hands caressed his bare shoulders as she kissed him again.

He pushed at the little cardigan she was wearing. It was white and flimsy and slid from her shoulders with ease. He found the hem of her red-and-white sleeveless top, and he pushed his hands up under the fabric. His fingertips skimmed along her rib cage and didn't stop until he cupped her breasts.

She arched into him, moaning softly into his mouth. Her hips gyrated against his so that he could feel her heat against the raging length of his cock.

He tugged her shirt up and broke their kiss so he could whip the garment over her head. He tossed it away and realized his office door was still open.

"Just a second," he said, his voice dark and full of gravel. He crossed to the door and closed it firmly, then locked it for good measure. He was pretty sure that Jamie was in his office and that Luke was in the vineyard somewhere.

When he turned to come back to her, he froze. She'd kicked off her sandals and was now shimmying out of her bra. She dropped it to the floor and gave him a torrid, come-hither look that momentarily turned his knees to water.

But then the savage beast within him that couldn't wait to be inside her stalked forward and drew her against him. "You are so beautiful." He bent her backward and shoved the items on his desktop to the side, some of them toppling to the floor. Thankfully, his primary workspace with his monitor was on the side that faced the window. Although in this moment, he wasn't sure he would've given a damn about any of it.

He laid her flat on the desk and turned her lengthwise so that the desk could support her comfortably. He stared down at her breasts, so full and perfect, their pink tips hard and beckoning. He cupped them firmly and lightly pinched her nipples. She came up off the desk, her eyes closing in ecstasy as she moaned again. Desperate to taste her, he leaned down and took one in his mouth, using his lips and tongue to drive her mad.

Her hands tangled in his hair, holding him to her. "*Cam.* Yes."

He stroked and kissed her for several minutes, moving from breast to breast—taunting one and then the other with his mouth and hands until she was writhing on the desk.

"You're torturing me." Her words came out on a gasp.

"Actually, I'm torturing myself." He wanted to prolong this time with her, but was also seething with impatience. "You're killing me."

She rolled to her side to face where he was standing and started to undo his belt. She quickly had his shorts unfastened and pushed them down, along with his boxer briefs. Her hands stroked his cock. He moaned as wave after wave of pleasure cascaded over him. He tipped his head back and closed his eyes, reveling in her touch. Then her mouth was on him and he had to grab the edge of the desk to keep his legs from buckling.

"Brooke. Good God. You are...amazing."

Her lips and tongue moved over him as her hand clasped the base of his shaft. She was fast and expert, utterly mind melting. He could barely think and soon his body was taking over, thrusting into her mouth in quick, relentless strokes. If she didn't stop he was going to pour himself down her throat, and that was not how he wanted this to go.

He moved back and kicked his shoes off before stepping out of his shorts. Brooke stared at him with slitted eyes and pushed herself up and off the desk. With slow, languorous, catlike grace, she slipped her skirt and underwear off until she was naked before him. Then she knelt, and he was sure she was going to finish what she'd started. He wanted to stop her, but the words wouldn't come.

But no, she was searching the pockets of his shorts. He watched her, confused. Then he realized. "Condom." Duh. It was a good thing one of them was thinking clearly. "My wallet's on the desk." He gestured toward where he'd tossed it earlier, near his monitor.

She moved stealthily behind the desk. He watched her movements, appreciating the slope of her hip and the curve of her back right above her ass. He was going to explore every inch of her. Maybe not today, but soon.

She pulled a condom from his wallet and came back around the desk. Was she moving more quickly now, or was that just his impatient hope?

Either way, when she reached him, she pushed him backward, making him take several steps until he felt the couch hit the back of his legs. Then she forced him down—not that he needed much coercion—and leaned forward with the condom.

He took it from her and ripped open the package. Surprisingly, he managed to get it on without assistance. At least his brain was partially working. And in the ways that counted.

She put one knee on the couch and swung her other leg up on his other side so that she straddled him. Her eyes found his and held them as she fondled his cock in long, agonizingly wonderful strokes. She held him to her entrance. She was all wet and hot and devastating as she lowered herself onto him.

He clasped her hips and pushed into her, his head falling back against the couch as he closed his eyes in rapture. When she'd taken him completely, she wriggled her hips and just rested for a moment. He felt every ragged breath she drew, every beat of her heart, every muscle stretch and contract around him and against him.

She cupped his neck, massaging his flesh before settling her hands on his shoulders. Then she began to move. Slowly at first, her hips rotating over his, pulling up just enough to tease him and not coming down quite enough to satisfy his need.

He let her play, his pleasure churning and mounting with each thrust. He tipped his head up and opened his eyes to feast on her. Her eyes were closed. She looked focused, her lips parted as soft little moans burst forth. He brought one hand up to her breast and held it captive for his mouth. She gasped as he sucked on her flesh, his fingers digging into her softness.

She clutched at his shoulders and began to move faster. She came down a bit harder, more fully, but it still wasn't enough.

He moved his hand up and cupped the back of her neck, drawing her head down so he could kiss her greedily. She tasted of heat and summer and bliss, and he couldn't get enough of her. He nipped at her lower lip. "Harder, Brooke. Ride me."

She ground down, taking him completely into her until

there was nowhere left for him to go. But it wasn't enough. He kissed her again, his tongue spearing into her as his cock did the same.

He grasped her hair and tugged lightly, not hurting her. She opened her eyes and looked down at him. "Ride me, Brooke. *Hard.* I'm yours. Now. Own me."

He pushed up, straightening his hips. Then he clasped her ass and squeezed her as he thrust up into her. He drove hard and fast, pulling sharp groans from her kiss-swollen lips. She did as he asked, riding him with a harsh frenzy that sent blood spiraling to his cock. He brought his hand around and found her clit, pressing and stroking her until she cried out, her eyes closing once more and her head falling back as her orgasm rocked her body. Her muscles clenched around him, and he moved even faster, holding her tight while he pulsed into her again and again.

His balls tightened as his orgasm crested and crashed over him. He yelled her name as he gave himself over completely.

They moved together for another minute, their hips eventually slowing and their labored breathing filling the air around them. She collapsed against him, her breasts caressing his chest. He ran his hands over her back, soothing her, soothing himself.

"That was quite a ride," he finally said.

"Yes," she murmured against his neck. He loved the feel of her against him. So soft, so warm. *So good.*

"I, uh, should get cleaned up," he said with great reluctance.

"Right." She pushed up off him, and he regretted not kissing her first.

She retrieved her clothing, and he went to the bathroom to take care of business. When he came back to the office, she'd already donned her skirt and bra and was just pulling her top over her head.

"That was fantastic," he said. "I'm so glad you came by."

She laughed, and he detected a bit of nervousness. Or shyness. Or both. It was adorable. And he was surprised to find he felt a little bit of it too. He liked her so much. He didn't want to fuck this up.

She found her cardigan and tugged it on. "I actually didn't mean for this to happen. I really did come to pick up wine and just say that I'd be open to seeing you casually."

If this was casual, he wasn't sure he wanted to see serious. No, he definitely didn't want to see serious. This was enough. This was great.

"Clearly, we were both excited by that development." He pulled on his briefs and shorts and didn't bother with his belt as he went to grab his shirt from where it barely dangled on the back of one of the chairs. "One of these days, though, I'd like to make love to you in a bed."

She slipped her feet into her wedges. "I'm sure we can manage that." She picked up her purse. "Where's my wine?"

He sat down and quickly put his shoes on. "I'll carry it to your car for you. Hayden left it out—you probably walked right by it."

She chuckled. "Probably."

They walked downstairs and found the wine. He was glad they didn't encounter his brothers. He wasn't going to hide their relationship, but he also wasn't going to put it out in front of them just yet. He cared for Brooke, and he wanted to take things slow. Okay, except for the crazy awesome sex they couldn't seem to keep themselves from having.

He smiled to himself as he hefted the case of wine onto his shoulder. He didn't care what speed they went, as long as they were going somewhere.

Brooke snuck a look at Cam's back as he lifted the case of wine. His muscles rippled beneath his shirt, muscles she'd caressed and madly clutched just a short time earlier. She'd meant what she told him—she hadn't expected that to happen. But she was glad it did.

She was also glad that they seemed to be on the same page. For the first time in years, she felt hopeful. She felt happy. And damn it, she deserved that.

In the parking lot, she unlocked her car with the remote and opened the back end. He deposited the case inside and shut the hatch. He turned, and the breeze tousled his dark brown hair, mussing it over his forehead. She reached out and brushed it back. He captured her hand and pressed a kiss to her palm. A shiver raced up her spine—a good shiver, the kind that was filled with anticipation and sprinkled with longing.

He pulled her against him and kissed her, his lips lingering over hers as she let her body relax into his. "I had a great time," he said softly. "I'd ask to see you this weekend, but you're busy."

"Yes, sorry." She almost wished she could tell her sisters that the condo had fallen through, but no, sisters before misters was a rule she didn't intend to break. "I'll be back Wednesday night."

He looked at her, his brow arching in seductive query. "Is that an invitation?"

She brushed her hand over his chest, relishing his solid warmth against her palm. "It's out there. What you choose to do with the information is your choice."

"I see." He lowered his head and kissed her again. "There's tonight, right? You're not leaving until morning?"

That was true. But she hadn't packed, and she still had some work stuff to do. But it was early, barely four, she could make some time later...

The sound of a car pulling into the lot drew them apart, but he didn't move away from her. They hadn't discussed whether they planned to be public, but she supposed it wasn't a secret.

It wasn't a car actually, but a king cab work truck stocked with ladders and a toolbox. They parked near Brooke's SUV, and a petite blonde climbed out of the passenger seat. "Hey, Cam!" She didn't come toward them but opened the back door and busied herself with something that Brooke couldn't see. The driver, a tall, dark-haired drink of water, came around the truck. Brooke could see instantly that he and Cam were related.

He came toward them. "Hi. I'm Dylan Westcott."

Cam's older half-brother and the construction guy. Brooke held out her hand. "Hi, I'm Brooke Ellis. I, uh, work with Cam."

Dylan's eyes narrowed infinitesimally as he scrutinized her briefly. His gaze darted to Cam with an equally assessing look. "Uh-huh. Nice to meet you." His demeanor said he wasn't entirely certain they were coworkers, which meant he'd seen them embracing. Oh well, it *really* wasn't a secret.

"Brooke is distributing our wine," Cam said. "And she's damn good at it."

The blonde came toward them, and Brooke saw why she'd been busy in the backseat—she carried a baby. The infant's chubby little legs stuck out from a ruffled romper, and she smacked her hand against her mother's chest, clutching at her shirt between thumps. Brooke's maternal instinct kicked into high gear, and she willed herself to keep it together. She could be around babies, for crying out loud—she had two nieces and a nephew.

Cam went straight for the baby, swooping her from her mother's arms. He lifted her up, much to the baby's delight. Her eyes shone as she giggled. He turned to Brooke. "This is my niece Emma. Oh, and her mom, Sara."

Sara snorted. "This is what happens when you have a baby,

you become a second-class citizen." She gazed lovingly at her daughter. "Not that I mind."

No, Brooke couldn't imagine she would. She'd gladly become a second-class citizen in exchange for a baby of her own. "She's beautiful. How old?"

"Five months," Sara answered, watching Cam while he made ridiculous faces and silly noises.

Brooke watched him too, and in that moment, any hope she might've nurtured for a future with him evaporated like water on a hot summer day. Despite the blazing heat of the sun, ice coated her veins and chilled her mood. Yet at the same time, she told herself this was stupid—she didn't want a future with him; she only wanted right now.

And *right now* he was snuggling his niece with adoring eyes.

Brooke urged a smile to her lips. "It was nice to meet you, but I should go."

"I hope we're not driving you off," Sara said.

"No, no, I was on my way out. I have work to finish." Brooke nodded toward Cam, feeling disjointed and irritated with herself. Maybe she'd drink one of those bottles of chardonnay when she got home. "See you later."

She made a point of looking at Cam and wished she hadn't. The picture of him with Emma in his arms would haunt her for a long time. He was an absolute natural as he held Emma's wrist and helped her wave. He even said, "Bye-bye, Brooke. See you later!"

Brooke smiled because she really couldn't help it—she loved children—and waved back. "Bye!"

She didn't end up drinking the chardonnay, of course, but she did throw herself into work and then packing. And when Cam's texts came and he asked if she was up for a visitor, she pretended she was already asleep.

Chapter Fifteen

After spending the weekend with her sisters, Brooke felt absolutely rejuvenated. She realized she'd been vulnerable Friday after being with Cam, and seeing him with Emma had triggered all of her worst anxieties. Rhonda and Tracy had restored her confidence and successfully reminded her that right now in her life it was okay to put herself first and live for the present.

So that was precisely what she was going to do.

Once her sisters had left early Monday afternoon, Brooke finalized her schedule for the next two days and completed some other work. By late afternoon, she was ready to get out for a bit, so she went for a walk on the beach. The day was cloudy and a bit cool due to the wind. By the time she walked back up to the front of the condo building, she was eager to put on some sweats and kick her feet up with a glass of wine.

But when she rounded the corner to the door of the condo, she stopped short. There, propped against the wall with a lazy grin, was Cam.

He pushed off and walked toward her. "Hey, beautiful."

She shouldn't have been surprised to see him. In fact, during her walk, she'd thought it might be nice if he were here with her tonight. A light, giddy feeling bloomed in her stomach and spread. A warning fired off in the recesses of her brain—this could move beyond casual so fast if she wasn't careful. "You're lucky girls' weekend is over."

He winced. "I took a chance. I hope that's okay."

While her insides churned with anticipation, she tried to maintain an outward air of composure. She shrugged. "Surprises are nice sometimes." She moved past him, catching the scent of his cologne, and managed to insert the key into the lock. Once she was over the threshold, she held the door open. "Come on in."

He exhaled. "Oh, good." The relief in his tone was evident.

She laughed. "Were you worried I'd send you away? After the other day?"

"Guys always worry about that kind of stuff."

She closed the door behind him and locked the dead bolt out of habit. "I'm sorry, but I have a hard time thinking an über-confident guy like you worries about that sort of thing at all. Nice try, though." She walked down the short hallway and turned to the kitchen, where she dumped her keys and purse on the island.

He came up behind her, his hands clasping her waist. "Maybe not usually, but you're different. Special. You know that, right?"

She didn't, actually, and the newfound knowledge sent tingles dancing over her flesh. She stepped away from him and turned, suddenly feeling shy. Or nervous. Or both.

"I didn't know that. But thank you." Part of her wanted to ask how she was special, but that would send them down a path she didn't want to take. She wanted now, here, nothing "special."

She moved around the island, putting space and the large slab of granite between them. "So you came down here to...?"

"Take you to dinner and...whatever else." He took a step to the corner of the island but didn't pursue her. "I really just wanted to see you. I was sorry we couldn't see each other Friday night."

She'd texted him back the next morning saying she'd already been asleep, but that she'd catch up with him when she was back in town. The whole time she repeated the word "casual" to herself over and over again. "Yeah, I'm sorry too."

"So, can I take you to dinner?"

That sounded divine. And like a real date. Once again, the word "casual" became a mantra in her brain.

She hadn't been on a real date in so long. The blind date with Justin didn't count. They'd met for drinks and, given the blind-dateness of it all, the conversation had been a tad awkward and slow. This would be different. She and Cam knew each other. *Well.*

And yet there were so many things she wanted to know.

Careful, Brooke, casual.

"Where should we go?"

He glanced at the clock on the microwave. "As it happens, I have reservations at The Bay House in about twenty minutes."

His thoughtfulness was awfully flattering.

"Oh, wow, I guess you really *were* worried that I wasn't going to show up!" She laughed. "They're on my schedule for tomorrow, but if Don's around, we can pitch your wines together."

He grinned, and his handsomeness rocked through her like a lightning bolt. "Sounds great. I like that—together."

She did too, but cautioned herself not to like it too much. "Let me freshen up real quick." She dashed back down the hallway to the master bedroom and checked herself in the mirror, fluffing her hair and spritzing on perfume.

When she went back to the living room, he was out on the deck, looking at the ocean. The sun was gliding toward the horizon, casting the water in a golden, shimmery glow.

She joined him at the railing, and a cool breeze made her shiver. She wrapped her arms around herself. "Fall's in the air a bit."

"It is. Just a few weeks away, really."

"I know. Crazy. I've lived here—well, in Ribbon Ridge—for almost two months."

He turned, leaning his hip against the railing. "And what do you think?"

She turned too, facing him, her arms still crossed. "I like it a lot. I've met some really nice people."

"I hope that includes me."

She rolled her eyes and pushed him lightly in the chest. "Don't go digging for compliments. That's obnoxious. Or so my mother says."

He captured her hand in his. "Let's go have dinner."

They left the condo, and he drove them south through town to the restaurant, which had a lovely view over Siletz Bay. They'd be able to watch the sun set from their table by the window.

"Is Don here?" Cam asked the hostess who sat them.

"Not tonight. He'll be here tomorrow, though."

She smiled at the hostess. "That's okay, thanks."

The hostess gave them their menus and said their server would be right with them.

Cam went for the wine list first. He groaned, and it reminded her of the noises he'd made the other day in his office. "So many great pinots from Eyrie."

Brooke forced herself to focus on the menu and not how

insanely attracted she was to Cam. "I think I want to try the tasting menu, and there's a wine pairing for it. What do you think?" It included a salad, three main courses to share, and a dessert trio.

"Looks great, and the wine pairings are spot-on. I'm game if you are—there's a chardonnay, you know." He looked at her in question, reminding her of the night they'd met and first discussed wine, including their mutual ambivalence toward chardonnay.

"I saw that, but I actually enjoy that one a lot."

"Me too." He glanced longingly at the wine menu.

Brooke laughed. "It's like going to church for you, isn't it?"

He smiled sheepishly. "A little bit. I'm rather passionate about it."

"I can see that. It's cool because I feel the same way—okay, maybe not *quite* as much as you."

When the server came, Cam ordered for them. A few minutes later, they had their chardonnay, and he proposed a toast. "To being on a real date. Thank you." He tapped his glass to hers.

She chuckled. "You're welcome. I notice this date is happening a long way from Ribbon Ridge. We didn't talk about whether this was a secret thing." She sipped her wine. "I recall you didn't want your mom to know you might be seeing someone."

He flinched. "That was stupid of me. I didn't want to be a piece of Ribbon Ridge gossip, but no, this isn't anything I want to hide." His gaze was warm and earnest and heated her in all the best physical and emotional ways. "And anyway, my brother totally saw us canoodling in the parking lot the other day and asked what was up. I told him we were dating—*casually*. I don't mean to diminish it by saying that. I just want you to know that I respect our plan."

She appreciated that and didn't take it any other way. They were on the same page, and that was great. "I'm fine with you telling him. Or anyone else for that matter. Because I told my sisters the same thing this weekend." Okay, she'd told them a bit more than *that*, but that was what sisters did.

He set his wine down after taking a drink. "Do I want to know what they said?"

She recalled her sisters' reaction and decided it would be funny to share. "Hallelujah?"

His eyes widened briefly before he dissolved into laughter. "That's funny."

"It had been a while since I...but you know that."

"Yes, but I don't know any specifics. Like about your ex. How long were you married?"

"Almost five years." She weighed what to say and decided to keep it simple. "We met in college and got married right after."

"Divorce sucks. My dad's divorce from Dylan's mom was pretty acrimonious. It was awful for Dylan—just be glad you didn't have any kids. What happened?"

Her brain tried to freeze up after his kid comment, but she willed herself to relax. He was right. Splitting up would be terrible if you had children, but in her case, the lack of them had been the cause. Or had it? She'd begun to think that their marriage wouldn't have worked out either way. If he couldn't stick with her through infertility, what other issue would've caused him to stray? "We just weren't meant to be."

It was like a weight lifted from her as she realized that wasn't a trite phrase but the truth.

He curled his hand around the bowl of his wineglass and swirled the chardonnay without lifting it from the table. He looked from the wine to her, his gaze probing. "That's a pretty romantic thing to say."

She wasn't sure what to make of that comment. "Well, marriage is romantic, isn't it?"

"I only meant that you sound like a romantic—like you have a nice heart." He smiled softly.

She recalled the conversation they'd had a couple of weeks ago at Taste when they'd danced around the topic of their past love lives. "What about you? Are you ready to confirm that you were in love once?"

He took a long drink from his chardonnay. "Yep, I was in love. Like you, we started dating in college. Unlike you, we did not get married, thank God." The sharp bitterness in his voice could've cut bone.

"And why was that such a good thing?"

One side of his mouth curved up. "We just weren't meant to be."

She narrowed her eyes at him. "I see what you did there."

"Only what you did." He took another sip of wine. "Look, that relationship is ancient history for me."

"And yet you haven't had any others since." She saw a darkness creep into his gaze and hoped she hadn't pushed too much. Especially when she wasn't in any hurry to talk about Darren and her...issues. She reached across the table and touched his hand. "Hey, it's fine. This is a casual thing, right? I'm with you because it feels good, and we're having fun. Are we still having fun?"

He took her hand and leaned forward to kiss the back. "I am."

Their salads arrived then, and they discussed food and wine pairings. The conversation turned to the wine dinner that was happening that weekend.

"Are you happy with how the final menu turned out?" she asked. "I know you were hoping for a salmon dish."

"Yeah, but Kyle won me over with his halibut. I think it'll be good. And we have amazing guests coming—thanks in part to you."

"I'm happy to have helped." She liked working with him. She liked talking wine with him. She could imagine going to France with him and showing him the places she'd been. "When are you taking that overdue trip to France?"

"No time soon. We've got the harvest coming up after this dinner."

"Next spring maybe?"

"Maybe." He looked at her as if he might say more, but didn't.

She'd been about to offer to go with him, but planning things six or eight months in advance was pretty much the antithesis of "casual."

The salad plates were cleared and the server brought dinner, which included beef, halibut, and duck dishes.

"Should I leave the duck for you?" she asked, recalling their first dinner together.

He laughed. "I guess, since you don't really like it."

"I'll try a bite. I like to be adventurous."

He raised a brow, and his gaze turned seductive. "I'll keep that in mind."

She shook her head, smiling. "I actually think that dinner was our first date. It was supposed to be a business meeting, but you rather manipulated the situation in your favor."

"I did, didn't I?" He showed absolutely no remorse.

She laughed. "Unapologetic, I see."

He grinned as he cut a piece of steak. "Completely."

"Oh, look!" She gestured toward the window and the magnificent sunset they'd been ogling throughout dinner. "The sun is just about to disappear. I love that moment when the orange sinks into the sea, like it's dissolving so it can rest before re-forming again tomorrow. Like it's home."

"Beautiful."

She turned her head to see that he was watching her. "The sunset, silly."

"You." His gaze was focused and intense, and she felt it all the way to her toes.

Their flirtation continued through dinner and dessert—what little of it they could eat. They had the remainder boxed up for later.

He drove her back to the condo, and they walked up the stairs and toward the door. She dug the key out of her purse and turned. "Thanks for dinner."

"Uh-oh, this sounds like a good-night. It's a long drive back to Ribbon Ridge."

"Only an hour. But no, this isn't good night." She unlocked the door and pivoted with her hand on the knob. "I didn't mean to be nosy at dinner. It just seems like...it seems like we've both been hurt, and I'm wondering if this is really casual or if we're just going very, very slow."

He caressed the side of her jaw and cupped her neck, his fingertips massaging her. "I'm not sure there's a difference. Anyway, like you said, this feels good."

It did. Especially the way he was rubbing her neck and how deeply he stared into her eyes—as if he could see right into her soul and the pain she kept inside. She tried to see into him, to understand why he needed to go slow.

But maybe he was right. Maybe it only mattered that this felt good.

She turned the knob and backed into the condo, pulling him with her. He closed the door behind him and locked the bolt. Then his hands came around her waist, and he kissed her. She reached out and dropped her purse, hoping it landed on the console table in the hallway, but heard it hit the floor.

He pulled back and bent to pick it up, then deposited it on

the table. He set the dessert box next to it before coming back to her.

His eyes found hers, and he just stood there a moment—promise and intent carved in every line of his face, burning in the depths of his stare. He clasped her sides gently and backed her to the wall, his mouth descending on hers. She expected an assault, but this was gentle, searching. And over too soon. But just so he could nip at her lips and kiss her jaw. He massaged her hip as he licked along the flesh beneath her ear. He held her there, pinned between him and the wall as he feasted on her neck. Brooke closed her eyes and let sensation take her away.

He scooted her along the wall until they hit the corner, then he guided her along the short hall to the bedrooms, turning right into the master. "Oh, look, a bed," he whispered before kissing her again. His mouth opened over hers, his tongue deftly sliding into her, eliciting soft moans from her throat.

She held him against her. He felt so good—his hands, his mouth. Everything he did sent need spiraling through her.

He pushed off the canvas jacket she'd thrown on earlier, letting it fall to the floor. His hands massaged her shoulders as he plundered her mouth. He was still gentle, his tongue caressing her in sweeping, delicious strokes.

He broke the kiss, surprising her. He held up a finger as if to say *hang on* and pulled his phone from his back pocket. He quickly typed into it, and soon music filled the room. It was something sexy. Justin Timberlake, she was pretty sure. He tossed the phone onto the nightstand, then kicked off his shoes.

She followed suit, losing her slip-ons. Her bare feet sank into the plush carpet, but only for a moment because he eased her back onto the king-sized bed. He shrugged out of his long-sleeved button-down and stretched out beside her, turning her so that they were on their sides, facing each other. "I've been looking forward to this. So much." Desire darkened his voice and filled his gaze with heat.

"Me too." She caressed the side of his face, from his temple to his jaw. He had the barest amount of scruff. It tickled her fingers as she traced along his flesh. She closed her eyes and leaned forward to kiss him.

He met her halfway, their lips connecting briefly before coming apart and finding each other again. They were playful kisses. Teasing and seductive. The kind that stoked your need into a steady burn.

He propped his head on his hand while the other hand traveled from her hip to her breast and back again. He pressed her back onto the bed, bringing his body over hers. He settled between her legs, his erection hitting the perfect spot and spurring her desire. His tongue dove into her mouth, and she felt absolutely devoured—but in the best way possible. She felt revered. Treasured even.

She clutched the hem of the T-shirt he'd had on beneath his button-down. He sat up and tore it away, then came back to her, his mouth finding hers as his hips ground down. She arched up into him, need pulsing through her. She ran her hands up and down his back, exploring every muscle, appreciating every plane.

He pushed her shirt up over her breasts and reached under her to unclasp her bra. Then he shoved that up too, impatient, apparently, to get to her. He knelt between her legs and used both hands to cup her. She loved how he touched her. He seemed to know exactly what would feel good.

He pulled on her nipples and caressed her flesh, using slow, deliberate strokes and light, gasp-inducing pinches to arouse her. Fire burned in her belly, and she ached to feel him naked against her.

She opened her eyes and saw the determination—the power

—in his gaze and gave herself over to him completely. She opened her legs farther and arched up to clasp his hips, but he pushed her back.

"My turn," he said. He stripped her shirt and bra away, then dropped over her, taking her breast into his mouth. The music, a new song now, but just as sexy, washed over her. Combined with the feel of his tongue on her and his familiar, delicious scent, she could barely keep herself together.

Moaning, she begged him not to stop.

He nipped at her flesh. "Never." Then he moved lower, his fingers working at her jeans until he had them open. She arched up, making it easier for him to tug them off her.

When he'd pulled them away, he turned her over to her stomach, surprising her. He pushed her thighs apart and knelt between her legs. "I've been obsessed with exploring your back."

He pushed her hair to the side, exposing her neck. His lips touched her flesh, then his tongue. He kissed her softly all along her nape and onto her shoulders, then traced his tongue down her spine to the middle of her back before using his fingers to continue all the way down, to just above her backside. "Here," he rasped. "This little concave place entices me. I want to pour wine in it and drink it from your flesh, but I think it would trickle everywhere, and then I'd just have to lick you clean."

His words enflamed her, and she couldn't keep from arching backward, seeking his touch between her legs. But no, he was torturing her. And she loved it.

"Another time," he said, his hands caressing her lower back and drifting to her ass. He massaged her flesh, arousing her with each caress. Sensation coursed through her and gathered in her core. "Should you kneel up and we'll do it like this? I'd love to watch this gorgeous back as I make love to you."

She gasped.

"Is that a yes?" He asked the question next to her ear before he tongued her there, sending shivers of delight down her spine.

"Yes. I don't care how...I just...need...more."

"Turn."

She did as he said, turning, but also feeling a little disappointed that he wasn't going to do what he'd suggested. And he was still wearing his damned jeans. She reached for the waistband, but he grasped her hand and held it up over her head. He kissed her again, his tongue probing deep. "You want more?"

She nodded. "Yes."

He tweaked her nipples and moved down, his lips and tongue skimming their way to her hips. She twisted and arched, her body crying out for release. "Cam, please."

He pushed her legs up, planting her feet on the bed on either side of him. She sensed what was coming next but wasn't completely prepared for the full brunt of his mouth on her. He sucked on her flesh, then buried his tongue inside her. She bucked up, her orgasm hammering for release. But not yet. He wasn't done torturing her. He pulled back and thumbed her clit, making slow, agonizing circles over her flesh. Taunting her, tormenting her. She opened wider for him and clutched at the bedspread, her fingers digging into the fabric.

"You like this?" he asked.

"I'd like you to go faster." She sounded harsh, her voice deep and needy. Foreign. But excitingly so.

"Really? I think this is good. But maybe a little more." He slipped a finger into her, and lights flashed behind her eyelids. She arched up, her muscles stiffening. No, she actually didn't want to come yet. She wanted this to go on and on.

"Yes, more. Please, Cam."

He pumped into her but didn't increase his speed. He

spread her folds wide and licked her, his tongue sweeping long, devastating strokes along her heated flesh. Want became desperate need as she writhed beneath him. When he entered her again, she was sure it was two fingers. More, but still not enough.

"Faster. *Cam.*"

"Like this?" He speared into her, his fingers filling her. Then his mouth was on her again, sucking at her clit. She was mindless with need.

"Come for me, Brooke." His voice was coarse and demanding. Thoroughly enticing. "*Come.*"

She couldn't keep it at bay any longer. Mind-numbing pleasure crashed over her. The lights behind her eyes dimmed to black as she tumbled headfirst into the abyss. Still, he didn't stop. His hand and mouth continued, drawing her orgasm out until she whimpered.

Then he was gone. She heard him take his pants off, then the sound of a wrapper. A second later, he was back between her shuddering legs. He didn't hesitate but drove into her, filling her at last. As he hit her G-spot, another wave of pleasure washed over her—a mini-orgasm she'd never had before.

He kissed her, and she tasted herself. This was a new experience, and, surprisingly, it didn't turn her off. In fact, it somehow heightened her desire for him. He sucked her lower lip and came to a stop between her legs.

"Open your eyes and look at me, Brooke."

She let her lids flutter open. The room was dark with just the light from the hall cascading through the doorway, but she could see him clearly. The tense, sexy set of his jaw, the dark intensity of his green eyes.

He brushed her hair back from her face. "I want to look at you when you come again, and I want you to look at me too."

He began to move once more, filling her, then withdrawing in easy, measured strokes. She rocked with him, meeting his thrusts and striving to keep this pace. Though it was slow, it was absolutely devastating in its power. She clutched at his back and his ass, feeling the muscles stretch and contract as he plunged into her.

She lifted her legs and wrapped them around his back. His eyes closed briefly as he slid in even deeper than before.

"Damn, Brooke." He moved faster, his hips snapping against hers.

Their gazes connected as their bodies moved, binding them together in a way that went somehow beyond the physical. Wonder filled her, heightening her pleasure.

"Now, *you* come for me," she said, watching him and loving the delicious agony in his expression.

"Together," he growled, his body picking up speed. He kissed her again, long and deep, their bodies moving in time. She closed her eyes again. He pulled back. "Look at me, Brooke. *Now*." He slammed into her, igniting her orgasm. She tried to keep her eyes open, but she was lost. Incoherent. Spent.

He thrust into her, prolonging the sensations shooting through her until he shouted her name. He held her tight against him, his hands digging through her hair and clasping her head as he let himself go.

He stopped moving but didn't leave her. He kissed her, his lips soft and coaxing, gently moving over hers. She cupped his head and kissed him back, loving this moment more than she ever imagined possible.

He drew his mouth away from hers, and she opened her eyes to see that he was watching her. "Wow," he breathed. "I... wow." He caressed her cheek, then abruptly stood and went to the bathroom.

She lay there, her body replete, her mind at peace, and wondered what in the hell had just happened.

Duh, sex.

Yes, sex. But something more. Something she wasn't sure she wanted to acknowledge.

Chapter Sixteen

Cam disposed of the condom and stood in front of the mirror, glad he'd closed the door. What the hell had just happened?

He turned the faucet on and splashed cold water over his face. Once. Twice. A third time. He shut the water off and stood there as droplets fell from his jaw to the sink.

He looked back into the mirror, a little afraid of what he might see. But it was just him. Familiar green eyes stared back at him. They didn't look different. But he felt different.

For the second time, he'd referred to sex with Brooke as making love. He hadn't done that since Jennifer.

Damn it. Jennifer didn't belong anywhere near him right now. Just a thought of her might poison one of the best nights of his life.

No, the *best*.

He'd never felt so aligned with someone, like he could sense her in his bones. He'd only been with her a few times, but he knew the rhythm of her body, and it called to him like none ever had. Even now, he wanted to hold her and kiss her and touch her, not roll over and go to sleep and plot how he would extricate himself from the bed.

He grabbed a towel and dried his face. He put his hand on the doorknob and hesitated. What if...what if that had been nothing special for her? Did he want to know?

God, he was acting like a noob.

He opened the door and saw that she'd crawled under the covers. She lay on her side, her blonde hair spread out on the pillow, her brilliant blue-green eyes fixed on him. "Hey," she said.

"Hey." He padded to the bed and climbed in beside her, drawing the covers over himself.

She snuggled closer, and he put his arm around her. "That was amazing." She sounded blissed-out. Utterly satisfied.

He smiled. "Totally." He leaned forward and kissed her forehead. Inhaling her scent, which now included his scent, he closed his eyes briefly and committed it to memory. He didn't ever want to forget how he felt in this moment. He smoothed her hair back against the pillow, loving its silky softness. Thick curls wound around his fingers, trapping him—only he was perfectly happy to be her captive.

"Can I ask you something?" This was stupid, and he was sure he knew the answer, but he couldn't keep himself from wondering. "That guy you went on a date with... Are you planning to see him again? Or maybe you already have."

She looked at him a moment, her lashes coming down just once before she touched his jaw. "I *was* planning to see him again, but not now."

A bit of tension—which he hadn't realized he'd been holding—seeped from his muscles. "What changed?"

Little pleats formed between her brows. "When I came to see you on Friday, I said I wanted to try this."

"You also said it was casual, and in my book, casual doesn't necessarily mean exclusive."

"I see," she murmured, dropping her hand from his face. "I guess I don't have your full rule book."

He captured her hand in his and squeezed. "I'm not sure my rule book applies here. Anyway, I'm not dating anyone else, and I don't plan to."

"Well, that's...good. But you'll need to keep me up to speed about these rules. Is there anything else I need to know?"

That he didn't trust women? That he didn't expect to find anyone he'd dare to commit to forever with? That he was as broken and damaged as they came with regard to healthy romantic relationships? Even before Jennifer had dumped him, their relationship had been toxic. He just hadn't realized it until much later.

"I'm not good at this." He shook his head and allowed a small smile. "No, I *suck* at this."

She looked at him with encouragement, her lips parted. "I'm not sure that's accurate."

"I haven't had a girlfriend in eight years. Not since the last one broke my heart."

She scooted closer and put her hand on his chest, her fingertips tracing over his skin. "I figured that's what happened. She was a moron."

"She was a bitch. And unfortunately ensured that pretty much every woman I met after her ended up in the same category before I even gave them a fair shot."

"That's understandable. How serious were you?"

"I was going to ask her to marry me." His gut clenched, and it felt like the world fell out from under him, like he was on a plane and suffered a sudden five-thousand-foot drop.

Her fingers stilled. Her hand skimmed up his chest and curled around his neck. "I'm so sorry. But...I guess it's good that things didn't work out. You could've ended up divorced like me."

"Count on it." If Jennifer hadn't found a better option then, she would've later. He had no doubt she would've kept looking, even with a ring on her finger. She was a self-serving leech. He'd thought they were so happy—discussing their life together, planning for the future, hell they'd even named *children* they'd have someday. The depth of her betrayal still stung, and damn that made him mad.

He rolled to his back. "Can we talk about something else?"

She kept her hand on him, her palm a comforting warmth against his chest. "How about my ex? He was cheating on me."

Cam immediately rolled back. "Asshole. Give me his address, and I'll go punch his face in."

She laughed, her eyes sparkling and her lips parted. "Thanks for the offer, but that's not necessary. I'm over him."

He believed her. God, when would he ever be over what Jennifer had done to him? When would he be able to entrust his love to someone else? Someone like Brooke. Yeah, he could love her. So easily. That hollow feeling in his stomach spread.

She stroked his neck. "You talked about exclusivity. I don't know what your rule is, but I don't date more than one person at a time. At least I never have, and I can't see myself doing that now. *Especially* not now."

Her words eased the ache inside him and shone a small, faint light into the darkness. He *had* dated multiple people, had slept with multiple people at the same time when he spent so much time on the road selling wine. Monogamy had felt like a fool's dream after his experience with Jennifer. But now he realized he'd grown tired of that sexually transient existence. He'd given up that lifestyle before he'd met Brooke and now, with her, he wished he could forget he'd ever done it.

He cupped her face and kissed her gently. Her lips were

still red from their kisses, but they were so soft, like ripe raspberries and just as sweet. "I have no plans to date anyone. I haven't dated anyone. Not in a long time. I don't want anyone else—only you."

God, had he said that out loud? Had he really put that much of himself out there? Panic nagged at his head, his stomach, and everything in between. He didn't want to regret this. Fuck, he hated that emotion more than any other.

She kissed him, stealing his insecurity and his doubt, at least for a moment.

He deepened the kiss, palming her nape as he swept into her mouth. She met him with lush precision, kindling his desire once more. His cock twitched, ready for her again. He gently rolled her to her back and nudged his thigh between her legs. She twisted her hips and threw her leg over his hip, bringing her wet heat against his thigh.

He moved his hand down her back and side until he reached her hip. He squeezed her flesh as she pressed into him. Her fingers curled into his neck.

Reluctantly, he pulled himself away and found a condom in his wallet. When he returned, she was waiting with open arms, her mouth claiming his in a delicious kiss.

They made love slowly, deliberately. He didn't think he'd taken the time and care to push someone—and himself—to the edge and beyond. By the time they came together, he was nearly brainless, his body simply moving in need and desperation. She felt like heaven against him, and he wasn't sure he deserved anything this good.

After disposing of the condom, he brought her some much-needed water and gathered her in his arms. He'd never done that. He'd never wanted to hold someone until he fell asleep.

He wanted to hold Brooke now. And maybe forever.

The buzzing of his phone on the nightstand jarred him from a deep sleep. He blinked at the light filtering through the window. It was early, but he didn't remember setting an alarm. Turning, he picked up the phone and saw that it was barely seven. And he had a text from Hayden.

Kyle and Maggie are parents! Ripley was born about twenty minutes ago. I'm about to go in and meet him so I'll send pictures in a bit. Soon it will be my and Bex's turn!

Cam smiled broadly, hearing his friend's excitement in the typed words. He knew how thrilled Hayden was to be having a kid of his own. He and Bex had lost a baby when she'd miscarried several years ago. They'd broken up soon after, and then found their way back to each other. Happy ever afters were possible after heartbreak—at least for other people. Could it be possible for him?

He felt Brooke's hands curl around his waist. Her lips caressed his shoulder blade. "Did you set your alarm?"

He rolled over and kissed her quickly. "No. Hayden texted me. His brother Kyle and his wife had their baby this morning. A boy—Ripley."

She pulled back and rolled to the side of the bed. "That's so great."

He frowned slightly. "You okay?"

She flashed him a ready smile. "Yep. Just going to brush my teeth."

Ah. Yeah, he should do that too. Except his toothbrush was still in the car. He'd brought an overnight bag in the hope that she'd invite him to stay, then had forgotten all about it. He'd been too caught up in her.

He jumped out of bed and pulled his pants on. "I'm going to run out to my car for a sec," he called toward the closed bathroom door. After throwing on his shirt, he slipped on his shoes and shivered his way to his car. Mornings on the Oregon coast were always chilly.

By the time he got back, he heard the shower running, so he made himself at home in the other bathroom.

He finished before she did and went to the kitchen, where he made coffee. His phone went off just as Brooke came in. Cam smiled at Hayden's text—a picture of him beaming while he held Ripley, all red-faced, wearing a tiny blue cap.

Cam held the phone out to Brooke. "Look at how goofy happy Hayden is. He can't wait to have his own kid."

Brooke smiled and turned toward the fridge. "I bet. I don't have much in the way of breakfast. I usually snarf down a protein bar or make a shake, but I didn't bring any shake stuff." She pulled out creamer and set it on the counter.

"That's okay. I'd be happy to take you to breakfast."

"The breakfast restaurant options in this town are awful. We'd be better off going to Starbucks."

He laughed, agreeing with her. "Then we can do that." Another text vibrated his phone. He looked down and this time it was a picture of the proud papa—Kyle—holding his swaddled son. The image of the former beach bum with a baby made Cam think that maybe the impossible wasn't impossible after all.

He stared at the picture and realized Brooke hadn't been all that excited. Didn't women typically fuss all over cute babies? He thought about her reaction to Emma the other night—also not quite what he might've expected. She hadn't even asked to hold her. Did she maybe not like children?

"So, uh, do you plan to have kids some day?"

She pulled two cups down from the cupboard and poured coffee into them. "I assume you want coffee since you made it." At his nod, she asked, "Cream or sugar?"

"Whatever you're having. My only preference is that it's strong. Okay, and bonus points for caramel."

She arched a brow. "I remember you like that. This is, in fact, caramel-flavored creamer."

He watched her pour a liberal amount into both cups. "Hmm, maybe you hoped I would surprise you here."

Taking a spoon from the door, she stirred both concoctions then handed one to him. "I actually didn't—at least not consciously."

"To caramel and the subconscious." He clacked his mug against hers. She hadn't answered his question. Was that on purpose, or had the coffee conversation simply derailed her? When she didn't answer, he decided to ask again. "So, kids, yea or nay?"

She winced. "Last night was great—and I like where we're headed. But that's a conversation for another time. A *way* other time."

She was right, of course, but something scratched at the back of his mind and gave him an unsettled feeling. He sipped his coffee and tried not to dwell on it. Things were great right now, and he wanted them to stay that way.

She sipped her coffee. "As much as I would love a Starbucks date with you, I need to drive south to Newport for the first part of my day. I'm going to finish getting ready, and then I should head out."

He exhaled. "If you weren't shilling my wine, I'd take umbrage and demand you stay, but I guess I'll let you go."

Her eyes widened, and she barked out an offended laugh. "Like you get to tell me what to do, mister. In bed, I'll allow it— as long as I get my turn. Out of bed? Not a chance."

The mention of a bed started his engines purring. He wished they hadn't gotten up so quickly. He'd fallen asleep planning round three for this morning and was disappointed it didn't look as though that was going to happen.

He set his coffee down and circled the island to take her in his arms. She still held her cup and didn't move to put it down. He found that a bit odd but didn't want to make something of it.

"Should I come back tonight?" he asked.

She shook her head. "I'm going to be working late and I've got an early start tomorrow. I need to catch up on my sleep—you kept me up pretty late last night."

Instead of going to sleep after making love that second time, they'd sat up talking about movies and television shows and music and bands. It had been fun, and they'd later fallen asleep in each other's arms. "I still can't believe you've never watched *The Walking Dead*."

She made a face and stuck out her tongue. "And I can't believe you have. Okay, I can, but ewww."

He smiled, glad that things were still good. Of course discussion of children was too soon. If he wasn't so damned out of practice, he would've known that.

She leaned forward and gave him a quick kiss. "Okay, I need to get moving. Stop distracting me." She winked at him as she stepped around him.

"I guess I'll take that as my cue to leave. Unless you're sure I can't help you get ready?" He looked at her suggestively, letting his gaze rake her from the top of her damp head to the tips of her turquoise colored toenails.

"You're a bad influence, Cameron Westcott. Get out of here." She bestowed him one last smile before presenting her backside and marching from the room.

He watched her go with a wistful stare. Damn, he was smitten. And while it felt better than he'd ever dreamed possible, he couldn't shake the sense that something was about to go wrong.

Maybe because in his experience, happy didn't have a shot at ever after.

Chapter Seventeen

Brooke stepped out of her car at the Ribbon Ridge Cemetery just as Kelsey drove up. They met in the gravel parking lot and exchanged greetings. A moment later, Crystal arrived.

She jumped out of her mini SUV and immediately apologized. "Alaina isn't coming, unfortunately. Alexa has a fever."

"Oh, that's too bad," Kelsey said. "I hope she's all right."

"It's minor, but she's cranky and sad, and only Mommy will do."

Brooke knew about this from experience. While she was babysitting her nephew when he was about a year old, he'd come down with a fever. He'd screamed until Rhonda had come home. "That's how it is."

"Poor dads," Crystal said.

Kelsey shrugged. "Or lucky, depending on how cranky the kid is."

Brooke shuddered. "Or if they're puking."

Crystal nodded vigorously in agreement. "Don't get me started on diarrhea. Alexa had a horrific episode when I was watching her one night. It was a terrible thing to do to one's godmother."

They all laughed, and Brooke felt a rush of relief. See, she could talk about children without suffering a pang of loss or a burst of anxiety.

Which hadn't been the case yesterday morning. The pictures of Kyle's new baby and the unadulterated joy on his father's and uncle's faces had pierced straight through her heart, leaving a hole the size of Jupiter. No, that wasn't quite right. It had been the glee in Cam's gaze that had nearly been her undoing. She had seen with her own eyes just how much the baby's birth had affected him. Then he'd asked her about kids and she'd just...faltered.

She'd hidden behind the coffee conversation, hoping the topic would just fade away. Then he'd pursued it, so clearly the issue was important to him. Her mind had stumbled and then shut down. She'd grasped at anything to keep him and that discussion at bay. In the end, she'd been relieved at his reaction —that he'd dropped it and said it was too soon to talk about it. Little did he know that it would be too soon pretty much forever.

"So where should we start?" Crystal asked. "We're looking for any tombstones with the initials BNR, right?"

"I think we should actually look for anything with a last name that starts with R. Take a picture of it with your phone."

"And what time period?" Brooke asked. "The brick said 1879, so anything between that date and...?"

"That's a good question," Kelsey said, looking from Brooke to Crystal. "What do you guys think? If BNR was a person who made that brick in 1879, he or she could've died anytime."

"Well, let's say they weren't over a hundred. So how about anything prior to 1970?"

Brooke nodded. "Okay, sounds good. Any ideas on how to tackle this?"

"Why don't we start at one end and each take a row?" Kelsey suggested. "That way we're still together in case we find something."

"Perfect," Crystal said, whipping her phone from her back pocket. "Let's do this."

They walked to the back corner and each took a row. The headstones were an amalgamation of sizes and shapes and conditions. This section was old, and some of the lettering was impossible to read due to weathering.

"How was your trip to LA?" Brooke asked Crystal as they walked.

"Busy," Crystal said from the row behind Brooke. "We crammed a lot of meetings in and a couple of interviews. Alaina doesn't like to invite people here, so she usually does that stuff in LA."

Kelsey, who was in the row in front of Brooke, turned and looked over at Crystal. "Any new movies coming out?"

"She's voicing an animated feature in a month or so. That'll be fun."

"Oooh, is it the sequel to *Frozen*?" Kelsey laughed. "I'm kidding."

Crystal laughed with her. "I wish! It's still cool, though. I'd tell you about it, but then I'd have to kill you."

"Of course. That's top-secret intel right there," Brooke said, smiling. She liked both of them and was glad they'd met. Forming connections made her think she could maybe stay in Ribbon Ridge long-term. Or maybe something else was making her think that...

She shrugged the thought away and focused on the head-stones. "I'm not finding any Rs yet."

"Me neither," Kelsey said. "Ironic given that the town is Ribbon Ridge." She rolled the Rs for emphasis.

"Totally." Crystal chuckled. "Wait, here's one. Joseph Rollins died 1889. Not a B or an N, but I'll take a picture."

Brooke saw the same name on the headstone in front of Crystal's. "This is a Rollins too. Ann Bedelia. There's a B, at least." She took a picture.

"And an N in Ann," Kelsey said. They continued for another minute in silence. "How was your beach trip, Brooke? Sell a lot of wine?"

"I did, actually." West Arch Estate had been quite popular. She'd shared her sales information with Cam earlier via text and was sure they'd talk about it later—assuming they'd get together.

"And how are things going with Justin?" Kelsey asked.

"Who's Justin, your boyfriend?" Crystal chimed in.

Brooke suddenly wished she hadn't overshared with Kelsey last week. But why? They were friends, right? "No, he's not my boyfriend. He was a blind date, and I told Kelsey I was thinking of calling him again."

Kelsey turned to look at her. "Uh-oh," Kelsey said. "You didn't?"

Brooke shook her head.

"What happened?" Crystal asked.

Brooke pivoted so that she could see Crystal too. "Uh, Cam happened."

Crystal came into Brooke's row. "Cam as in Cameron West-cott? Are you two a thing? Wait, I think I heard he was seeing someone. That's like major news in the Archer circle." She rolled her eyes, grinning. "Small towns. You gotta love 'em. I come from one in North Carolina."

Kelsey moved closer so that she was just on the other side of a headstone. "Did you have sex again?"

"Yes. He came to the beach." Where they'd had sex. But

he'd called it making love. Did he always call it that, she wondered?

Crystal's grin didn't fade. "Sounds hot."

"It was…romantic." Aside from the baby disaster, she'd felt incredibly close to him. He'd been an amazing and thoughtful lover—as gentle as he'd been aggressive in their other encounters. She'd loved seeing that side of him.

"Uh-oh, sounds like you're falling for him." Crystal's tone was teasing, while Kelsey was watching her skeptically. But then Kelsey knew a little about Brooke's history and Crystal didn't.

"Are you ready for that?" Kelsey asked, her gaze laced with concern.

"I don't know." Brooke turned her head toward Crystal. "I got divorced a couple of years ago, and it was kind of ugly. Cam's the first guy I've dated—the first guy I've paid *any* attention to really—since then."

Crystal nodded. "I get it. And that sucks. Sorry about your ex."

"I hope you're taking it slow," Kelsey said.

"We are. Very. It feels…good. A little foreign, like a pair of shoes I forgot about in the back of my closet, and putting them back on is a little strange."

Crystal chuckled. "Good analogy. That happens to me all the time." When both Brooke and Kelsey stared at her, she added, "With shoes! I'm a total shoe whore. I, uh, actually don't date that much. Too busy with work."

"Even since Alaina's career has slowed down?" Kelsey asked.

"Yep. Always tons to do. I do get a little more sleep now." She winked at them. "Back to the grind." She returned to scanning headstones, and Brooke and Kelsey did the same.

A few minutes later, Crystal called out to them. "Guys, here's Benjamin Archer's headstone."

Brooke and Kelsey walked over to where Crystal stood. Ribbon Ridge's founder had a large, rather new and fancy headstone, as did his wife next to him, though hers was a bit smaller.

"The family replaced his headstone a while back because the original was so decrepit."

"How awesome to have founded a town," Crystal said, her tone glazed with reverence. "I love history like this. My grandpa was a Civil War reenactor. I can't tell you how many battles I attended when I was a kid."

Kelsey smiled, her eyes lighting. "Now, *that's* awesome. Were your ancestors rebels?"

"Ha, rebels! You're such a northerner. Actually, my family was both Confederate and Union. All dirt poor and fighting for their state. That's what it was about to them back then. My family comes from North Carolina and Pennsylvania."

"It sounds like you know a lot about them," Brooke said.

"I do. My grandmother was really into genealogy. I'm a member of the Daughters of the American Revolution too."

Kelsey shook her head. "So cool. I can only trace to my great-great-grandparents. Someday I'd love to go back further. I guess that's why I find this project so fascinating. It's silly, but I can't rest until I know who BNR is and why he had that brick."

Crystal nodded. "I completely understand. The less we learn about those initials and that date, the more I want to find the truth!"

"You guys should start your own show—solving small-town historical mysteries." Brooke chuckled. "Reality show, buddy comedy, with a bit of Indiana Jones thrown in."

Crystal howled. "*Yes*. I'm so pitching that to Alaina and Sean for their production company."

"I'm game," Kelsey said, smiling. "But so far, we suck at solving this one."

"True." Crystal's tone was wry. She looked back at Benjamin Archer's headstone. "Hey, any chance the B is for Benjamin and the N and R are just other people? Like maybe they were a trio and the brick was something they made?" She shook her head. "I know that sounds like a longshot."

"Any idea is a good one," Kelsey said. "Let's keep that in mind as we look. Maybe we'll see an N or an R first name with dates that are similar to Benjamin's."

A few headstones down, Brooke got a little excited. "Guys, here's an R—Reginald Carver."

Kelsey and Crystal moved to stand beside her, and they all took in the fading letters of his name. There was no birth date, but the death was listed as April 2, 1879.

"This has the year and one of the letters," Crystal said, her tone hopeful.

Kelsey took a picture. "Just in case." She glanced around. "Let's keep looking, particularly for an N."

They fanned out and scoured the surrounding area for several minutes. Kelsey was a few rows away when she called out, "Anything?"

Brooke looked up and saw Crystal shake her head. "No," Brooke answered.

They continued with their search and found a few more single B, N, and R names, but no N first names and nothing else that sparked an idea. They gathered back near their cars.

Crystal frowned. "So it looks like Reginald is our only lead."

"At least it's something," Kelsey said. "We can go back to the records and zero in on him and look for N names."

Crystal nodded. "Good plan. It's not a lot to go on, but it's something. Do you want to set up a time to look through the records together? Alaina and I should bring them to the library anyway in preparation for the exhibit."

"Sounds great. Just this past weekend, I finally got the upstairs cleaned out enough," Kelsey said. She turned to Brooke. "Do you still want to help, or has your interest in this waned—I wouldn't blame you."

On the contrary, Brooke was as intrigued as ever. The mystery of BNR had bitten her too. Or maybe it was their enthusiasm that was contagious. "Oh no, you're not getting rid of me now."

Crystal grinned. "Excellent! Okay, I'm off. See you guys soon."

As Crystal jumped in her car and drove away, Kelsey turned to Brooke. "Hey, I didn't mean to be negative earlier. I'm sorry if I came off that way."

"About Cam?" Brooke shook her head. "Not at all. I appreciate your wariness, actually. I'm feeling cautious too, but optimistic. For now, it's casual and slow, and we're just enjoying each other's company. There would be...issues if we wanted to make a go of it, but I'm nowhere near that yet."

"I think you're being very smart. And I'm glad it's going well. Maybe even a tad jealous, but when I think of starting something..." She shuddered.

Brooke sensed genuine fear, not just anxiety from a bad breakup. "Kelsey, are you okay? I definitely don't want to pry, but if you ever want a shoulder—a confidential one—I'm here."

Kelsey smiled, but there was sadness in the lines around her mouth. "Thanks. I really appreciate that. It's tough to open up about it. I was pretty stupid. He...wasn't very nice."

Brooke knew right then that he'd hurt her—emotionally and physically. She also knew Kelsey wasn't ready to talk about it, and Brooke both understood and respected that. "I'm so sorry. And now I'm going to hug you. Not because I think you need it, but because I suddenly do." Hearing even this much about Kelsey's past reminded Brooke of the struggles she'd been through, of the pain of Darren's betrayal and the agony of her dream life breaking into tiny impossible-to-put-back-together-again pieces.

Brooke squeezed Kelsey tight and was happy that Kelsey squeezed back.

"Now we're BFFs," Kelsey said, smiling and offering a wink.

"Definitely."

Kelsey pulled her keys from her purse. "I'll be in touch about our next research session."

"I hope it's soon. I'm anxious to find some answers!"

"Me too!" Kelsey waved before turning toward her car.

Brooke climbed into her SUV and pulled out of the parking lot. As she turned onto the main road back to town, her phone rang and she answered it via the Bluetooth in her car.

"Hello!"

"Hey," Rhonda's voice sounded from the speakers. "You have a minute?"

"I'm driving, what's up?"

Rhonda exhaled and hesitated. Brooke instantly knew something was wrong. Her muscles tensed, and she gripped the steering wheel tightly, her knuckles whitening. "Rhonda? Is everything okay?"

"Yes. I just wanted to tell you something before you saw it on social media or something. Darren and his home-wrecker girlfriend are getting married."

Brooke's insides wavered for a moment—like they turned to jelly and then went back to normal again. It didn't matter to her that he was getting married again. She took a deep breath. "Well, good for him. I hope she doesn't expect him to be faithful."

"There's, uh, more."

Brooke had loosened her hold on the wheel, and that fluttering feeling came back to her. What more? She suddenly knew...

"They're having a baby," Rhonda said, confirming Brooke's fear.

Brooke's vision blurred. She blinked madly to keep her focus on the road. She wrapped her fingers around the leather wheel as if it was the only thing keeping her from drowning in a sea of black emotion. "Of course they are," she choked out.

It wasn't that he hadn't wanted kids—she knew he did. It was that he hadn't seemed to care that she couldn't have them. All during her infertility battle, he'd been supportive, but in a very hands-off way. As the medical bills had mounted and her anxiety increased, he'd started to change his tune. He'd said having kids didn't matter, especially if it meant spending a fortune and her losing her mind. She'd realized much later that she hadn't been "losing her mind." She'd been understandably devastated. All the while, he'd been sleeping with his coworker and then blamed Brooke for driving him away.

"He's such an asshole," Rhonda said, as if she'd read Brooke's train of thought. But then she probably had. They'd discussed his betrayal at length last weekend.

He was going to get his happy ever after—the life they'd planned together. The injustice of it curled Brooke's stomach into a heavy knot.

She drove into town and willed herself into a sort of numbness. She wasn't going to break down. She couldn't—she had to get home.

"Brooke, you okay?" Rhonda asked tentatively. "I'm so sorry. But I wanted you to hear it from me."

"I'm glad." This was hard, but anything else would've been much worse.

"Hey, I think you should talk to Cam."

What the hell? "Why? We're in a fledgling relationship."

"I know you say that, but I spent the weekend with you. I saw how your eyes lit up when you talked about him. And you said your beach date was spectacular."

Brooke had texted her sisters yesterday during lunch and told them about him surprising her. She hadn't, however, told them about the baby situation that had derailed her yesterday morning.

Gah, there were babies everywhere!

Brooke turned toward her loft and pulled into the parking garage. "I can't talk to Cam about this. He totally wants kids someday. There's no future with him."

"Damn it, Brooke, you're being so shortsighted! Just because *you* can't carry a kid or even make a kid doesn't mean you can't be a mom or have a family someday. You guys could use a donor egg and a surrogate, you could adopt—you have options!"

"Not for someone whose mother can't wait to have a grandchild with 'her' blood." Bile churned in Brooke's stomach as she thought of what Cam had said about his mother.

Rhonda made a sound that sounded like an angry gargle. "You are so stubborn. Sometimes I think you like to wallow in your circumstances. This doesn't define you. You're an amazing aunt, and you'll be an amazing mom. Not *if* but *when*."

Brooke pulled into her parking place and started to shake with her anger and frustration and sadness. "It must be nice to call the shots from the sidelines. You have no idea what this feels like or how painful this journey has already been. Yes, there are options. Expensive options with zero guarantees."

"There are no guarantees in life, period." Rhonda sounded cold and dispassionate. "Come on, Brooke, you know better than that."

"Yeah, I do. Which is why I prefer to err on the side of no

risk, no pain. I've been down that road, Rhonda, and right now, I can't do it again. Cam is not The One."

Except as soon as she said those words, something opened up inside her. The wobbliness, the uncertainty faded, and she felt a clarity. But just for a moment. It was gone almost as quickly as it had come.

"Fine. I just hope you aren't screwing up a good thing."

"I'm not screwing up anything. We're having fun, and we'll continue to have fun. Thanks for letting me know about Darren." Brooke thought about all the passive-aggressive, snarky ways she could congratulate her ex. That gave her a small bit of satisfaction. Of course, she wouldn't do any of them.

"Will you please call me if you want to talk?" Rhonda asked. "I'm sorry I upset you. I love you."

Brooke closed her eyes briefly. "I love you too. I'll talk to you later." She disconnected the call before Rhonda replied.

Suddenly weary, Brooke leaned her head against the steering wheel. Her mind churned from Darren to Rhonda to Cam. Part of her wanted to tell him the truth. She wanted to believe he'd understand, that he'd stand by her when Darren hadn't. But how could she know that? She'd been with Darren for several years and she'd only known Cam, what, five weeks?

It seemed clear to her that he wanted kids given the way he interacted with his niece and his reaction to the new baby yesterday, and then he'd asked her about kids. You didn't ask about kids unless they were important to your future. And yes, she realized it could be that he didn't want them, but that just didn't seem to be the case based on her observations.

And if that were true...she'd be doing him a favor if she walked away now. Before things got complicated and messy. Before it hurt too much to walk away.

Oh, who was she kidding? It was going to hurt either way. She wasn't completely sure, but she suspected she was in love with him. She loved his sense of humor. She loved the things they shared in common. She loved the way he looked at her, the way he touched her, the way he made her feel like the best woman in the world.

Which was no small feat given how he'd been hurt in the past. More than anything he deserved to be happy, and she wanted that for him. She was just afraid she wasn't the woman to make it happen.

Chapter Eighteen

Cam finally relinquished the sleeping Ripley to his father. "Kyle, he is one cute kid. You sure he's yours?"

Kyle smacked him in the arm. "Don't be a douche bag." But he was smiling. In fact, Cam hadn't seen him not smile in the hour he'd been at the hospital visiting.

Cam waggled his eyebrows. "It's part of my charm." He leaned toward Kyle. "And yours too, unless you're going to get all responsible and normal and shit."

Maggie cleared her throat from the hospital bed. "He already has. It was called marrying me if you recall. You might consider it."

Cam peered over at her, marveling at how together she looked despite giving birth the day before. "What, marrying you? Last time I checked, bigamy was against the law."

Maggie looked at the others in the room—Bex and Hayden. "Will somebody please throw something at him now that he's not holding my son anymore?"

"Hellooooo!" A singsong voice carried through the doorway as Maggie's mother came in. Cam had met her only a couple of times, but she was incredibly distinctive with her henna-tattooed arms, long flowing skirt, and lack of bra. He hated that he noticed that, but it was hard *not* to.

She waved at everyone. "It's a party! But then I expect nothing less with so many of you Archers." She turned to Cam. "But you're not one of them."

"Nope, just a friend."

"Hey, we're related by marriage," Kyle said. "You're much more than a friend." His eyes conveyed gratitude and camaraderie. Yes, Cam supposed they were more than friends.

Cam clapped Kyle's shoulder. "Ditto, bro." He turned and went to the bed to kiss Maggie's cheek. "Good job, Mama, he's gorgeous."

She clasped his arm briefly. "I'm serious. You need to settle down. Or at least get a girlfriend."

"He has one," Hayden offered. "Kind of."

Cam inwardly groaned. Just what he needed—everyone weighing in on his recently resurrected and still feeble love life. "And on that note, I'm out of here!" He waved to everyone in the room and took his leave.

Hayden caught up with him in the hallway. "Sorry, dude. I'm just really happy for you."

Cam looked at him askance. "We only started dating like a week ago. Not even."

Hayden shrugged. "I guess it seems longer since you guys have been dancing around it for weeks. You seem pretty smitten."

Smitten. Hadn't he used that same word? He didn't respond.

They got to the elevator, and Cam glanced at Hayden. "Are you following me?"

"Just walking you out."

Cam pressed the Down button and exhaled. "What do you want?"

"I want to know what's going on. You went to the beach, you came back with a shit-eating grin. I haven't seen you like this since..." He shook his head. "Nope. Haven't ever seen you like this. Dopey almost. Did you get any work done yesterday? I think I saw you puttering around the tasting room about ten times."

He *had* been distracted. And yeah, dopey wasn't the worst word to describe him.

The elevator arrived, and he stepped inside. Hayden joined him. "So spill. You gave me such a hard time when Bex came back to town."

Cam pushed the button for the lobby. "Yeah, because I didn't want you to get your heart broken again. I'm a cynic, remember?"

Hayden studied him a moment, crossing his arms. "You *were* a cynic. I think that's changed."

It had...but how much? Cam thought about what Hayden had just said—that he didn't remember seeing Cam like this. And he was right. Cam had never felt like this. Maybe it was his age and experience compared to what he'd felt for Jennifer, maybe it was that Brooke was just completely different. Jennifer had never been The One, no matter how much Cam had thought so at the time. Brooke, on the other hand... Could he let himself go down that path? Damn it, he just felt *good*, and he wanted it to continue.

"Okay, I'll admit my cynicism has lessened." He cracked a smile at Hayden.

Hayden dropped his arms with a laugh. "There you go. That's a step in the right direction. Would you guys be up for a double date, maybe next week?"

"Sounds fun. I'll check with Brooke, but I think she'll be fine with that." They'd been very up-front with each other, and they were definitely dating. Exclusively. His heart skipped a beat. "I think I have a girlfriend."

The elevator doors opened, and he didn't move.

Hayden clapped him on the back and steered him into the lobby. "Yes, I think you do." The grin was evident in his voice.

"I gotta go." Suddenly, Cam was desperate to see Brooke. To hold her. To call her his girlfriend and see if the light burning inside him was reflected in her eyes.

"Take her flowers," Hayden called after him.

That was a good idea. Cam stopped at the florist before heading to her loft. Armed with a dozen red roses and one white one, he buzzed up to her.

"Hello?" she answered.

"Hey, it's Cam. Can I come up?"

"Um, sure." She sounded a bit hesitant, but maybe he'd caught her getting out of the shower or something. He *hoped* he'd caught her getting out of the shower.

The buzzer sounded, and he let himself in. A minute later, he was stepping off the elevator and striding to her loft at the end of the hall.

She opened the door just as he got there. She was dressed in khaki shorts and a dark red tank, and her feet were bare. He clutched the flowers and smiled at her. "You should consider taking a shower right before I get here. It's worked well for me." He looked at her suggestively, but she didn't respond. Her gaze was fixed on the flowers.

"You brought roses."

"Yes." He held them out. "For you."

"Red roses." She took the bouquet, her brow creasing. "What's the white one?"

"Friendship. I love that we're friends, and I hope we always will be."

She blew out a breath and looked at him, but only briefly. "I hope so too." She turned and walked down the short hall to her kitchen.

He closed the door and followed her. Her demeanor was not what he was expecting. Every muscle in his body tensed. "Is everything okay?"

She set the flowers on the island and turned to the sink, where she bent down and opened the cupboard to pull out a vase. Setting it in the sink, she filled it with water. "I'm okay. Why'd you bring me red roses?"

He heard the shakiness in her question, and his skin turned glacier cold. "Why do you think?" Because he was falling in love with her. And he'd allowed himself to let that stupid emotion rule his brain. He should've gotten all white roses.

"I can guess." She set the vase next to the flowers but didn't put them in the water.

He reached for the roses. "I'll take them back."

She didn't stop him. "You can, if you want. It's just... You're throwing me for a loop here. I thought we were going slow."

He picked up the bouquet and clenched it in his fist. "I get it. I fucked up. No red roses." Right now, he wasn't sure he wanted anything with her. Her mood, her detachment was all too reminiscent of the day Jennifer had shown up at his apartment and told him about Aaron. Her fiancé. The guy with the house in Eastmoreland, a BMW, and a rock the size of Gibraltar that he'd put on her finger.

Cam hadn't thought the horrible shock of that day could be repeated, but he now realized it could. If this went bad...

He coughed. "What's going on here?"

She met his eyes, but only briefly. "I've been thinking about...us, and while I really like you, it seems like it's moving too fast, whether we want it to or not. I mean, you brought me red roses." The bridge of her nose scrunched up. "Yesterday you asked if I wanted kids, and I kind of brushed you off. I don't want kids. Does that change how you feel about me? And please don't lie, because I can see that you love children."

God, he'd suspected this, but hadn't really considered how he might feel. It was as if he'd been punched in the gut. Hard. He managed to find his breath. "I do love kids. I haven't thought about it that much because I didn't expect to get married." He hastened to add, "Not that we're talking about marriage here."

No, right now, he wanted to pretend he'd never met her. It was going to be Jennifer all over again—precisely what he'd been afraid of and what he'd tried to avoid. It would serve him right. First time he let down his guard and *bam*.

"No, we're not." She sounded so distant, so unlike the fun and warm person he'd come to know.

"So tell me what you're saying here." He tensed and prepared himself for the worst.

Her gaze found his, but it didn't carry the warmth he'd grown accustomed to. "I don't want to keep doing this. I don't see a future, and the longer we continue, the more awkward things will get."

He could say that he'd prepared himself, but the truth was that there was nothing he could've done to deflect the agony that was now tearing through him. Not just at her, but at himself for being such a colossal fool. "You think things are going to get awkward?" His voice climbed. "They're going to be fucking impossible, Brooke. I can't work with you anymore. Hell, I don't even want to *see* you anymore, and you live right across the goddamned street."

She flinched. "I'll find someone else at Willamette to take over the account."

"I don't care about the damn account." He threw the flowers

on the counter and turned away from her. He wiped a hand over his face. This couldn't be happening again.

He told himself he hadn't been about to propose, that this wasn't as bad as Jennifer. Except it was. He'd finally let someone in, and she was the wrong one. His desire to trust withered and completely died. He apparently didn't know how to pick someone who wanted him forever.

He spun around and glared at her. "Thanks for doing this now. No, really, I mean it. Yeah, I'm mad and hurt, but it could've been a lot worse. So thanks. Just have the new rep e-mail me. I do care about the account—and it can't be you."

Her gaze was steady, but her throat was working, the muscles contracting. "I understand."

"See you around, I guess." He turned and left, silently vowing to never open himself up again.

Brooke heard the door close and went to lock the bolt. She placed her hand on the wood. If she opened the door now and called his name, she could ask him to come back, tell him that she loved him. Because she did.

Straining, she listened for the elevator. When it was gone—when he was gone—she just stood there, numb, for what could've been an hour but was probably only a minute or two.

What had she done?

Legs shaking, she turned and went back to the kitchen. Her gaze fell on the roses. God, he'd brought her red roses.

Tears welled in her eyes, and she covered her mouth with her palm. Pain and regret tore through her. She could go after him, but to what end? It didn't change the facts. He wanted children. She couldn't give them to him.

And those unfixable truths didn't change the fact that she

loved him, and given the color of the roses he'd brought her, maybe he loved her too. The red roses weren't even the worst part—that single white one...that had nearly broken her.

Now it did. She sank to the floor and cried. She didn't know how long she sat there with tears streaming down her cheeks, her shoulders shaking, her throat clogging.

Her phone vibrated on the counter, and she jumped up thinking, stupidly, that it was maybe him. But no, it was Rhonda. On FaceTime. Brooke didn't want to talk to her. And she sure as hell didn't want Rhonda to see her like this.

The vibrating stopped for a moment, then started again. When it stopped for the second time, Brooke picked up the phone and sent her a text.

I don't want to talk right now.

Rhonda: *You okay? I feel bad about earlier.*

Brooke stared at her phone. She wanted to say, "Yeah, I'm fine." But she'd never been good at lying to Rhonda.

Brooke: *No. I ended it with Cam.*

The phone showed that Rhonda was typing. And typing. And typing. Finally: *I'm sorry to hear that. Did you tell him why?*

Brooke: *If you're asking whether I told him about my infertility, no. I told him we were a dead end. And we are.*

Rhonda: *So you didn't trust him with the facts and give him a chance to decide for himself?*

Brooke's tears had stopped when she'd started typing. Now they dried completely as she glared at the phone. She set it down on the counter and walked into the living room. That was a mistake. All she could see out the window was Cam's townhouse.

She pivoted and went right back to the kitchen, where her phone was vibrating as Rhonda tried calling again. Picking it up, she hit Ignore. Then she texted Rhonda again.

Please leave me alone. I know you think you're helping, but you're not. This is my life and I'm not going to live it the way you would.

Rhonda: *From where I'm sitting, you're barely living it at all. What's the worst that could happen if you told him the truth? He'd leave you and you'd be no worse off than you are now. But what if he didn't? What if he's everything Darren wasn't and you find a way to be together—happy? I can't believe you don't even want to try.*

Brooke turned her phone over on the counter and walked to her room in a fog. She sat down on the edge of her bed and stared, unseeing, at the wall.

Rhonda was right. Logically, anyway. There was no way Cam could hurt her more than Darren had. But he could still hurt her. And she knew she couldn't give him what he wanted. Questions pinged in her brain:

What if you really don't know what he wants?

What if he stands by you and builds a future with you?

What if he is your happily ever after?

Those were a lot of what-ifs. She wasn't sure she could chance them. She told herself this was for Cam, that she was saving him from heartache when he learned the truth about her. The reality, however, was that she was protecting herself because she was too scared to risk him leaving her. Better to be the one to do the leaving.

If only she hadn't fallen for him so hard. She got up and went back to the kitchen. Ignoring her phone, she went to the flowers and unwrapped them. One by one, she took them out of the plastic and snipped the ends of the stems. She sprinkled the food packet into the vase and arranged them one rose at a time, adding in the baby's breath and greenery as she went. When she got to the last flower, the white one, she knew she'd made a terrible mistake.

He was her friend, and she hadn't treated him like one. Friends trusted each other, and friends were honest. She owed him at least that much.

And maybe, just maybe, Rhonda was right.

Now she had to try to make herself look presentable, which meant a bunch of cold water and some makeup.

Chapter Nineteen

The sun had long dropped from Cam's view as he sat on his back porch, but the brilliant streaks of orange and yellow and pink from its setting streaked the sky. They were beautiful and warm and happy—in complete opposition to the way he felt.

He lifted his beer bottle to drink, and when nothing hit his lips, he recalled that he'd finished it. He set the empty on the table. He should get up and get another. Or ten.

Only he was rooted to the chair. The breeze stirred, rustling through his hair, but he didn't feel the temperature. It could've been ice-cold, and he wouldn't have noticed.

He'd done a good job over the past however long he'd been sitting here keeping Brooke from his mind, but without the beer to occupy him, like it had really been the beer, thoughts of her assaulted him.

Her laugh. The sparkle in her eye. The lilt of her voice when she gave him great snark or cried his name as he made love to her.

Ha, *made love*. It had been that for him but clearly something completely different for her. The ease with which she'd terminated their short-lived relationship cut right through his heart and battered his soul. He'd kept himself closed off for nearly a decade. And it hadn't been long enough.

He stood up. Time for another beer or maybe something stronger. He grabbed the empty from the table and went into the house. After dropping it in the recycle, he went to his liquor cabinet and perused his choices. Tequila? No, too celebratory. Gin? Not hard enough. Thirty-year-old Highland malt whiskey? Hell, yes.

He pulled the bottle down and went to grab a glass. It was then that he heard his phone vibrating on the counter where he'd tossed it earlier. He didn't think it would be her. What more could she want to say to him? She didn't seem particularly vindictive, even if she was a heartless bitch.

He set the bottle down and picked up the phone as the call dropped. Four missed calls. From an unknown number. Southern Oregon area code. Like Brooke's area code.

But not her number.

The phone vibrated again, this time with FaceTime. The picture that appeared on the screen wasn't someone he knew, but she looked familiar. The shape of her face and the set of her eyes screamed Brooke. One of her sisters?

His first instinct was to ignore the call—he couldn't imagine why either of them would want to contact him. But something picked at the back of his mind, and he decided to answer. Maybe they were trying to reach Brooke and couldn't. Maybe something had happened to her.

Despite what had transpired earlier, he didn't want to contemplate that. He answered the call and didn't give a shit about his rudeness. "Who are you?"

She smiled, but it seemed strained. Her eyes held a nervous glint. "Hi, Cam. You are Cam, right? You look like your picture."

"Yeah, I'm Cam. Who are *you*, and why are you calling me?"

"I'm Rhonda Markwith—Brooke's older sister."

Score a point for him, not that it mattered. "Still waiting for the why you're calling." He knew he sounded obnoxious, but he didn't care. Especially with one of Brooke's relatives.

She set the phone down and straightened in her chair. Behind her, he saw a wall with photos. He didn't look too closely but saw kids. They must be hers.

"My sister's an idiot."

That wasn't the word he would choose. "She's something, all right."

Rhonda winced. "Yes, about that. I'm going to break her confidence and tell you something I probably shouldn't because I think it's important. It might not matter in the great scheme of things, but if somebody doesn't fight for what they really want here, it would be a tragedy."

Cam stared at her for a moment, torn as to whether he wanted to hear whatever she had to say. He supposed it couldn't be worse than anything Brooke had already said to him. "I want to be intrigued, but I don't think I can muster that right now."

She nodded. "I get it. Just listen. Brooke can't have children."

Of all the things he might have been expecting, that hadn't been it. She didn't say anything more, probably to let this sink in. But he was having trouble processing. "She told me she didn't want children. If she doesn't want them, what difference does it make?"

"Because she lied to you. She *does* want children. Desperately. She tried—for years—with her ex, and it just wasn't possible—"

Cam cut her off. "She lied to me? Why would she lie to me?" He'd been lied to before, and it had hurt. This time was no different. His insides curled in on themselves, like someone was peeling him away layer by layer. He shouldn't feel this strongly given the amount of time they'd known each other. But damn it, he did. He loved her. And she'd lied to him.

Rhonda had started talking again, but he didn't hear a word of what she said. Well, he heard *sound*, but the meaning? Absolutely no idea. He couldn't process past the anger and hurt thundering in his head.

"Thanks for calling." He disconnected the call without noticing if she'd stopped talking and definitely without caring.

He turned and stalked out of his townhouse, slamming the door behind him. He barely looked before crossing the street. At the door to Brooke's loft, he hesitated. He had to buzz up, and she wouldn't let him in. Probably.

Clenching his fists, he swore violently. Maybe someone would come along. She'd asked him not to come in that way, but right now he didn't give a shit what she wanted. She owed him the truth.

He paced in front of the building and froze a moment later at the sound of her voice.

"Cam?"

He turned and saw her standing just outside the door. Had she seen him out here? His gaze flicked up to her window as if he could assess her view. It didn't matter. She was here. And he was livid.

"Your sister just called me. I think I deserve an explanation."

The light from the lamp on the outside of the building splashed over her face. She was pale and her eyes were red, as if she'd been crying. *Good.*

"What did she say?" Her voice was low, and it trembled like a leaf on a blustery day.

"That you can't have kids, but that you want them. Is that true?"

She squeezed her hands together. "Yes. I was just coming to tell you."

"Because you were hoping to beat your sister to it? How big of you."

"I didn't know she was going to call you. I'm sorry she did—not because I'm mad she told you. It's just... This is between us."

"There is no *us*."

She flinched. "Can I explain?"

"No. Maybe. But I'm talking first. You had a chance to tell me the truth, but you chose to lie instead." He advanced on her. Her eyes darkened with trepidation, but she didn't move. "Do you know what I hate more than anything? People who lie to me. My ex lied to me. All the time. All while I was so in love with her and planning to ask her to be my wife, she was fucking some other guy and getting engaged to *him*. So lying isn't something I can tolerate. *Ever*."

She paled even further, her eyes looking dark and huge in her face. "I'm so sorry. I didn't realize—"

"And would that have changed anything?" He took another step toward her until he could reach out and touch her. He caught her familiar scent—that damn vanilla and bergamot—and hated it. "If you'd known I'd been utterly betrayed, you would've told me the truth? I don't think so. Tell me why you lied."

"I just..." Her lip quivered, and she looked away, turning her head. "It hurts too much. I saw you with your niece, and then when Kyle's baby was born... You should have children." She turned her head back to look at him. "I can't give you any."

For the first time, his brain slowed and relinquished a bit of his anger. "Why? What's...what's the problem?"

"I don't have viable eggs, and my uterus isn't hospitable. I

245

had a surgery to try to fix it, but it didn't work, so I can't even carry a donor egg." She smiled then, and it was the saddest expression he'd ever seen. Nearly all his ire fled. "So you see, I'm pretty worthless when it comes to procreation." A tear snaked down her cheek, and he stared at it, trying to understand what this meant for her.

"I'm sorry."

She wiped at her face with the back of her hand. "Yeah, it sucks." She tried another smile, this one a little better but still wobbly. "You'd think I'd have come to terms with it over the past few years, but I really, really wanted to be a mom."

The ache in her voice sliced into his heart. And he learned something vital about himself right then: "I really want to be a dad."

She nodded and another tear escaped. "I know. I can see that about you. I love that about you. I wish...I wish things were different. I'm so sorry about earlier. If I wasn't in love with you, I could've just kept going as we were."

In love with him. She was in love with him.

"I love you too. But—" That single word fell out of his mouth before he could censor it. He loved her, but she was standing here telling him she couldn't give him children, some-thing he realized he wanted. The future he'd denied himself out of the hurt and anger he'd nurtured the past eight years unfolded before him—a dream he hadn't known he'd harbored. Until now.

And it was more than the kid thing—*that* he'd have to process. He just didn't know how he felt *at all*. None of that changed the fact that she'd lied to him. She'd made a decision to end their relationship without giving him a fair shot. Just like Jennifer had done.

"But what?" she prodded, sounding small and uncertain.

Part of him wanted to reassure her, to hold her, to tell her everything would be all right. He didn't hate her. He didn't want her to hurt. Not when she'd clearly been through hell. The other part of him, however, was in defense mode. He'd worked so long and so hard to protect his heart from further damage and right now, it was hanging on by the tiniest of threads.

"But I need to go. I have to think about...everything. I honestly don't know where we go from here. I'm sorry."

He turned and hurried across the street because he didn't want to see her cry.

Silent tears slithered down Brooke's cheeks as she watched him go. This was what she'd expected, what she'd known would happen, what she'd tried to shield herself against. But it had been no use—she was as hurt and broken as she'd ever expected to be.

She turned and trudged back into her building but didn't go upstairs. She sat on one of the chairs in the lobby and just stared through the glass doors toward his townhouse.

She could go over there and beg him to forgive her. But no, he'd said he needed to think. She owed him that much at least.

His hurt and anguish washed over her, and she realized she was going to completely lose her shit. She bolted up and pounded the Up button for the elevator. She just managed to keep herself together until she was back in her loft. As soon as the door was closed and the lock turned, the tears fell in earnest.

What had she been thinking? Certainly not of him. Shielding him from future heartache had been a lie she'd told herself. She'd wanted to protect herself, and it had royally backfired.

They'd both tried to keep their hearts safe, but in the end, it hadn't mattered. She remembered some stupid Internet meme she'd seen: the heart wants what it wants. And hers wanted Cam. His had wanted her too, but would that be enough?

She understood that he needed to process. It had been slightly different with Darren because he'd already been married to her. He couldn't just walk away. He had *eventually*, but that had come over time. As she'd undergone procedure after procedure and received bad news and more bad news. How much of that had been her fault, just like this? Yes, Darren had cheated, but she'd pushed him away. She'd burrowed herself deep under the weight of her depression and shut him out. Was it any surprise that he'd found someone else?

Not any more surprising than it was for Cam, a young, healthy man who wanted a family, to walk away from her. She didn't really deserve anything different.

She'd turned her phone off but imagined Rhonda was madly trying to reach her. She found it, turned it back on, saw a ton of missed calls and all-caps texts, but she didn't read any of them. She typed in a simple message and sent it to her sister.

I'll be fine. I'm going to bed. I'll talk to you tomorrow.

Yes, she'd be fine—the new definition of fine she'd created after starting the new no-kid chapter of her life. The kind of fine that left the edges of her soul feeling frayed and the weight of her heart too heavy to bear.

Chapter Twenty

Too much whiskey had made Cam's head feel like an anvil. He walked into the winery Thursday morning and didn't bother taking his sunglasses off. Maybe he'd just go up to his office and sleep on the couch.

"Yo, there you are." Jamie leapt down past the last stair as he came down into the main room. "I have like a billion questions about Saturday."

Cam held a finger to his lips. "Shhh. You don't need to yell."

Jamie cocked his head to the side and studied him. "Dude, I can't see your eyes, but I'm guessing you're hungover."

"Maybe." Abso-fucking-lutely.

"What are your billion questions? And can you please whisper them?" He walked past his little brother and started up the stairs to his office. Slowly. Climbing each one felt like scaling an entire rock wall. By the time he reached the top, his stomach was churning and his head was throbbing. Had he forgotten to take that Tylenol?

He made it into his office and collapsed onto the couch, instantly closing his eyes. Maybe coming to work had been a bad idea. But he *had* to be here. The biggest event of their fledgling winery was happening in just two days.

"Cam?"

"Mmm?" He'd forgotten about Jamie entirely.

"Are you all right? Well, aside from your ghastly pallor. Should I bring you a garbage can?"

"Probably not a terrible idea." Cam didn't think he was going to puke, but it was maybe better to be safe than sorry just now. "Lying down is an improvement, though."

"Anything you want to talk about? I mean, why the hell are you so hung?"

Cam lifted his hand to wave at him but didn't think he raised it very far. He kept his eyes closed. "It's no big deal."

The "no big deal" crept into his mind for the first time since he'd gone back to his townhouse and drunk half of that bottle of whiskey. He shoved her from his thoughts.

"Hey, what's up?" That was Hayden's voice. "Holy hell, you weren't kidding. He looks like hammered shit."

He and Jamie were apparently discussing him as if he couldn't hear them. "I can actually hear you, despite my, uh, deteriorated state."

"Did you actually drive here?" Hayden asked, his voice incredulous.

"Yep. I'm not drunk. But you know, that's not a bad idea either. Little hair of the dog, maybe." He opened his eyes and tried to sit up. The room tilted sideways, and he fell back against the couch with an "oof."

"Maybe we should let him sleep for a while," Jamie said.

"Yeah, probably." Hayden sounded concerned.

"Don't worry about me." Cam was already fading. "I'm goooo..."

Cam startled awake and knocked his sunglasses off his face. They fell to the floor as he rolled to his side. His office was dim and blessedly empty. His heart had sped up but now began to slow as he realized where he was.

He swallowed. Damn, his mouth was dry, and his teeth felt like they were wearing furry slippers. Gross.

He pushed himself up and was instantly rewarded with a sharp pain in his head. Awesome.

After a moment in which he gathered his equilibrium, he found his footing and stood. Right on his sunglasses, crushing them. Not awesome.

He stumbled to the fridge and pulled out a bottle of water. Opening it seemed harder than normal, but he blamed his fuzzy, still mildly hungover state. He downed half the bottle in one gulp and made his way to the bathroom, where he brushed his teeth practically out of his mouth.

The rest of the bottle of water went down nearly as fast, so he got another one. After taking a healthy swig of that, he sat behind his desk and started up his computer. Judging from the number of messages in his Inbox, Jamie wasn't the only one with a billion questions.

This was good, though. Busy was good today. No, busy was great.

A couple of hours flew by before his stomach started to grumble with hunger. Finding a decent place to take a break, he went downstairs to grab some food.

As soon as he rounded the corner on the landing of the stairs, he saw his partners sitting in the main room. Like they were waiting for him. He took the rest of his descent slowly.

Luke stared at Cam's feet. "I realize you're the most fashion forward of us, so I guess mismatched shoes are the latest thing?"

Cam looked down at his feet and saw that he was indeed wearing two different shoes. Well, that was pretty fitting for this shit show of a day. "Yeah. It's totally a thing. Saturday night, you better not wear a matched pair."

Cam went into the kitchen, hoping that was going to be the end of the interrogation. He was dead wrong, of course. All three filed in behind him.

Opening the fridge, he kept his back to them. "You guys don't have to babysit me."

"Oh, we're not babysitting. We're being nosy assholes," Hayden said. "Spill. I don't remember the last time you came in looking like death. Probably because you never have."

That was true. Cam loved wine, but he wasn't a big liquor drinker. At least, not of the half-bottle-of-whiskey variety. "I opened a really great bottle of Scotch last night. Sue me."

"Are you going to tell us your deal?" Luke asked. "Or are we going to have to call Brooke and ask what's going on?"

Cam closed the fridge and turned to scowl at them. "Why do family think they have the right to butt in?"

He was simultaneously glad that Rhonda had called him last night but also annoyed that she'd stuck her nose in. Brooke had come around—if he believed that she'd really been coming to see him. Since she'd come outside and looked so...anguished, he decided he did. Even if she had lied to him before that. And maybe that made him an even bigger fool than he already was.

"Because they do," Hayden said grimly, speaking from very specific experience. His family had meddled in a major way, enticing Bex into coming back to town with her dream job in the hope that she and Hayden would get back together. It had pissed Hayden off to the point that he'd left town, but in the end, it had worked.

Cam suddenly felt weary and defeated. "Brooke and I broke up. We just weren't going to work out. Satisfied?"

Jamie leaned back against the kitchen counter and crossed his arms. "Hell no. Why?"

"The particulars don't matter. Anyway, they're her business, not mine." He wasn't sure it was his place to tell them all that she couldn't have kids.

And just like that, what little wind he had completely left his sails. His heart ached for her, just as it ached for his own loss. He loved her. More than he thought he'd ever love anyone again. She was a gift, but not the one he'd expected. He could only imagine how she felt. He could walk away from her, and he could have children of his own. She could not.

"Sounds like a cop-out," Hayden said.

Cam bared his teeth at him. "Damn it, Hayden, it's not. She's infertile, okay? I finally fall in love with someone—someone I can think about spending my life with—and it's not what I expected."

All three of them wore identical expressions—pitched brows, wrinkled forehead, semi-frowns.

"What are you saying?" Luke asked.

"I know you all think I'm a committed bachelor, and I guess I was. No, I was a hurt bachelor. And it just took me a long time to find my footing. Contrary to all the shit you give me, I've practically been a monk since we started this winery."

"We know," Jamie said. "And I'm sorry we gave you shit."

Luke nodded. "Me too. But dude, you're in love with her. That's gotta count for something, doesn't it?"

With a sigh, Cam slouched back against the counter next to the fridge. "I don't know. She lied to me about not being able to have kids. I had to hear it from her sister."

Hayden crossed his arms over his chest too. "Ah, now your meddling-family rant makes sense."

"That can't have been easy for you," Luke said softly. "After Jennifer."

"No, it wasn't."

"Can you forgive her?" Hayden asked. "I know a lot about

253

forgiveness—it's not for her, it's for you." He did know a lot. He'd had to forgive his parents for interfering.

He wasn't sure, but... "I want to. I just don't know about the other." He hated saying this out loud. He felt like such an asshole. "The kid thing. I didn't realize how much I wanted to be a dad until she said she couldn't have children."

"Oh, hell." Hayden dropped his arms to his sides and crossed the kitchen and stood next to him. Both Luke and Jamie came closer too.

"It's not like I had this Big Plan. Like I said, I didn't expect this. Then I met Brooke, and I just fell for her. Hard. Somewhere in the recesses of my consciousness, I had this idea of a house and a wife and kids here in Ribbon Ridge."

"So she can't have kids at all?" Jamie asked.

"Nope. No eggs, dysfunctional uterus. Nothing happening." His heart twisted. He wanted to punch her ex-husband more than ever now. How could he have walked away from Brooke?

The same way Cam had walked away from her last night and was thinking of doing permanently.

Except, a tiny voice in the back of his head argued, *you aren't married. Your commitment isn't the same. You can walk away...*

But could he? He loved her, and the thought of turning his back on what they'd stumbled upon made him feel like he'd been hit by a Mack truck. And backed up over and run over again.

"What about adoption?" Luke asked. "Or a surrogate? Can't you use someone else's egg for that? I admit I know dick about this."

"Yes, that's possible," Hayden put in. "Bex and I researched different options when she had trouble getting pregnant." He looked at Cam apologetically, as if he were sorry they *had* gotten pregnant.

Was that what happened to Brooke whenever she told people she couldn't have children? She got pitying looks and sympathetic comments? That had to get real old real fast. Not that Cam thought that Hayden pitied him. Still, it was a delicate subject and completely new to Cam. If he was going to be with Brooke, he needed a crash course.

"What are you going to do?" Jamie asked. "And can we do anything to help?"

"Besides getting completely up in my grill?" Cam smiled. "No, you can't do anything. I'm still not sure, but I think I need to figure it out with the person who matters most."

"You really do love her," Hayden said. His lips curved into a broad grin. "I knew it. I'm so happy for you." He gripped Cam's shoulder and gave it a squeeze.

Cam's achy head twitched. "Yikes, Hay, I'm still not feeling that great."

Hayden pulled his hand back with a laugh. "Understandable. You sure you can function? Maybe you should take the rest of the day off?"

"With the dinner on Saturday?" He shook his head. "Way too much to do. I need to find something to eat and get back to it." Even if he was ready to talk to Brooke right now, he really didn't have time. There were far too many things that needed his immediate attention. He supposed he needed to make sure that she was still coming. She'd invited that critic from *Wine Enthusiast* and really ought to be here for networking purposes. She'd come. She was a consummate professional.

"Okay, but don't overdo it." Luke moved past him and opened the fridge. "Can I make you a sandwich at least?"

When they'd been younger, Cam, as the oldest, had often made them sandwiches for lunch. "Sure, thanks."

Later, when Cam went back to his office, he was tempted to pick up his phone and call Brooke. But what would he say? His thoughts still weren't organized, but he felt better than he had last night. There was a lingering pain from her lack of trust in him, but he wanted to believe they could get through it. No relationship was ever going to be easy. He just wanted to be damn sure he didn't put all his heart into someone who would cut it out. Been there, done that.

He hoped Brooke was who he thought she was. He'd find out soon enough.

The last two days had passed in a blur in which Brooke focused harder than ever on work. She'd stealthily avoided actually talking to her sisters, limiting her contact with them to text only. She thought they understood, but Rhonda still sent apology texts at least five times a day.

It had felt great to spend this afternoon with her new circle of friends. She'd met up with Crystal, Alaina, and Kelsey at the library—rather, upstairs from the library. They'd been poring over their stockpile of records for the elusive N name, assuming that was even the missing piece. So far they hadn't found anything, but they had piles left to go. No way would they make it through everything today.

Brooke was grateful for this project. It kept her mind occupied, and that was the best thing possible.

"Whoa," Crystal said from her table, where she sat next to Alaina, papers spread out before them. "I just found a guy named Nathaniel."

Alaina leaned over and looked at the paper in Crystal's hand. "Nathaniel Danforth, died 1903."

"Death certificate?" Kelsey asked. She and Brooke were sharing a table pushed up against Crystal and Alaina's.

Crystal nodded. "Place of birth is St. Louis in 1835. Parents are Warren Danforth and Margaret Tobin."

They sat there and looked at each other for a moment.

"Okay, so not super helpful, but it's something." Crystal set the paper in a blank space toward the middle of the tables. "I'll just set this here."

They continued on for a while, music streaming from the Internet playing in the background as they worked. "Ugh," Alaina said, standing. "I need to stretch." She arched her back and bent to touch her toes.

Brooke turned the page in the diary she'd started reading a little bit ago. So far it had only managed to distract her. She'd tried to skim it, but it was fascinating. It had been written by one of the Archers' ancestors, someone named Maribel Walker. She wrote stories about her children, about their daily tasks, about things going on in town. She reminded herself to stop reading and just look for N names or BNR, but suddenly something jumped out at her:

Bird's Nest Ranch.

There it was: BNR. The initial letters leapt off the page at her. She read the entry from the start.

August 8, 1881

The clouds finally moved in today for a bit of respite from the heat, though it didn't rain. Working to irrigate the fields continues to be the focus of so many in Ribbon Ridge. Thomas went up to Bird's Nest Ranch today to lend a hand. It doesn't look too good for them, but hopefully Hiram will recover. I worry for Dorinda if he doesn't.

The next paragraph talked about harvesting berries and

making jam. Brooke looked up from the diary. "Hey, Crystal and Alaina, did you see this Bird's Nest Ranch?"

All three heads popped up and pointed toward Brooke. "What's that?" Crystal asked.

"Bird's Nest Ranch—the initials. I was just thinking what if they aren't a person's name."

Crystal blinked. "Well, damn."

Kelsey leaned over and looked at the diary. "Who are Thomas and Hiram and Dorinda?"

"Thomas is Maribel's husband. This is her diary," Brooke said. She looked around at all three of them. "I'm guessing Hiram and Dorinda own the ranch. Maribel writes about how Thomas went to help them, but that things don't look good— Hiram is sick or something."

"When is that?" Alaina asked.

Brooke rechecked the date. "August 8, 1881."

"Well, don't leave us hanging," Crystal said. "Keep reading!"

Brooke chuckled. "Okay." She returned to the diary and looked for mention of the Bird's Nest Ranch. Every few minutes, someone would ask if she found something until Kelsey said they should knock it off. They all laughed, but the room was quiet until Brooke closed the diary.

"Nothing else," she said dejectedly.

"That's too bad," Alaina murmured. "But I think I might have something. This is a death certificate for Hiram Olsen." She looked up at them, her expression grim. "Date of death is August 14, 1881."

Kelsey briefly put her hand to her mouth. "Oh, that's terrible. Does it have a cause of death?"

Alaina glanced down. "It just says fever. His wife is listed here—Dorinda Foster."

Crystal put down the paper she was reading. "I don't know

if the Bird's Nest Ranch is what we're looking for, but I want to know what happened to it and Dorinda after Hiram died."

"Me too," Kelsey said. "I just keep thinking that it makes sense for the brick with the date on it to be associated with a place. I wonder if the brick was part of the ranch—the house or something."

Alaina nodded enthusiastically. "Yeah, me too."

Brooke thought about the diary passage. "In the diary, Maribel said Thomas was going 'up' to the ranch. The brick came from a house built up on the hill at the winery. Maybe Bird's Nest Ranch was on the hill?"

"It's a good theory," Crystal said. "Especially with a name like Bird's Nest—like it's up above the town maybe. It would be great if we could find something about the ranch with the 1879 date on it. Too bad they didn't have building permits then."

Kelsey smiled. "Very true."

Crystal looked around at them. "Are there any town records? Like from the church or the town hall? Something that might list events or... I don't know. I'm grasping at straws here."

"No, you're not." Kelsey stood up and went to a bookshelf in the corner. "I borrowed this book from the McMinnville Library. It has some early photos. I thought it might be helpful." She sat back down and thumbed through it. Brooke craned her neck to see over Kelsey's shoulders. They were photographs of places in the county. She turned page after page, but there was nothing in Ribbon Ridge.

"There's something!" Brooke declared as the words Ribbon Ridge jumped out at her.

"That's Main Street. It looks so different."

Alaina and Crystal got up and joined them on their side of the tables. Soon all four were huddled over the book, looking at the old pictures of the town. Kelsey turned another page, and the sound of their breaths catching filled the room.

There on the page was a photograph of a man and a woman in front of a clapboard farmhouse. The caption read: Bird's Nest Ranch, 1879.

"Well, I'll be damned," Crystal whispered.

Kelsey looked around at them, beaming. "I think we found the origin of our brick."

They began to laugh and shout and high-five.

After a minute of exuberance, Alaina stood with her hands on her hips. "Great work, ladies."

"Oh, but it's not finished," Crystal said, looking down at the photo. "I have to know what happened to the ranch and Dorinda."

"Absolutely." Kelsey flipped through the rest of the book, but there was nothing more about the ranch. She turned back to the picture and left the book open on that page. "I haven't been up to the winery. Does this look like the house is in the same place?"

Brooke studied the photograph. It was hard to tell since images from that period weren't terribly clear, but it did seem that there was a slope behind them. "It could be. I think we have more research in front of us."

"Does that mean we're all on board?" Crystal asked.

"I am, definitely," Brooke said without hesitation. She was as intrigued by the mystery of Dorinda Olsen as the rest of them.

"Me too, obviously," Kelsey said.

Alaina put her hand on Kelsey's shoulder. "Count me in!"

"Excellent!" Crystal glanced at her fitness tracker on her wrist. "Geez, is it that late? No wonder my stomach is grumbling. I think it's time to call it a day. At least for me."

"Yeah, I need to get home to Alexa and Evan," Alaina said. "I didn't realize it was that late." She went around the table and gathered up her purse and jacket.

Crystal did the same. "Is it okay to leave everything out like this?"

"Definitely," Kelsey said. "I hope you guys don't mind, but I'll probably sneak up here as much as my schedule will allow. I'll let you guys know if I find anything."

Crystal pulled out her phone. "Sounds good. Should we set up our next group time?"

"Yes, let's do that," Alaina said.

Brooke pulled out her phone. It was terrible, but every time she looked at it since the other night, she kept hoping there was a text or call from Cam. And each time there was nothing, with now being no different.

"Brooke?" Kelsey asked. "Does Monday night work for you?"

Brooke mentally shook herself. "Probably. Let me look."

She opened her calendar and saw the winery dinner tomorrow night. She hadn't decided if she should go. But somebody for Willamette should. She'd told her boss yesterday that they needed to assign West Arch Estate to someone else, but they hadn't done it yet.

Kelsey nudged her, and Brooke realized she'd lost track again. She looked at Monday and said, "Yep, I'm good."

Crystal peeked around Kelsey and asked, "You okay? You've seemed a little off today, but I don't know you too well, so maybe I have no idea what I'm talking about."

"I'm fine... Just a little off my game."

Kelsey's gaze took on a knowing glint. "Is it what I think it is?"

Brooke laughed nervously, not at all sure she wanted to tell them what had happened. But she supposed she had to tell Kelsey since she thought Brooke and Cam were dating. Plus, Kelsey was her friend. And so were Crystal and Alaina.

"It might be," Brooke said. "Cam and I aren't seeing each other anymore."

Kelsey touched her arm. "I'm sorry to hear that. But wow, that was quick."

"We want different things." She squeezed her eyes shut for a moment. Was she going to hide this forever? It was who she was, and it was time she learned to live with it. "No, that's not quite right. We'd like the same things, I think, but it isn't in the cards for us. I can't have children, and I think that's a deal breaker for him."

All three women gasped and immediately hugged her. The people Brooke had told had reacted similarly, but this felt different. Maybe it was the fact that it was three of them. It was like empathy in surround sound.

Alaina went and got her chair and brought it around next to Brooke's. "Sit and tell us all about it."

Brooke wasn't sure what to do with the attention on such a sensitive subject. She didn't regret telling them, yet she wasn't sure she was ready to open up completely. "You need to get home. It's okay."

Alaina shook her head firmly. "Not a chance. You need some shoulders, and here's six of them."

Kelsey turned her chair to face Brooke's and moved Brooke's so that it was facing out. Crystal fetched her chair, and soon the three of them were seated in a semicircle.

Crystal pointed at the empty chair. "Sit. We're not going anywhere. Unless you really want us to."

Surprisingly, Brooke found she didn't. She dropped into the chair and summoned a smile. "Thanks."

Alaina reached over and patted Brooke's knee. "We had a child-related situation before we got married—Evan and I. I was actually trying to have a baby on my own—that damned biological clock was killing me—and inadvertently got pregnant with him. Oops. Happy occurrence, right? Only if the baby daddy wants to be a baby daddy, which Evan didn't think he did. No, he was damned sure he was never going to be a father."

Brooke relaxed listening to Alaina talk. It soothed her own anxiety. "Why?"

"Maybe you don't know, but Evan has Asperger's syndrome. He didn't think he'd make a very good dad, and he didn't want to chance passing that on to his kid." She exchanged a smile with Crystal. "Lucky for me, he decided he loved me enough to give it a try, and you know what? He's the best damned dad Alexa could ever have. And no, she doesn't have Asperger's, but that doesn't mean our next kid won't. Yes, we're trying for another one, and I think we may have been successful. But shhh, don't tell anyone. We haven't spilled the news to his family yet."

Crystal smiled smugly. "I knew, of course."

Alaina laughed. "Of course. Anyway, I know this story doesn't really have much to do with yours, except that sometimes even in the face of certain adversity, things can work out."

"I'm so glad they did for you," Brooke said. "I just don't know if that will happen here. Cam and I just started dating. I'm not sure there's enough between us to make it worth fighting for." Saying that made her throat constrict because she loved him, and she'd come to realize over the past couple of days that she wanted to fight for a future with him, but she couldn't if he wasn't invested too.

Alaina crossed her legs. "So, when I was looking into my own baby-making options, I was amazed at how many ways there are to have a family without a man. Not that you don't want a man, but you get me." She winked at Brooke. "I'm sure you've researched everything, but if you ever need a sounding board or want help hunting down information, I'm your girl."

"We're all your girls," Crystal said. "Just look at what researching badasses we are."

Everyone laughed again, and Brooke felt better than she had in ages. She also felt like she belonged here, something she'd begun to doubt heavily over the past few days. She'd even looked at other jobs within Willamette that were far away from Ribbon Ridge.

"Can you use a surrogate?" Kelsey asked.

"Not with my eggs. I don't have very many, and the ones I do have are all nasty and useless." For once, she was able to say that without feeling like she might be overwhelmed with grief again.

"Stupid eggs," Crystal said. "I don't know that I'll ever use mine, and as far as I know, they're peachy. Wish I could give them to you."

Alaina's eyes widened, and she turned her head toward her best friend. "Are you offering to be her surrogate?"

Crystal laughed. "Uh, no. Part of my probably not having children comes from an aversion to all the disgusting side effects that came along with your pregnancy. No, thanks."

"Hey, there were lots of good things too."

Brooke expected Alaina to apologize for saying that, and when she didn't, Brooke realized she was glad she hadn't. Talking about this with them was the most normal conversation she'd ever had. She didn't feel pitied or condescended to. She just felt understood.

"You guys are the best," Brooke said. "I can't thank you enough for your support. Really."

Alaina turned her attention back to Brooke. "I meant what I said about being here for you. You have options—you don't need a kid of your own blood to be a mother. You don't even need a baby. There are so many older kids who need loving parents."

Brooke knew that, but it would take a special partner to

agree to that kind of journey. Was Cam capable of being that partner?

They all stood and hugged again. Kelsey stayed to tidy up a little, and Brooke walked out with Crystal and Alaina, who squeezed her hand before they walked toward their car down the block.

Brooke strolled back to her loft, feeling better than she had in days. Maybe she'd even work out tonight. Yeah, some yoga sounded great.

She went into the lobby of her building and nearly tripped.

Standing up from the chair with a manila envelope in his hand was Cam.

Chapter Twenty-One

Cam watched the surprise on her face fade to confusion and then wariness. "Hi, Brooke. Before you yell at me for having someone let me in, I didn't. I was waiting for you outside, and your neighbor insisted I come in and sit down."

"Okay. Why are you here?" Her tone was as guarded as her gaze.

He missed the glow that usually emanated from her, that light that had drawn him to her weeks ago at the salmon bake. When she'd given him the brush-off.

"Did you know that I have a three-strikes rule?" he asked. When she shook her head, he continued. "I give myself three shots with a woman. If she shuts me down every time, I'm out."

"Like baseball."

"Exactly. I figure with you, I'm on about strike ten or something."

She cracked a smile, and some of the tension left his frame. She inclined her head toward the envelope in his hand. "What's that?"

"Oh, I'll get to it. Can we maybe go upstairs?"

She hesitated, but only briefly. "Sure."

He went ahead of her to press the elevator button. Once they were inside, he said, "I meant to text you about tomorrow night. You're still coming, right?"

"Yes. Unless you don't want me to."

"Of course I want you to. You've been a huge asset."

"Thanks." She glanced at him with a small smile as the doors opened.

He gestured for her to precede him and then followed her down the hall to her loft.

Once inside, she set her purse on the counter and turned to him. "Can I get you anything?"

He stood on the other side of the island from her and shook his head, suddenly nervous, his throat going dry. He didn't want to screw this up. "I messed up the other night. I'm afraid I might do it again."

She shook her head too, but with more intensity. "No, *I* fucked up. Not you. I should've told you the truth. I was scared you'd leave."

He wanted to kick himself. "Which is exactly what I did."

"Yes, but I don't blame you. Especially given your experience." She took a deep breath. "Besides, you came back. With an envelope. I have to admit I'm very curious about that."

He laughed and set it on the counter, sliding it across to her. "Open it."

She picked it up, looking at him, and then tipped her head down to pull back the flap. She reached inside and pulled out infertility pamphlets and papers he'd printed from the Internet. Slowly, she sorted through them, setting them on the counter as she glanced over each one.

When she looked up at him, her eyes were wide and such a clear blue-green, he would've sworn he could see himself in their depths. "Where did you get all this?"

"Some of it I printed at home." He'd stayed up until four this morning reading everything he could about infertility, surrogacy, adoption, everything he could find that might be pertinent to their situation. Yes, *their* situation. "The rest I picked up in Portland at a fertility clinic."

Brooke stared at him. She opened her mouth but didn't say anything. He waited another moment to give her a chance to find her words, but when she remained quiet, he continued.

"I've looked at a lot of options—probably not all of them—and I think there are avenues we can explore. If we get that far. I mean, you might tell me to get the hell out when I'm done rambling."

"I won't," she whispered. "Not ever."

His chest expanded with emotion. "I'm so sorry about the other night."

"You have nothing to be sorry for. It was my fault. I can't—" She looked away for a moment, and when her gaze found his again, there were tears in her eyes. "What are you saying?"

He came around the counter, and she turned to face him. He moved as close as he dared, close enough that he *could* touch her, but not close enough that they were touching. "I'd like to give this—us—a try."

"Even...even knowing what you know?"

"Especially knowing what I know. I didn't realize I wanted a family until I met you. And now that I know I *do* want one, I don't think I want it without you."

She made a sound, a broken sob, and brought her hand to her mouth. A tear fell from her eye, and he reached out and caught it on his fingertip. "Don't cry, sweetheart. Not about this. We're going to be okay. I hope. I'm going to try."

She nodded and hugged him, her fingers digging into his back. She suddenly pulled back and looked up at him. "Are you sure? This isn't going to be easy, and everything we try might fail."

He'd thought about this intermittently during his nearly all-night research session. "I know. There are no guarantees in life, as much as we want them. I wanted to be sure no one would ever get close enough to hurt me again. But here you are. I nearly let my own hurt and distrust keep me from something wonderful, and I don't want to live like that. YOLO."

She laughed. "Did you just say YOLO?"

He shrugged. "You do only live once. I've spent eight years drowning in regret, and I don't want to do that anymore. I want to be happy and feel good, and with you, I get both of those things. I can't make you promises for how this will go, but I can tell you that I love you. I've been in love before, and it wasn't like this. Once I got my head back on straight, I thought about moving on without you, and I just didn't want to do it. And before you ask me again—yes, knowing what I know. You're who you are, Brooke, faulty reproductive system and all. And I love every piece of you."

She stood on her toes and kissed him, her lips soft and gentle and so sweet. "I love you too. So much."

He kissed her back, deepening the connection as he claimed her mouth with his. She twined her arms around his neck and held on tight.

When they came up for air a few moments later, she beamed up at him. "I have no idea where we're going, but I'm so glad I'm going there with you."

Cam swept her into his arms. "I know exactly where we're going. The bedroom." He carried her around the island before stopping short. "Shit. I left my wallet at home. I don't suppose you have condoms?"

"Nope, and you don't need one. Not really."

He grinned at her and planted a fast kiss on her lips. "Well,

I'm just going to consider that a little bonus." He carried her into the bedroom and set her on the bed.

She looked up at him, her eyes searching. "You're certain this is what you want?"

"More than anything."

———

The Arch and Fox restaurant hummed with conversation and a palpable excitement. Brooke stood with Cam as they talked with the critic from *Wine Enthusiast*. She and some others in the industry had come for a special tasting that afternoon and had been enthusiastic in their praise.

Brooke could tell that Cam was flying high. Dressed in an impeccable navy pinstriped suit, he looked good enough to eat. She'd never before considered the pride in having arm candy but had to admit she enjoyed the envious stares of the women who darted him interested glances. Glances that turned to disappointment as soon as they saw him touch Brooke's back or put his arm around her waist, which he did often.

All in all, it was a magical night. She'd been floating on air since Cam had come to see her last night, and she never wanted to come down.

She still couldn't believe the time he'd spent researching her infertility and possibilities for the future. Darren had never done that. As if she'd needed any reminders that Cam was *not* Darren.

No, Cam was sensitive and caring and the most supportive man she could ask to have in her life. They'd made love and stayed up far too late talking about all of the procedures she'd tried and, to a lesser extent, his experience with his ex-girlfriend that had hurt him so badly.

Brooke found she wanted to look Jennifer up and punch her

face in, much as Cam wanted to do to Darren. She smiled at that thought.

As the wine critic excused himself, Cam leaned his head close and whispered in her ear, "What are you smiling at?"

"You. Us. Last night. Later. Pick something."

"All of it. I pick all of it." He brushed a kiss against her flesh, sending a shiver down her neck.

Hayden and Bex approached them. Hayden smiled at Brooke, then looked at Cam. "You ready?"

Cam nodded, and they went to stand in front of the stone fireplace. Luke and Jamie joined them.

"Don't they all look so handsome?" Bex asked. She was showing now, the gentle slope of her belly just visible beneath her dark purple dress.

"Very. Jamie and Luke better watch out. There are a lot of single women here. I've had to direct several death stares at a few of them because they wouldn't stop checking Cam out."

Bex laughed. "Oh, I still have to do that with Hayden. But you have to admit it's kind of satisfying to have such a hot guy."

Brooke watched Cam signal for everyone's attention, and her heart turned over. "Definitely."

"Thank you, everyone, for joining us tonight." Cam looked around the room. It was filled with industry professionals, Ribbon Ridgers, and a lot of family. Brooke had come early and been introduced to every Archer and Westcott. She was pretty sure she'd need a flow chart later.

"As many of you know, this winery started as a bit of a dare." Cam nodded toward his partners. "The four of us grew up together and never actually planned to do this. We were sitting around a table at The Arch and Vine, and we realized that each of us could contribute something valuable to a winery."

Jamie piped in. "It was me, actually. It was my idea."

Everyone laughed and no one louder than Cam. "That's true. Yes, it was wee Jamie's idea."

Jamie rolled his eyes but grinned.

Cam turned to his youngest brother, and Brooke could see the warmth in his eyes. "And a damn fine idea it was." He looked back out over the dining room. "So this idea somehow managed to find its footing. We were lucky enough to score this incredible vineyard, and Luke has turned it into something special."

Luke glanced down but smiled. "Still working on it, but it's coming along."

"See what I have to deal with?" Cam said. "One brother who wants to hog the spotlight and another who wants to dodge it." He shook his head, smiling. "But none of this would work at all without the winemaking skills of my best friend, Hayden Archer. Without further ado, I'll turn it over to him because I know he has a ton of stuff to say."

Hayden stepped forward, but Cam didn't back away yet. "One more thing," he said. "I want to thank everyone here. Your support and friendship means a lot to us." His eyes found his parents, whom Brooke had met earlier. "Mom and Dad, thank you." Then his gaze settled on her. "And Brooke—I can't wait to see where this adventure takes us." He winked at her, then took a step back. "Okay, I'm done."

Hayden gave him a look of mock exasperation, then grinned. "Thank *you*, Cam, for dreaming up this event tonight. And to my sister Sara, who coordinated it." He continued with more thank-yous, then briefly talked about the wine they'd be pouring with dinner.

Soon after, they all sat and partook of the fabulous meal that Kyle's staff had prepared. Kyle had felt bad that he couldn't attend, but newborns kind of decimated one's social calendar.

At the end of the night, after everyone had left, Brooke sat in a corner where she took off her shoes and massaged her aching feet. She wasn't sure where Cam had gone but knew he was finishing up somewhere.

Just then he came from the kitchen, his hand behind his back. He walked to her table and sat down.

She was curious what he was hiding, but didn't ask. "You must be exhausted." He didn't look it; his eyes were still bright.

"I am. We can go. In just a minute. I have something for you."

"Behind your back?" She craned her neck, fruitlessly, to look.

He brought his hand around and handed her a bouquet. A dozen white roses and one red one in the middle.

Brooke's throat knotted. After a moment, she managed to speak. "They're beautiful, and they mean so much. Thank you."

"Do you know what the red one is for?"

"Because you love me?"

He grinned and scooted forward in his chair until he was at the very edge. "Well, yes, but that's not all. That red rose is our child. I don't know where he or she will come from or when he or she will come, but they're out there waiting for us. I know it."

Her breath caught, and she just stared at this amazing man who'd captured her heart, her trust, and her dreams so completely. "When you say it, I believe it."

He leaned forward, his mouth inches from hers. "Good." He kissed her, and she wrapped her free hand around his neck, pulling him.

He fell off the chair and into her lap.

"Ack! My flowers." She giggled.

He rolled away and fell to the floor, sprawling at her feet. "I think I'm going to stay here. I *am* exhausted."

She set the flowers on the table and lay down next to him, curling against his side. "Okay." She splayed her hand over his chest. He'd long ago shed his coat and tie, and it wouldn't take much to divest him of his shirt...

He wrapped his hand around hers. "Oh, you don't have to stay, but I appreciate the offer."

"Wherever you go is where I want to be. You're stuck with me."

He turned to face her. "Good."

Then he kissed her, and she knew that nothing had ever been *so* good.

Epilogue

Late September, West Arch Estate

The vineyard was bustling with people and activity on this first day of the harvest. Every Westcott, Archer, their significant others, and even Brooke's family were here to help. They'd hired some workers, but not many since everyone wanted to pitch in.

Luke was overseeing everything, which meant he was running this way and that, with Hayden acting as second in command. Cam supposed he should be helping to manage things, but he was content to just pick grapes and make out with Brooke when no one was looking.

He looked at her backside as she bent to pick fruit and wished they were alone in the vineyard. He thought back to the midnight picnic they'd had up here a couple of weeks ago. They'd drunk Riesling and made love under the crescent moon. Up here, the sky seemed so close, like you could wrap yourself in the stars. Actually, that was how he felt when he was with her —as if he were embraced by the heavens. Wow, had he turned into a lovesick sap.

And it felt great.

She stood up and glanced back at him, then turned fully toward him. "What?"

"What what?"

She set her hand on her hip. "You have this weird look in your eye."

"Weird, really? Not lustful or infatuated?"

She laughed. "Okay, those too. But intensely so."

"Well, I was checking out your ass." He moved toward her and slipped his hand around her waist. "And thinking about that night we came up here to stargaze." He leaned forward and nuzzled her neck, but she didn't melt into him as he'd hoped.

Instead, she cleared her throat and whispered, "We have company."

Cam didn't let go of her waist but came around to stand by her side.

Evan Archer, Alaina's husband, stood there, his gaze inscrutable, as it so often was. "Sorry to interrupt, but it's lunchtime."

"Thanks," Cam said. "I'm hungry, as it happens." He tightened his grip on Brooke's waist, tickling her.

She tried to dance away, laughing, but he held her close.

"Yeah, well, if you want to stay up here for some alone time, I can try to make sure no one comes this way." There was no innuendo in his tone, no teasing, just a straightforward offer to give them some privacy. He turned and left without another word.

Cam pivoted and pulled Brooke against him. "Evan is such a great guy."

Brooke pressed her mouth to his. "Mmmm-hmmm. I like him and Alaina a lot." Her stomach rumbled against his, and he laughed.

"I guess we should go eat."

She pulled back and smiled at him. "Please? I'm starving."

He grabbed her hand. "Let's go."

They walked down the hill to where tables had been set up under massive canopies. Bex and Sara and some others had put out lunch in addition to wrangling children. There was quite a spread of food and drink.

Cam and Brooke filled their plates and sat down at a table where his parents and her parents were getting to know each other. Brooke leaned toward him and whispered, "Is this weird?"

"Kind of, but it's also sort of cute."

Their dads had bonded over fishing and were even talking about taking a weekend trip together next summer.

"I guess we have to be in this for the long haul," Brooke said as she scooped a bite of pasta salad.

"I wouldn't have it any other way, would you?"

She turned her head and her eyes were full of love. "Nope."

Rhonda sat down opposite them. "Hey, guys. Thanks again for inviting all of us up this weekend."

"Where are Isla and Will?" Brooke glanced around for Rhonda's two children, who Cam had met last night.

"Will's asleep inside. Sara and Bex set up a day-care situation with a couple of teenage sitters. And Dave's got Isla." She nodded toward her husband seated at another table. He sat beside the four-year-old Isla, who was busy trying to help Alaina and Evan's daughter eat.

Cam watched Brooke for her reaction to all of this kid discussion. She seemed fine. Of course she was fine. They'd talked at length about her feelings of loss and inadequacy, and she'd told him that his support and love had given her the missing piece she'd really needed to move on and embrace the life she had. No, it wasn't what she'd planned, but she felt better equipped now, with him at her side, to face the future, whatever it held.

And while they hadn't specifically discussed getting married, they seemed to have formed a tacit agreement that they were headed in that direction. He knew that was what *he* wanted. Last night, he'd talked to her parents about his intent—not asking their permission per se, but making sure they knew how much he loved and valued their daughter and how integral she'd become to his life.

All he had to do now was find the right moment to give her the ring he'd picked up yesterday.

"Cam?" Rhonda said his name loudly, as if she'd been trying to get his attention. Maybe she had.

"Sorry, just thinking. What did I miss?" He looked between her and Brooke.

Rhonda rolled her eyes and grinned at the same time. "You two are so in love, it's disgusting. I'll bet money your mind was completely hung up on my sister."

Cam looked over at Brooke, who wore a faint blush. "No one would take that bet, because duh. My mind is irrevocably hung up on her."

Brooke's blush deepened, and she reached over and squeezed his thigh, which sent a jolt of lust straight through him. Now he really wished they'd followed Evan's suggestion up in the vineyard. After lunch maybe...

Kelsey joined them, sitting on the other side of Brooke. She and Brooke had become good friends, and they spent a lot of time working on the Ribbon Ridge exhibit for the library, which they were hoping to open early next year.

Brooke introduced Kelsey to her sister, and they shook hands over the table.

"What's this I hear about some sort of excavation around

here?" Rhonda asked. "Brooke told me a little—and that you're working on it together—but didn't finish the story last night."

Kelsey swallowed a bite of food and nodded. "Yeah, we're looking for the site of the original building on this property. A clapboard farmhouse built in 1879."

"Problem is, we're not entirely sure where to look," Brooke said. "Fortunately, we're in the process of working with the county historical society to find out where it might've been. They're going to try to find maps from that time period, provided they have them among their records."

Rhonda leaned her elbow on the table, her fork dangling from her fingers. "That's so fascinating. I can't wait to hear what you find."

"We just hope we find something!" Kelsey said, laughing. "We'll all be so disappointed if we come up empty-handed."

Cam knew she spoke the truth. She and Brooke, along with Alaina and Crystal, were completely committed to this research project. He loved how immersed Brooke had become in Ribbon Ridge. For a guy who never planned past tomorrow, Cam had been surprised to realize he had dreams for his future, and he was even more shocked to see them start to come true.

After a bit, Cam stood to get water for himself and Brooke. He was waylaid by his parents, who gushed over how much they liked Brooke's folks. He knew his mother wanted to ask when they were going to get married, but he hadn't told her he planned to propose. She was a mix of shock and glee when it came to their relationship. She'd never imagined that he would be the first of her boys to settle down. Cam couldn't quite believe that either.

As he headed back toward the table with a couple of waters, his brothers and Hayden corralled him to the side.

"Hey, this is pretty crazy, right?" Jamie asked.

"What, you mean everyone here?" Hayden shook his head. "We have big, meddlesome families. Of course they'd want to come help." He grinned. "They're also pretty awesome."

Luke looked at Hayden. "Did I hear your dad say he wanted to intern with you when you blend?"

Hayden chuckled. "Yeah, the master brewer has decided he's interested in winemaking."

Cam laughed along with him. He'd known Rob Archer almost his entire life, and he was a beer man through and through, as evidenced by his incredibly successful chain of brewpubs and now line of beers, which they'd started bottling last year.

"That's pretty cool," Cam said. He knew how much it had to mean to Hayden that his dad was so interested. Rob had been disappointed when none of his children had taken up the craft of brewing beer. He was, however, delighted that his daughter-in-law Bex was keeping it in the family.

"I'm just amazed at how well this is all doing," Jamie said. "Really, when I first brought this up that day at The Arch and Vine, I never foresaw this."

Cam remembered that day vividly. He now realized it was the moment in which he'd decided his disconnected, ambivalent existence wasn't good enough. It was the moment he'd turned a corner and started on his way to finding Brooke. To finding happiness. "I did. At least, I hoped it would be this."

Hayden clapped his shoulder. "Me too, bro."

"Well, I didn't doubt it," Luke said. "I mean look at us. We're total studs." They all laughed. "And right now, this stud needs to get back out to the vineyard."

"Yeah, we all do," Hayden said, and they all took off.

Cam went back to the table and said he was heading back up the hill. Brooke immediately stood to join him. Hand in hand, they hiked back up to where they'd been picking.

Once they were back between their rows of grapes, Cam pulled her into his arms and kissed her. She tasted of the wine they'd had at lunch and something chocolate. "Did you have dessert?" he asked against her delicious mouth.

"Emily Archer brought brownies, and I couldn't resist."

Cam knew from twenty-five plus years of experience that Hayden's mom made the best brownies around. "Somehow they taste even better on your lips."

She giggled, and he kissed her again, taking her joy into himself and basking in its glow. After a minute or maybe two, she pulled back with a sigh. "We should really get back to work."

"Yep." But he didn't take his hands from her waist.

"You're going to have to let go."

"Never." Without thinking, he dropped to his knee in front of her.

Her eyes widened, and she brought her hand to her kiss-swollen mouth. "*Cam.* What are you doing?"

He couldn't contain his grin even as a thread of nervousness snaked through him. "Like you don't know." He pulled the ring from his pocket and unwrapped the tissue he'd placed it in. Taking her hand, he looked up into her eyes. "Brooke, you know how much I love you. I try to tell you multiple times every day." He smiled. "And I'm sure this isn't a surprise, but I'm ready to make it official, and I hope you are too. There's no one else I'd rather spend my life with. Will you marry me?"

"I never imagined I'd find someone who'd love me so completely and so unconditionally." Her smile faded. "You're sure? I know we've talked about it so much—"

He knew she meant her infertility, and they had talked about it a lot. "My love, no doubts, no second-guessing. I'm more sure of this than I've been of anything in my life. And I'm more than ready to start our journey together."

Her smile came back, lifting her lips and deepening her dimples. "Given that I rarely stay at my loft anymore, I think we already have." She tugged at his hand. "Stand up and kiss me, Cam. Yes, my answer is yes."

Joy burst through him, lighting every corner of his soul. "First things first. He slipped the diamond on her finger, happy that it fit perfectly.

She looked down at her hand and exhaled sharply. "It's gorgeous."

He rose to his feet. "It pales next to you."

She wrapped her hands around his neck and pulled him down for another kiss. When they came up for air, she held her hand up and looked at the ring again. "My sisters are going to be jealous. Oh man, everyone's going to be ecstatic. I think they'll likely throw an impromptu party."

He kissed her neck. "So long as I get you to myself at some point, it's all good. Actually, we're alone right now..."

She laughed low and seductive in her throat. "We are, but it's hot and bright and not that private. I can hear your mother laughing two rows over."

He reluctantly stopped licking the salty-sweet flesh beneath her ear. "Well, damn."

"Later," she promised.

He lovingly stroked her cheek. "I can't wait."

Thank you so much for reading! Grab the next book in the Ribbon Ridge series:

Sexy vineyard manager Luke Westcott and sweet librarian Kelsey McDade are workaholics who decide to make time for friendship, but when their

relationship heats up, the ghosts of Kelsey's past could send everything up in flames.

Don't miss Luke and Kelsey's story in *So Right*!

Ribbon Ridge is a fictional town based on several cities and towns dotting the Willamette Valley between Portland and the Oregon Coast. It's pinot noir wine country, very beautiful and picturesque, and a short drive from where I live. My brother actually dwells right in the heart of it in a tiny town with no stoplights. There is, however, an amazing antique mall in an historic schoolhouse (and apparently seven Pokestops).

Would you like to know when my next book is available and to hear about sales and deals? **Sign up for my VIP newsletter** which is the only place you can get bonus books and material such as the short prequel to the Phoenix Club series, INVITATION, and the exciting prequel to Legendary Rogues, THE LEGEND OF A ROGUE.

Join me on social media!

Facebook: https://facebook.com/DarcyBurkeFans
Facebook group: Darcy's Duchesses
Instagram at darcyburkeauthor
Pinterest at darcyburkewrite

And follow me on Bookbub to receive updates on pre-orders, new releases, and deals!

I hope you'll consider leaving a review at your favorite online vendor or networking site!

I appreciate my readers so much. Thank you, thank you, *thank you.*

Also by Darcy Burke

Contemporary Romance

Ribbon Ridge

Let Go (a prequel novella)

Get Lucky

Sparks Fly

Fall Hard

Can't Stop

Break Free

Hold Me

Turn On

So Right

This Love

Historical Mystery

Raven & Wren

A Whisper of Death

A Whisper at Midnight

A Whisper and a Curse

A Whisper in the Shadows

A Whisper of Secrecy

A Whisper in Darkness

Historical Romance

Rogue Rules

If the Duke Dares

Because the Baron Broods

When the Viscount Seduces

As the Earl Likes

Until the Rake Surrenders

Since the Marquess Demands

What the Scoundrel Desires

How the Devil Sins

The Phoenix Club

Improper

Impassioned

Intolerable

Indecent

Impossible

Irresistible

Impeccable

Insatiable

Marrywell Brides

Beguiling the Duke

Romancing the Heiress

Matching the Marquess

The Matchmaking Chronicles

Yule Be My Duke

The Rigid Duke

The Bachelor Earl (also prequel to *The Untouchables*)

The Runaway Viscount

The Make-Believe Widow

The Untouchables

The Bachelor Earl (prequel)

The Forbidden Duke

The Duke of Daring

The Duke of Deception

The Duke of Desire

The Duke of Defiance

The Duke of Danger

The Duke of Ice

The Duke of Ruin

The Duke of Lies

The Duke of Seduction

The Duke of Kisses

The Duke of Distraction

The Untouchables: The Spitfire Society

Never Have I Ever with a Duke

A Duke is Never Enough

A Duke Will Never Do

The Untouchables: The Pretenders

A Secret Surrender

A Scandalous Bargain

A Rogue to Ruin

About the Author

Darcy Burke is the USA Today Bestselling Author of sexy, emotional historical and contemporary romance. Darcy wrote her first book at age 11, a happily ever after about a swan addicted to magic and the female swan who loved him, with exceedingly poor illustrations. Join her Reader Club newsletter for the latest updates from Darcy.

A native Oregonian, Darcy lives on the edge of wine country with her guitar-strumming husband, incredibly talented artist daughter, and imaginative, Japanese-speaking son who will almost certainly out-write her one day (that may be tomorrow). They're a crazy cat family with two Bengal cats, a small, fame-seeking cat named after a fruit, an older rescue Maine Coon with attitude to spare, an adorable former stray who wandered onto their deck and into their hearts, and two bonded boys who used to belong to (separate) neighbors but chose them instead. You can find Darcy in her comfy writing chair balancing her laptop and a cat or three, attempting yoga, folding laundry (which she loves), or wildlife spotting and playing games with her family. She loves traveling to the UK and visiting her beloved cousins in Denmark. Visit Darcy online at www.darcyburke.com and follow her on social media.

facebook.com/DarcyBurkeFans

instagram.com/darcyburkeauthor

pinterest.com/darcyburkewrites

goodreads.com/darcyburke

bookbub.com/authors/darcy-burke

amazon.com/author/darcyburke

threads.net/@darcyburkeauthor

tiktok.com/@darcyburkeauthor

www.ingramcontent.com/pod-product-compliance
Lightning Source LLC
Chambersburg PA
CBHW020357110726
47899CB00006B/1749